# Readers Love Amy Lane

## *Swipe Left, Power Down, Look Up*
"A dose of much needed sweetness, humor, and an excellent HEA…"
—Rainbow Book Reviews

## *Under Cover*
"I have never been let down by Amy Lane and this one keeps that record going…I love a good thriller and this one kept me on the edge of my seat!"
—Love Bytes Reviews

## *Weirdos*
"The 80 pages is just as sweet as you think and pulls on your heart strings…It did mine."
—Paranormal Romance Guild

## *Shades of Henry*
"If you want emotions, character drama without it translating into a third-rate show and a romance that makes you feel tingly, go ahead with Shades of Henry."
—Leer sin Limites

## *Bonfires*
"This book is for everybody, for the gay and the straight, for the open minded and the close minded, for the brave and for those who are afraid! Everybody."
—OptimuMM Book Reviews

By AMY LANE

An Amy Lane Christmas
Behind the Curtain
Bewitched by Bella's Brother
Bolt-hole
Christmas Kitsch
Christmas with Danny Fit
Clear Water
Do-over
Food for Thought
Freckles
Gambling Men
Going Up
Hammer & Air
Homebird
If I Must
Immortal
It's Not Shakespeare
Late for Christmas
Left on St. Truth-be-Well
The Locker Room
Mourning Heaven
Phonebook
Puppy, Car, and Snow
Racing for the Sun
Hiding the Moon
Raising the Stakes
Regret Me Not
Shiny!
Shirt
Sidecar

Slow Pitch
String Boys
A Solid Core of Alpha
Swipe Left, Power Down, Look Up
Three Fates
Truth in the Dark
Turkey in the Snow
The Twelve Kittens of Christmas
Under the Rushes
Weirdos
Wishing on a Blue Star

BENEATH THE STAIN
Beneath the Stain
Paint It Black

BONFIRES
Bonfires
Crocus
Sunset

CANDY MAN
Candy Man
Bitter Taffy
Lollipop
Tart and Sweet

COVERT
Under Cover

Published by DREAMSPINNER PRESS
www.dreamspinnerpress.com

## By Amy Lane (cont'd)

DREAMSPUN BEYOND
HEDGE WITCHES
LONELY HEARTS CLUB
Shortbread and Shadows
Portals and Puppy Dogs
Pentacles and Pelting Plants
Heartbeats in a Haunted House

DREAMSPUN DESIRES
THE MANNIES
The Virgin Manny
Manny Get Your Guy
Stand by Your Manny
A Fool and His Manny
SEARCH AND RESCUE
Warm Heart
Silent Heart
Safe Heart
Hidden Heart

FAMILIAR LOVE
Familiar Angel
Familiar Demon

FISH OUT OF WATER
Fish Out of Water
Red Fish, Dead Fish
A Few Good Fish
Hiding the Moon
Fish on a Bicycle
School of Fish
Fish in a Barrel
Only Fish
A Perfectly Sonny Daye

FLOPHOUSE
Shades of Henry
Constantly Cotton
Sean's Sunshine

GRANBY KNITTING
The Winter Courtship Rituals of
Fur-Bearing Critters
How to Raise an Honest Rabbit
Knitter in His Natural Habitat
Blackbird Knitting in a Bunny's Lair
Weddings, Christmas, and Such
The Granby Knitting Menagerie
Anthology

JOHNNIES
Chase in Shadow
Dex in Blue
Ethan in Gold
Black John
Bobby Green
Super Sock Man

KEEPING PROMISE ROCK
Keeping Promise Rock
Making Promises
Living Promises
Forever Promised

Published by Dreamspinner Press
www.dreamspinnerpress.com

By AMY LANE (cont'd)

*Published by DSP Publications*

**LONG CON ADVENTURES**
The Mastermind
The Muscle
The Driver
The Suit
The Tech
The Face Man

**LUCK MECHANICS**
The Rising Tide
A Salt Bitter Sea

**PRINCETON ROYALS**
Riding Shotgun

**TALKER**
Talker
Talker's Redemption
Talker's Graduation
The Talker Collection Anthology

**WINTER BALL**
Winter Ball
Summer Lessons
Fall Through Spring

**ALL THAT HEAVEN WILL ALLOW**
All the Rules of Heaven

**GREEN'S HILL**
The Green's Hill Novellas

**LITTLE GODDESS**
Vulnerable
Wounded, Vol. 1
Wounded, Vol. 2
Bound, Vol. 1
Bound, Vol. 2
Rampant, Vol. 1
Rampant, Vol. 2
Quickening, Vol. 1
Quickening, Vol. 2
Green's Hill Werewolves, Vol. 1
Green's Hill Werewolves, Vol. 2

*Published by Harmony Ink Press*

**BITTER MOON SAGA**
Triane's Son Rising
Triane's Son Learning
Triane's Son Fighting
Triane's Son Reigning

Published by DREAMSPINNER PRESS
www.dreamspinnerpress.com

# RIDING SHOTGUN

## AMY LANE

Published by
DREAMSPINNER PRESS

8219 Woodville Hwy #1245
Woodville, FL 32362 USA
www.dreamspinnerpress.com



Riding Shotgun
© 2024 Amy Lane

Cover Art
© 2024 L.C. Chase
http://www.lcchase.com
Cover content is for illustrative purposes only and any person depicted on the cover is a model.



Trade Paperback ISBN: 9781641087803
Digital ISBN: 9781641087797
Trade Paperback published October 2024
v. 1.0

*This book took forever to write—not because it was hard but because my health went to hell during production. So this one is dedicated to Mate, who stuck by me and makes sure I never end up back there, and my bestie Mary, who sent me cookbooks to make sure I stay out of the hospital, and to my kids who all gathered for Mother's Day in an effort to make me know I was loved.*

# Acknowledgments

So one night about eight years ago, Kim Fielding sent me an article about a shipment of bull jizz that got stolen somewhere near Turlock and abandoned in a nearby field. Heh heh heh. I wrote a terrible epic poem about it, and we've been giggling about the incident ever since. So, yeah. I finally wrote a book about bull jizz—and it's all Kim's fault.

# The Royal Family Meeting

**Laure:** You guys! You guys! Family conference, *now*.

**Prock:** Is everybody okay? Because if everybody's *not* okay, we need to talk about your approach, big sister. The last time you did this it was because Mom was changing the carpet.

**Sal:** It was shag carpet, Prock. You straighties might think that's okay, but the rest of us can assure you it is not.

**Chance:** It has nothing to do with being gay—his standard is with or without baby vomit, so give him a break.

**Reg:** Wait—Val's not on the list. Why is Val not on the list? *Is he dead?*

**Prock:** She would have led with that.

**Chance:** Would she, though?

**Laure:** Yes, you assholes, I would have led with that.

**Reg:** Then what's wrong? Why are we freaking out about my second-favorite brother?

**Sal:** Who's your favorite?

**Reg:** Now *that* is the real mystery, right?

**Sal:** Well played, bitch, well played.

**Prock:** It's obviously me until he says so. Now c'mon, Laure, what's the damage?

**Laure:** He's lonely. You guys, Val is *lonely*.

**Chance:** FFS—I've got finals!

**Prock:** Sis....

**Sal:** I've got a date. I'm out of here.

**Reg:** How do you know?

**Laure:** He said so.

**All:**....

**Laure:** You guys?

**Reg:** Was he being facetious?

**Sal:** Does it *matter*? Laure, I take it all back, you're right, this is a problem. If Val even mentioned he had a feeling, it's a big deal.

**Prock:** I assume you or Reg have a plan?

**Reg:** I might, but Laure just called me too, remember?

**Prock:** Sorry, Reg. You two usually plot the best.

**Laure:** My only plan hasn't joined in the chat yet. He's probably too busy being a big important feeb.

**Reg:** Should we all text him separately too?

**Laure:** Sure—okay, guys—everybody at the same time—let's make his phone into a sex toy—

**Reg, Sal, Laure, and Prock:** Dean! Dean! Dean! Dean! Dean!

**Chance:** Wait a minute, what do you mean a sex toy?

**Reg, Sal, Laure, and Prock: Dean**! Dean! Dean! Dean! Dean!

**Dean:** Because it's vibrating, Chance. The rest of you assholes, has it occurred to you that I'm busy?

**Chance:** Heh heh heh… sex toy!

**Laure:** It's an emergency, Dean. Quick, give us the name of somebody we can set Val up with.

**Dean:** Contrary to popular opinion, law enforcement is not filled with closeted gay men. Or uncloseted gay men.

**Sal:** Oh, honey, that has *not* been my experience.

**Reg:** Dude, every "straight guy" you've brought home to meet Mom and Dad has hit on me.

**Chance:** I legit thought you were bringing them home to match them with us. Marcus was beautiful. I wanted him so bad.

**Sal:** Oh, honey….

**Reg:** Oh, honey….

**Laure:** Oh, honey….

**Dean:** See, Laure I knew about, but it's because I thought he was straight.

**Chance:** I can't believe he didn't hit on me. Prock, did you know?

**Prock:** I'm so sorry. He was legit surprised when I told him I was the one married to a woman.

**Chance:** *Am I a troll?*

**Laure:** You're a sweet summer child too beautiful for this world. Now can we move on to Val? Dean, do you have any friends who might work for him? He's the oldest, and he's cranky and getting mean.

**Dean:** He's always been cranky and mean.

**Laure:** And he told me he was lonely.

**Dean:** Fuck. This *is* an emergency.

**Laure:** *See?*

**Dean:** Wait. Was I the only one who was going to sit shotgun with his next shipment?

**All:**….

**Dean:** I'll take that as a yes. Okay. Actually, yeah. My old shooting mentor. He's retired now, working security.

**Chance:** Is Val that old? I mean, retired and all? This guy's gotta be, what? Sixty? I mean, that's *Dad's* age, right?

**Laure:** Dad's sixty-five and Val is forty. My God, Chance—are you sure you're in college?

**Chance:** I forget about the gap.

**Laure:** Mom was having seven of us, Chance—it wasn't like they were taking time off.

**Chance:** Whatever. How old is this guy, Dean? Is he old and warty with hair growing out his ears?

**Dean: He's** fortysomething and hot, and if he does have hair growing out his ears, he knows how to groom.

**Sal:** Hello, Daddy.

**Dean:** And he's discreet and likes bears.

**Reg:** Too bad Prock's taken.

**Prock:** Har, har. It's baby weight—my wife says so.

**Laure:** If he can help Val with security, he's perfect.

**Dean:** I swear to God I'm not setting him up with my brother if that's all we expect Val to need.

**Reg:** Seriously, somebody's got to get laid. I need the vicarious thrills.

**Sal:** Would you like to hear about my weekend?

**All:** *No!*

**Sal:** You bitches are just jealous.

**Laure:** Dean, back out of doing security. Give me your guy's number and I'll recommend him when Val comes asking. We've got to have some finesse here, or Val will know he's being played.

**Reg:** What's the gig? What does Val need security for?

**Dean:** Heh heh heh….

**Laure:** Don't say it.

**Dean:** But it's too funny!

**Laure:** Please? God, Dean, it's hard enough being the only girl.

**Chance:** But I want to know.

**Reg:** So do I, now.

**Sal:** Seriously.

**Prock:** Don't leave me out!

**Dean:** Well if you *really* want to know….

# BULLDOOKIE

Valedictorian Princeton Royal had a headache the size of a diesel engine, and its name was Dean.

"Goddammit, little brother, you *promised*," he snapped into the phone. "I asked you this *a month ago*."

"I know, Val. I'm sorry. If it's any help, I asked Laure if she could find someone to help. I gave her a list of my old contacts. She's running someone down."

Val stalked the lot of his independent long-haul business and made careful note of which units were out and which ones were due back. Unlike many other long-haul businesses, Val had built his reputation on safe practices and paying his employees a living wage without forcing them to work overtime or keep double logs. It was tough—the competition cheated—but one of Val's signatures was offering a security caveat on his clients' most valuable cargo. A month ago, he'd accepted a fifty-thousand-dollar bond on the promise to get this shipment from Elite Cattle Incorporated in Bakersfield to Conti & Sons Cattle Ranch in Texas, and it had to be timed and shipped perfectly, without incident, and with speed.

Dammit, Dean had been perfect. He knew how to drive a rig, he had his fancy FBI badge, and Val could stand his company, mostly. Together, they could take turns driving and make the twenty-hour trip from Bakersfield to Austin in twenty-four hours or less travel time, thus ensuring that Vinnie's in-season, rare, longhorn-hybrid cows could be inseminated and gestating at optimum speed.

And for the return trip, they'd be bringing Vinnie's prize bull to Elite Cattle Incorporated so he could spend a week fucking his balls out on the collection dummy before returning the poor guy, replete and probably just a little bit dizzy, back to Vinnie's ranch. The whole dance and cow-jizz exchange had taken months to negotiate. Geneticists had been consulted to make sure that Elite Cattle Incorporated's "right stuff" would mesh well with Vinnie's prize cows' "right stuff" without contaminating the bloodline at Vinnie's ranch, while invigorating and adding to the stock at Elite Cattle Incorporated.

Before his high school buddy Vinnie had called him, banking his entire family's stock and future on Vinnie's memory of the kid who didn't lie, wouldn't back down, and always had a buddy's back—coupled with the solid business reputation Val had built since—Val had no idea that bull jizz could be such a serious business.

But it *was*, and not only *serious*, but serious enough to be *dangerous*.

"You don't get it," Val said now to Dean. "Vinnie's had two shipments already that have been stolen and abandoned. By the time the authorities tracked down the trucks, the refrigerator units had been turned off and *hundreds of thousands of dollars* of bull sperm had gone bad."

"Ew," Dean said, and Val grunted. Dean was usually pretty stoic, but, well, yeah.

"The ew isn't the point," Val persevered. "This is Vinnie's family ranch, Dean. And he's got a narrow window. The cows hit their cycle, he calls Elite, they transfer the straws of sperm into the refrigerator car that night, and we move out the next morning. We're heading to Austin in two days, tops. Vinnie's getting his straws retested at the geneticists again, so I've really got to hustle. We have to get optimum fecundity. This is a big fucking deal, and I need somebody to *literally* ride shotgun in case somebody tries to steal the shipment. Do you understand?"

"Did you just say 'fecundity'?" Dean asked suspiciously, and Val actually *snarled* at his little brother.

"*This is a big deal!*" he roared, and before Dean could defend himself—or better yet, promise Val he'd get the time off like he promised—Val's phone beeped.

"It's Laure," he said, still irritated. "What's Laure doing on my phone?"

"Probably calling with my replacement," Dean said. "Text me if it's suitable. Love ya big brother. Bye!"

And Dean was gone, and Laure was there.

"Laureate, this had better be good," Val snapped when she'd connected.

"I run the best headhunting firm in central California," Laure told him evenly. "I'm not good, I'm *great*. So you apologize."

Val grunted. She really *was* good. The fact that Dean had called her when he'd been assigned somewhere in Texas instead of Sacramento during what should have been some accrued time off meant that Dean was as dependable as he'd always been, but being part of a bureaucracy had taught him to delegate.

"Can he drive a rig?" Val asked, because his plan depended on one of them driving and the other sleeping.

"He can. And he's good with a weapon. In fact he was Dean's shooting instructor, and he's been part of several joint FBI/ATF stings for transporting goods over state lines. He's retired now and does the odd security gig. He's bonded, fingerprinted, and I've got three people vouching for him, including Dean and Dean's SAC, so, you know, he's as pedigreed as your bull jizz, okay?"

Val grunted. "Dean told you, didn't he?"

Laure's chuckle was a direct result of being raised with six boys and now the mother of two of her own. She appreciated a dirty joke and could tell them with the best.

"Of course he did," she said, and he could picture her, long dark hair pulled into a ponytail, cat-shaped brown eyes glancing sideways. Laure had been the second oldest of the seven of them, and if she couldn't laugh at all the assholes around her, she never would have survived. "I have so little in my life, Val. Did you think he'd deprive me of knowing you were making a living as a cow pimp?"

"I hate you," Val muttered, but that was family code for "I love you so much I'd kill you in your sleep."

"I hate you too. You're looking for Rory McCauley, retired FBI—"

"He'd better not be too old to hold a rifle," Val muttered.

"Age forty-eight," she continued, as though he hadn't spoken.

"That's young. What happened?" he asked suspiciously.

"He got injured and took medical leave," she said. "Dean tells me he enjoyed contracting as security so much, he took the early out. Runs a gun range when he's not out on jobs, has a son who works it for him when he is. I'm saying, Val, the guy's creds are solid."

"Married?" Val asked. Sometimes married guys were the best, like his brother Proctor. A happy homelife tended to make people more even-keeled, better-tempered. Val, who had always been grumpy at best, might not have been able to *act* mellow, but that didn't mean he didn't *appreciate* it when somebody else did.

"Divorced," Laure replied mildly. "Amicably by everything Dean tells me. Look, I know this is last minute, Val, but all my sources say this guy's a keeper."

Val grunted. "Great. Tell him to meet me—"

"At your business office in five minutes," she said, her voice a wicked purr.

Val narrowed his eyes. "How do you even know—"

"I knew you'd be at the lot today," she said, sounding innocent. "I figure you need today to outline the job for him because you'll get called in the next few days, right?"

"Tomorrow or the day after," Val conceded. God, he really *had* been counting on Dean.

"Well, meet this guy, shake his hand, establish that you won't kill him during the haul, and you can get a good night's sleep before you start. That way if you don't leave tomorrow, I can be by early afternoon to drop off some supplies for your drive the next day. How's that?"

Val had reached the end of the fence line for the truck lot, and in the distance he could see a battered pickup truck turning down the road that would lead past the hurricane fencing and eel wire to the business office itself.

"Apparently it's peachy," he grumbled, "although you know I'm a grown man and can shop for myself—"

"Yeah, but the boys will both be gone tomorrow night and I'm making lasagna tonight. I can bring you dinner too."

He sucked in a breath. His sister's lasagna was decadent heaven. He knew it was probably a ploy to get him to soften up toward this new development, but he was suddenly salivating and didn't care if he didn't get lasagna until the next day. "Fine," he agreed, knowing he was weak even as he watched an unfamiliar vehicle pulling around the eel-wire and chain-link fence to the entrance to the lot. "But I gotta go now because he's here and I gotta go meet him."

"Play nice," Laure warned.

"Oh sure," Val told her. "I'm a *sweetheart.*"

She started cackling in his ear then, and he hung up on her, saving his wind for the trot back to the double-wide that served as his office.

As he jogged, he put together a mental picture of his new work partner. Probably short, he thought sourly. Dean was the shortest of his siblings, with a slender build that made his classic G-man suit look good on his neat frame, so this guy, this Rory McCauley, would probably be short too—but not slim like Dean. He'd worked at the bureau for what? Twenty years? Dean claimed that he did a lot of paper pushing, so this guy had probably gotten pudgy, or at least a little stolid. He'd been injured, too, and that was hard to come back from. So injured and slow. Graying, pudgy, saggy jowls probably—he was pushing fifty, right? Not that Val was that much younger. Val could own it. If he didn't keep his diet like God's watch, he'd be saggy and jowly too. It also helped that he ran or swam as often as possible and stayed on his feet and walked the yard when he wasn't the one running cargo. He liked to stay fit. His frame was heavier, stockier than Dean's, and he knew he had to work that much harder to not fall into unhealthy habits.

Proctor, his married brother—his one heterosexual brother, for that matter—had put on twenty pounds in his first year of marriage, and he and his wife had become absolute health-food fanatics ever since she'd given birth to their third child, in an attempt to lose that weight.

The girls, cherubic little hellions that they were, loathed anything organic or flavored with applesauce. Prock had been a picky little shit when he'd been in grade school, and Val firmly believed God had a sense of humor in these matters. It sort of helped that Val and Sal fed them things like Lucky Charms and Pop-Tarts whenever the girls were at their parents' because while Val was dour and growly and Sal was campy, bitchy goodness, they were both dicks who would mess with "sweet little Proctor" every chance they got.

*Ah, sibling politics*, Val thought with satisfaction. Best hobby known to man. His mental image of McCauley was coming along nicely. Squat, jowly, maybe some broken blood vessels from a little too much scotch, and a graying buzz cut rounded it out. He wasn't sure why. Someone with experience, with a "Don't worry, son, I got this" swagger but few personal complications. Someone Val could play poker with but who wouldn't expect the conversation to get too personal.

Oh yeah! This guy would be *great*. Val was looking forward to meeting him already.

With a little *whoof* of breath, he hit the ramp up to his portable office and stood for a moment, checking his wind to make sure the job hadn't taken too much out of him. He got there in time to see the battered pickup that he'd assumed belonged to Rory McCauley pull into one of the office parking spaces and turn off.

The man who got out of the pickup could not *possibly* be Rory McCauley.

For one thing he was tall. Tall and lanky in jeans and a western-cut plaid shirt and cowboy boots, swaggering across the parking lot, cowboy hat in hand. The jeans and boots were worn, and the boots were dusty—although the jeans were clean—and Val noticed he had the slightest hitch in his step as he strode toward the ramp.

This man was not short, he was not fat, and he was not gray.

Sure, he had some threads of silver in his shaggy brown hair, but they went with the crow's feet and those grooves in his lean cheeks, near his mouth, that indicated this was a man who smiled a *lot* and even knew how to laugh.

He grinned up at Val from the bottom of the ramp.

"This the office for Royal Trucking and Transport?" he asked, thumping his hat against his thigh.

Val fought not to get lost in those squinty brown eyes because… whew. Damn. He did not need this now.

"Sure is," he said, proud of how he kept his voice clipped.

"You Val Royal?"

"Yessir, what can I do for you?" *Please don't say you're—*

"I'm Rory McCauley. I got a phone call from Lori Royal—"

"Laure," Val corrected him. "No e sound at the end. You cannot possibly be Rory McCauley."

"Beg your pardon." The man's grin amped up at the corners. "And I most certainly am."

"But you're… you're… you are *not* fat, retired, and ugly," Val burst out, so incredibly *offended* by this man's good looks he wanted to go hit something. Divorced. With a son. Oh fuck, why would his sister, knowing he was hard up, pair him with somebody this… this *tall*, this *rangy*, this *goddamned handsome* when Val had to keep his head on business. It was no goddamned fair!

The man's expression altered subtly. He'd been smiling up at Val in obvious good humor, but at Val's blunt words he gave a bark of laughter. His good humor was still there, but it went… lazier. Coiled, like a bullwhip. His eyes, a bright nut brown, went from being wicked and intelligent to hot and assessing, and he raked those eyes up and down Val's muscular body like a touch, leaving Val sweaty and *very* uncomfortable.

"Nossir," Rory McCauley all but purred. "I am not fat, I work hard to not be ugly, and I do not work for law enforcement anymore, but I am not, strictly speaking, retired. Were you looking forward to someone like that?"

Val closed his eyes, took a breath, and tried to still his suddenly galloping heartbeat.

"I was hoping for a professional who was not a distraction," he said, hoping for dignity.

He was not prepared for Rory McCauley's low rumble of a laugh, the kind that seemed to vibrate right up the ramp of the office, through the soles of Val's shoes, and straight into his thighs.

"I am the soul of professionalism," McCauley promised, although Val's libido was waking up and saying things that were *by no means* about work. Then McCauley winked, and Val had to grip the handrail to keep his knees from going weak. "Don't worry, son," he added. "I got this."

Oh no, Val thought faintly. Oh no, oh no, oh no.

Odds were very good he was in *so* much trouble. This was his business. This was his *friend's* business. This was his *reputation* that was at stake.

From far away, he heard himself say, "Do you have your paperwork?"

Rory waggled his eyebrows and produced a sealed manila envelope that had been folded in half lengthwise and stuffed in the back pocket of those worn, tight jeans.

"I do. Does that mean I can come in now?"

Oh God.

But Val was in need. So very many kinds of need, and he wasn't sure if it was common sense or self-destruction that made him say, "Sure. Let's get your paperwork filed, and I can fill you in on the job."

# Truckin'

RORY BENT over the old army surplus desk, filling in his paperwork, and purposefully stretched his legs to bump them into Val Royal's. Royal startled and pulled his legs back, sucking in his stomach and glancing left and right to see if anybody had noticed his reaction.

Heh heh…. Rory had noticed his reaction.

Mm… nice.

Rory had been Dean Royal's shooting instructor in the Federal Law Enforcement Training Centers academy and had appreciated the younger man's competence and efficiency—and his sneaky little moments of wit and humor. Dean had been a looker too, with rich brown hair and dark hazel eyes, much like his brother, as well as high cheekbones and a square jaw—but Rory didn't hit on students, or coworkers for that matter, particularly not back in his feeb days and *particularly* not when they were scarcely older than his son.

But Val was a different kettle of fish.

For one thing, he was a good ten or so years older than Dean, which made the age gap *much* less uncomfortable, and for another, as a private contractor, Rory and Val were on more equal footing. Either one of them could break the contract if they needed to. But Rory definitely didn't want to *now*.

But that was one thing. The other thing—signaled by Val's deeply etched scowl, the V in his forehead so pronounced Rory had to wonder if it was tanned as evenly as the rest of Val's face—was just so delightful! Rory had met a lot of just-the-facts-ma'am G-men in his time at the bureau, but he'd never met somebody so very serious about….

He had to check the paperwork twice.

"Bull jizz?" he asked, the chuckle bursting out of him before he could stop it.

"The cattle business is a multimillion-dollar industry," Val said with dignity, but Rory caught it. A tiny tick at the corner of a tightly compressed, lean mouth.

"I know it," Rory drawled. "The hat and boots aren't just for show. Grew up in Texas, so I know me some cows."

And now there were two tics—one at *each* corner.

"Although, you know, not as intimately as some of my compatriots," Rory continued, eyeballing some of the language on the shipping manifest. "Given that I don't rightly remember seeing a bull with a prick small enough to come in a straw."

And now Val's *forehead* was twitching, like that deeply etched V was struggling to *un*etch itself from Val Royal's forehead.

"The, uhm, material is collected and then separated into straws," Val said as though reciting something he'd had to learn for school. "The straws are either frozen or chilled, depending on when they're going to be used to inseminate the cows." He paused and swallowed. "I, uhm, have no idea if that's done in vitro or in utero, but, uhm, I have no desire to see a goat fuck, and I extend cows the same courtesy."

Rory almost choked on his own tongue. "You little shit," he said, laughing at his new working partner. "You had me thinking you had no sense of humor about this at all."

Val was holding his hand up to his mouth to hide his grin, but the subtle shake of his shoulders—not to mention the relaxation of the tension in his forehead and the crinkles at the corners of his dark hazel eyes—gave him away.

"Yeah, yeah," he said with a sigh, dropping his hand and relaxing against the back of his chair. "I get it. A shipment full of bull jizz has the makings of high comedy." He sobered, although his scowl hadn't returned. "But I wasn't kidding the first time. It's a multimillion— perhaps *billion*-dollar industry, and my friend Vinnie, the guy in Texas, is *depending* on this shipment. He's trying to diversify his herd. He's got your standard Texas Longhorns, and he wants to make a Longhorn/ Limousin hybrid."

"Limousin?" Rory asked, intrigued. "That's a breed of cow?"

Val snorted. "It's got a—" He closed his eyes. "—a lower proportion of fat and bone, I guess? So, you know. One cow, more juicy meat. And longhorns are good, but mixing that up with a breed that does better free range, he can carve a niche in the boutique meat industry, I guess. You know, high-end restaurants, farm-to-table places. I mean, it's not Wagyu beef, but it's cheaper, and it's got the, you know, *novelty* thing going, and once people realize it tastes good...."

"He could increase his profit margin by a lot," Rory agreed.

"He could. But…." Val shook his head. "It should have been an easy thing, you know? Vinnie's smart. He proposed this business plan, he got backers, he insured the first shipment. And then somebody stole the shipment, detached the trailer from the rig while the driver was catching his mandatory shut-eye and left it out in the desert to rot. Vinnie got the insurance money, arranged for another shipment, and *this* one was sabotaged—again while the driver was asleep in the cab at a truck stop—and by the time the rig got to Texas…." He grimaced.

"Ew," Rory said succinctly.

"I mean, spoiled bull jizz. Yeah. That's gotta be a truly special cologne, you think?"

"You'd have to burn what you were wearing," Rory agreed emphatically. He touched the brim of his hat, sitting upside down on the desk next to him, for comfort. Hopefully it would never come to that, but, well, yuck.

"So," Val continued, "Vinnie calls me last week and offers me the contract. He's scraped together the last of his backers' money and insurance money, and he can't *get* this insured through the livestock investors after the last two tries. He had to take out a bond through *me* and…." Val shook his head, and Rory suddenly got it.

He'd seen the modest yard—ten trailers? He probably had four or five dedicated drivers with their own rigs. This was a *tightly* run operation.

"This could break you," he said softly.

"Or make me," Val agreed, just as serious. "We've secured loads for years, but nothing this expensive or with this sort of… *jinx* on it, you know? So yeah, this could bankrupt my company, or it could absolutely cement my reputation for small loads that absolutely positively must get to where they're going. But first…." He indicated Rory with two open palms, face up.

"I've got to come through," Rory said, understanding. "So, yeah, bull jizz is funny, but this job is no laughing matter."

Val nodded soberly, but then the corners of his mouth turned up. "Mr. McCauley—"

"Rory," Rory said, and had the thrill of watching Val swallow almost like a high school kid.

"Rory," Val repeated, that V in his forehead trying to make an appearance again. "If you met my brother Dean, you'll know my family has got a puckish sense of humor. My mother never could resist a dirty joke or an awful pun, and if nobody would laugh at it, she'd giggle at it herself. I *know* how to laugh at a truck full of bull semen, trust me. And if this job gets done, I will be telling that story at bars for free drinks—how bull come made me the man I am today."

Rory manfully blocked a snicker, and Val nodded appreciatively.

"But first, my best friend from high school is trying to save his family's business, and it sure does look like somebody's got it out for him. I promised. You just signed all the right paperwork to earn a hefty commission for this job. Please tell me you can help my friend make his fuckless cow dreams come true."

Rory *did* snicker then, but he'd stopped by the time he met Val's eyes and extended his hand over the desk. "I promise, Val. I won't let you down."

Val shook his hand firmly, and Rory, mindful that he could be asking for a broken jaw, didn't let go of that broad-palmed, blunt-fingered hand right away. Val tugged gently at his hand and swallowed again. "I appreciate it," he mumbled, and Rory kept hold.

"You want to appreciate it over a beer with me?" he asked, and Val grimaced, finally reclaiming his hand while looking gratifyingly regretful.

"I'm afraid not," he said. "Vinnie's herd needs to be fertilized in the next two weeks so he can make his production schedule. I've got tomorrow to get my shit together here at the yard so Stacy, my office manager, can take over for me while I'm gone, and odds are good we move out at six in the morning, the day after tomorrow. That means you and me leave *here* at four in the rig to go pick up their trailer, do the inspection, and take off. Son, I'm *booked*, and beer is not on my schedule."

Well, that was disappointing, but Rory was not easily dissuaded. "How about a burger, then," he said and crinkled his eyes at Val in a way that he'd used to charm both men and women his whole life—although usually it was the men who had followed him to bed. "Everybody needs to eat. C'mon, Val. What's that short for, anyway? Valerie? Valerian? Valiant?"

Val grunted. "Oh God. No. No. I'll have a burger with you, but I am *not* explaining the name thing."

Rory's eyebrows went up. "Now I'll take that as a challenge. Where we eating?"

Val seemed chagrined for a moment and then gave him directions from the main road in front of the business lot to—in his words—"the best burger joint in central California that nobody ever heard of" and promised to meet him there in half an hour.

"If I'm leaving the office," Val told him, "I need to lock up."

"I'll help," Rory said smoothly. Val had his cell number after all that paperwork, and Rory could sense an impending blow-off—or so he thought.

"It won't take a minute," Val said, rolling his eyes. "You got me, McCauley—"

"Rory."

"Rory. I'm on for dinner. I'm looking forward to it, even, just like I'm looking forward to my little house and a swim before bed and these *really soft* bamboo cotton sheets that my sister got everybody for Christmas. You have no idea. They get softer with every wash. If you want, order for me. I like their third-of-a-pound mushroom swiss burger, midrare, and a pitcher of root beer. You heard that right, don't give me shit. I promise I'll be there before it lands on the table."

Rory eyed him evenly. "I don't like broken promises," he said.

"Maybe order the fried pickles as an app, then," Val said. "That'll give me an extra five minutes."

Rory chuckled, relenting. "Fine. But if you don't show up, I'll be here at six in the morning tomorrow with your food for breakfast, and I'm making you eat every bite."

Val quirked one eyebrow with an uncomfortable sort of perception. "Don't worry, Rory—you're not the only one who can keep his word. Now shoo and let me get busy."

Rory did, heading back to his truck just as the wind swept the bare plain of Bakersfield, making Rory shiver a little. The April breeze was probably the last bit of cool left in the old dust bowl. Bakersfield from May through September was almost unrelentingly hot and dry, so Rory savored it and glanced around the trucking yard as he approached his vehicle. The place was clean and spare, surrounded with razor wire and designed to throw as much heat up as possible, like a lot of such places, but the gravel was clean and unlittered, and there were no oil spots or industrial spills to mar the tarmac. Rory caught the pale glint of sand near the repair bay, and realized that if there *were* mechanical spills, Val Royal took care of them before they were an eyesore.

It wasn't pretty—but then transportation and shipping often *wasn't*. Still it was the kind of place that showed pride and neatness and a certain sense of order.

Val Royal was probably a good boss. An exacting one, but a generous one. Once he'd let his scowl drop, Rory had enjoyed the man behind the stony front very much.

And he had *really* enjoyed watching Val shift in his seat as the air charged between them. Rory knew Dean was gay, and Dean had mentioned once that the gene had "thrown true" for most of his sibling pool. Hitting on Val Royal had been a risk, but a calculated one; the odds had been in Rory's favor, and even if he'd crapped out, he was pretty sure he wouldn't have gotten into too much trouble. He sure had called that puckish sense of humor right.

As Rory made his way toward a low-slung building on the outskirts of town, he got a whiff of brisket, and there was a trail of smoke coming over the top of the stained boards and flat roof that could only be a slow-cooker barbecue setup in the back.

There were places like this in Texas—often out in the middle of rolling fields. A slow cooker, a small kitchen, a generator for lights, some picnic tables, some pop-up tents in case of cloudbursts—or to fend off the merciless sun. Rory maintained some of the best food in the world was served under the diamond-studded skies of rural Texas, and this place… well, this place looked like a slice of home.

A part of him settled. This could be worth it even without the company, he thought happily, and went inside to stake out a table and place his order.

A draft, a root beer, and a basket of fried pickles had just arrived when Val walked in, wearing a worn denim jacket over his dark blue work polo. The waitress who had served Rory gave him a grin and a wink, and he nodded his chin to where Rory sat.

She nodded back, and he slid his fit body across from Rory's, giving a particularly decadent sigh as he took his first sip of root beer.

"You know," Rory said, taking a sip of his draft, "I thought that maybe the root beer thing was, like, your consolation prize. I had no idea you were really excited to drink that."

Val's smile was appreciative—and, Rory noticed, a little bit weary. "I could drink root beer twenty-four seven if it wasn't, you know, pure sugar and bad for my kidneys. So I drink water at work, but afterward?"

"A man likes to relax," Rory said, liking him more with every exchange.

"And still wake up in the morning," Val agreed. He took another reverent sip of root beer from the iced mug. The waitress had poured it out of a bottle—it appeared to be local brew, and Rory had to laugh at himself. He'd been thinking Val was kidding, had even anticipated him drinking with a sort of martyred sigh. But this was a *treat* for the man, and he'd let Rory be part of it, and Rory was impressed.

"So," he said, after one more sip, "what'd you order?"

"Brisket burger," Rory told him. "I hope the meat is as good as advertised—"

"Oh it is," Val said. "Sylvie, the waitress? She's married to a man who learned barbecue from his parents in Oklahoma. Some of the best I've ever had."

Rory grunted. "I am *offended* that it's not Texas," he said, and Val laughed at him.

"I know it. But you know us Hollywood types—we don't know good barbecue from vegan meatballs. You can always tell your Texas friends how sad it is out here."

Rory laughed, feeling a shaft of homesickness. "Yeah, I probably would if I ever planned on going back for more than a visit."

"I thought you liked Texas," Val said, looking surprised. "You certainly like to cowboy it up."

Rory shrugged. "There's a lot of stuff I like *about* Texas," he said after a moment. "But my business is here. My son is here. A lot of my old FBI contacts are in California."

"Like my brother?" Val asked.

"Yeah. God, he's a gifted little shit. One of the best marksmen with a pistol I've ever trained."

"Mm," Val said. "See, he doesn't tell the family that. Likes to pretend he got into the FBI for the paperwork. It's cute, really, because Mom still tells all her friends about her son the federal agent. She's so proud."

"She's not proud of all of you?" Rory asked, curious.

Val snorted. "Of course she is. My mom is like… like *the best*. We go to visit her and Dad on the weekends, right? As many of us as possible. And she's hoarded leftovers for the whole week, knowing we'll raid the fridge. She plans dinner Sunday knowing there will be at least two kids at her table, possibly more. And Dad is just as bad—saves stuff for us that we don't need. Television sets he finds in the neighborhood, furniture from friends giving it away. Laure took a collection for a rental space a couple years ago. We all put our junk from Dad in it, and then Laure had her two teenaged sons truck it all to the nearest swap meet and make their gas and car money for the following year. They've been doing that for three years. The youngest, who's graduating from high school, is buying himself a used SUV for college. It's *amazing*."

Rory was laughing by the time he was through. "Does your dad know?" he asked.

"Mom does," Val confessed. "She said it was a good system, and she was proud of Laure's boys and told us to carry on."

Rory laughed some more. "Dean used to tell family stories too. I swear it makes me want to meet them."

Val shrugged and dipped a pickle fry in some ranch before taking a bite. "Our folks are good people," he said after chewing. "Not perfect. I'm sure every one of us has an 'Oh my God, *Mom*! or *Dad*!' story. I think Dad actually chewed Prock out for bringing home a girlfriend and not telling him. He was like, 'I don't know why gay is the normal for my sons, but it is, and I just would have liked a little warning is all.'"

Rory burst out laughing, and Val nodded, munching another fry.

"You see what I'm saying? We've been trying to figure out for *years* whether that was appropriate or not. Vote's still out, but since this is the man who bought my brother Sal guyliner for his prom on the way home from his factory job, we're going to give him a pass."

"I love the man already," Rory said mildly, wiping out the last of the pickle fries with some help from the ranch dressing on the side. "My mom… I hope she would have been accommodating."

Val raised his eyebrows. "Of what?" he asked, except the waitress showed up at that moment with a plate for each of them with two of the biggest burgers Rory had ever seen.

Rory, who'd had coffee for breakfast and skipped lunch so he could drive from his last gig in LA to this one in Bakersfield, suddenly lost the thread of the conversation as he tumbled headfirst into the siren song of brisket and cheese and mushrooms and….

He came up for air—with half the burger still in his hands and a sort of blissful haze of food saturation filling his bones—when Val ordered another root beer for himself and a to-go box.

"You're leaving me?" Rory blurted after he'd swallowed his current mouthful and wiped his mouth.

Val snorted. "No, I'm taking this home for breakfast. My God, you can eat." His laughter subsided, and his eyes crinkled warmly in the corners. Rory was really starting to like that. "Been a while?" he asked kindly.

Rory nodded, a little embarrassed. As much as this wasn't *supposed* to be a date, he'd been hoping to charm the man across from him, and it was hard to do that when you were shoving half a cow down your maw.

"Finished a job down in Burbank this morning," he said. "Got your sister's call and drove out before lunch."

Val nodded. "Well, I appreciate it." He looked vaguely uncomfortable. "You cannot read a damned thing into my next question. Do you have a place to stay?"

Rory nodded. "Oh yeah. My place is outside of McFarland. It's less than an hour away, and the gun club my son and I run is about fifteen minutes from there, in traffic. I'll get home just fine, don't you worry."

"Glad to hear it," Val said.

And now that Rory was down to eating like a human and indulging in some conversation, he said, "So, uhm, what was your alternative if I wasn't close?"

"A guest room," Val said. "I've got a three-bedroom house in a little residential neighborhood nearby. Frankly, Laure found it for me and *made* me get a house with a spare bedroom and a den. She seemed to think I'd have siblings galore staying in fucking Bakersfield to be with me."

Rory chuckled again; it seemed as if Val's company was like fungus, because it grew and grew and grew on him. "Do you?" he asked.

"Yeah," Val muttered. "I have no idea why. I mean… *why*? Not that we don't all live in California, but why? Why would they *choose* to stop through Bakersfield?"

Rory took a guess. "Because they have a big brother who isn't as grumpy as he pretends to be?"

"I blame the pool," Val said with disgust. "Now that it's raining again, the thing is full, and I can't seem to shake my relatives."

"You have a *pool*?" Rory said, batting his eyelashes like the ingenue he never had been. "Oh, then I take it back. I'm going home with *you*, cowboy, and you'll have to haul me out of the pool with a *backhoe*."

Val cackled. "See? I told you it wasn't my winning personality!"

At that moment the waitress brought Val the check, which he took care of so smoothly Rory was caught by surprise. He was starting to realize that Val's grumpy persona was just that—a way to keep people from seeing the protective gentleman underneath.

"Nicely done," Rory said with approval after she'd left to run Val's card and collect his to-go order. "Do I get a chance to return the favor?"

Val regarded him with an expression that was surprisingly serious.

"This was for driving straight up when my family asked you," he said with a nod of his chin that indicated dinner. "Like I said, it's appreciated. If Dean and Laure vouch for you, your security services are much needed."

"And my shameless attempts to hit on you?"

Val's eyes narrowed. "Well, that depends," he said. "On how serious you are with those."

"I wouldn't have done it if I didn't think you were mighty tasty," Rory said, feeling a little stung.

Val shrugged. "Yeah, but maybe I'm searching for courtship, not a hookup."

"Who says I'm not?" Rory asked, now feeling a *lot* stung.

But Val didn't take offense. "Nobody," he said mildly. "I'm just thinking that if you *really* were looking for a real thing, this whole conversation wouldn't have been about me, or my family, or even my pool. I got some stories to tell—and I got no problem with that. But I don't sleep with strangers, Rory McCauley, no matter how good a game they talk."

Rory was still gaping at him when the waitress came back by with Val's boxed leftovers, including a small box of what appeared to be dessert in the bag.

"Thank you, darlin'. Make sure you get my friend his own slice of peach crumble, y'hear?"

"'Course, Val," she said with a flirty wink. The woman was in her late forties, with bleached hair and lots of black makeup around the eyes and, Rory noticed, wide hips and a chest that would make a straight man look twice. When Val winked back, Rory got the distinct impression it was because they were friends and not because she was hitting on him, and Rory was suddenly jealous.

Apparently he'd failed the first test to cross the bridge into Val Royal's inner circle, and he wasn't sure whether to be mad at himself for not seeing the openings Val had given or dismissive of Val's apparent acid test for a lover. Rory was a first-rate bedmate, if he said so himself, and as a friend and colleague he had been known as a stand-up guy. How important *were* his innermost thoughts anyway?

"See you next time, Sylvie," Val said before turning back to Rory. "I'll see *you* at the lot, four o'clock sharp, morning after tomorrow. I'll have plain coffee in a giant thermos, but I do not object to something with caramel, ice, and a whole lot of sugar if you're driving by one of those places. I'll leave it up to you."

"I'll see you there," Rory said, thinking he'd have a *case* of the biggest coffee frappes the world had ever seen.

Val's lips were doing that quirking thing in the corners again that indicated amusement, and he took a step to turn away.

"Val," Rory added, suddenly irritated at himself for giving up so quickly.

"Yeah?"

"I wouldn't have spent *all* the time in the pool," he said, his own smile playing with the corners of his mouth.

"Think a lot of yourself, do you?" Val asked and then laughed in response to his own question before turning away and heading for the door.

Rory resisted the urge to bang his head softly against the table before turning determinedly to his last few bites of burger. As he chewed steadily and swallowed, he was aware of the persistent throbbing in his groin and the way his cock had swelled up against the inseam of his jeans.

Well, shit.

He had two days there, two days' rest, and two days back to convince Val that even a one-night stand with Rory McCauley was worth the effort.

Either that or be convinced that a many-night stand with Val Royal was worth risking his own damned heart.

"Here you go, hon," said Sylvie, breaking him out of his moody thoughts.

He looked up, took the bag holding the boxed cobbler from her, and smiled. "Why thank you, Miss Sylvie. This was kind."

Her eyebrows went up. "Oh no, hon. This wasn't kind. This was the same brush-off I've seen Val Royal give a dozen times before." She shrugged. "For some reason he seems to think the dessert will make it go down sweeter."

Rory felt his eyes narrow and his gaze go flat and calculating. "Oh does he?" he asked.

"Mm-hmm," she said. "But you know, I think that's because none of those other guys were smart enough to know the secret to his heart."

"You gonna tell me, darlin'?" he asked, thinking it couldn't be that easy.

"Well, since I've got my own man, I don't know everything," she said, "but I do know it involves not being so taken with food that you forget your end of the conversation."

Rory all but groaned, because she had him there.

"I'll remember that," he said earnestly.

"You do that," she replied. "You might also remember he comes from a big, tight-knit family that believes in happy ever after. You don't get that by being an island, hon." She cracked her gum and winked. "And don't worry about a tip. Tonight that's my job."

And with that she swung around and va-va-voomed off, leaving Rory with a full stomach, dessert to go, and the feeling that he'd somehow irrevocably blown off a good thing.

Oh, he had not counted on this in the *least*.


"So," ANTHONY said the next morning as he flipped Rory's veggie omelet. "You had a brisket burger without me?"

"It was some of the best barbecue I've had outside of Texas," Rory praised, knowing it would make his son jealous—and maybe it would make him stop at the place, now that he knew it existed. Anthony looked a lot like Rory—almost as tall, longish brown hair, hazel eyes developing their own crinkles, and a small, almost pretty, nose. But he was uniquely Californian about food. He wanted to try *everything*.

"So you didn't bring me any is what I'm saying," Anthony needled before plating Rory's food and setting it on the table in front of him with ketchup and sriracha because some things just *were*.

"Sorry, son," Rory told him, diving into the gruyere, chive, and mushroom omelet with glee. "Someone else picked up the tab. It didn't feel gentlemanly to ask for another burger." But he *had* brought his son the peach cobbler, which was why Anthony had been on for breakfast.

"Ooh, did you get lucky?" Anthony asked, getting to work on his own breakfast. His had ham and tomatoes in it.

Rory grunted. "Sadly, no."

"You got shot down?" Anthony asked, and although he sounded gratifyingly surprised, the next bite of omelet went down hard. Rory hadn't realized that even his *son* thought he was a player.

"Not completely," Rory defended. "He's a busy guy with a lot to do before the haul to Austin is all." Sure it *sounded* good, but Rory was still a little stung by the thought that Val took guys to the burger place all the time to let them down easy.

Anthony regarded him steadily as he savored his breakfast. "There is…." He frowned, and Rory got a shiver of embarrassment. Rory's son had always held the empathy gene—it had surprised Rory, because his mother had been, like, able to see into his heart even when he was at his absolute worst as an adolescent. Anthony's mother, Connie, was a nice woman—the best—but this extra little sense of what a person was feeling? That was all Rory's mama.

"There's what?" Rory asked, trying not to be defensive.

"This is the guy you're working for, right?"

Rory felt a blush coming on. "Yeah, he's the one with the contract. Val."

"Mm. You like this guy," Anthony said, cocking his head. "You said that. Said he'd be easy to work for, smart, fair, even a little fun. And you're put off because he didn't invite you home?"

Rory shrugged. "He's just looking for something long-term is all," he said.

Anthony blinked. "And that's… bad?"

Oh, how embarrassing. "Tony—"

"Don't 'Tony' me like I'm twelve, Dad. You're the one who seems to think one-and-done is the be-all and end-all of your existence."

"I'm not the settling down type!" Rory protested. "You know that!"

"You mean besides the settling down you've done my entire life? Your house being half a mile from Mom's until I hit college? That wasn't settling down? You coming to dinner once a week when you weren't on assignment—that wasn't settling down? Jesus, Dad. You and Mom have worked for twenty-five years to make my life 'settled' and happy. You can't take a little of that for yourself?"

Rory scowled at him. "You are *ruining* my *omelet*," he complained. "Do you know how hard it is to find this cheese in the damned supermarket nearby?"

Anthony scowled back. "It's like living with a fifth-grader," he announced. "Go ahead, enjoy your omelet. But if this guy gives you another chance—this smart, fair, funny guy—I think maybe you should take it." Anthony took another bite and chewed in the silence. "Unless he's a troll," he said thoughtfully. "I mean, I don't want a stepdad who's a troll."

"That's not very enlightened of you," Rory retorted, pouting because his grown son might very well be more mature than he was.

Anthony raised his eyebrows in challenge, and Rory had to concede the point.

"He's not a troll," he mumbled, taking another bite and savoring.

Anthony kept up his quiet regard.

"He's about forty, and he's really frickin' cute," Rory admitted through a full mouth. He swallowed. "I mean…." Rory sighed. "Yeah. He's a snack, as you young people say."

"Well, if he's looking for settling down, he's apparently the full meal," Anthony said mildly. "Got any plans to redeem yourself?"

"June's place still open at gawdawful a.m.?"

Anthony had dated June's son for a while, and then he'd moved on to a young woman who'd been on summer break from a school down south. Unlike Rory, his son liked women and men equally—and didn't mind looking for a long-term thing. But Anthony was picky, and he had a quiet string of happy exes, cheering him on to true love.

"For coffee and breakfast sandwiches? Yeah," Anthony said.

"You got the app for the place? I think Val's got a weakness," Rory admitted, already thinking ahead.

"That's the stuff, Dad." Anthony pulled out his phone. "Let's git 'er done."

Rory regarded him with narrowed eyes even as his phone buzzed. "Are you trying to get rid of me?" he asked suspiciously.

Anthony rolled his eyes. "Look, one of the best features about this guy is he's less than half an hour away. I could both have the house to myself *and* see my beloved father figure on a regular basis."

Rory laughed—he had to. "So yes, but with love."

"Lots of love," Anthony reassured him. "Now finish up. We both have lessons to give today."

Rory did as ordered, because Anthony was right. Rory reserved two days a week to give shooting lessons to their best clients. His word was a cornerstone of their business.

But he did make a little bit of time to order a coffee-drink breakfast of champions from McFarland's best coffee shop. Val Royal was looking more and more worth it.

# Miles of Lonesome Road

"Oh my God," Val muttered as he got home the next day. It was late—well, five o'clock, but since he was getting up at 3:00 a.m., it was late enough. He had just enough in him to raid his refrigerator, drink the last of his milk, and feed his fish so Laure's oldest, Shaw, could take care of them in two days. Shaw and his brother Russell had become the family's go-tos for housesitting. They were smart, resourceful, trustworthy, and Laure hadn't been able to afford the pool when she'd bought *their* house, so they were always really good at taking care of that and using it responsibly.

Yes, Val loved his family, but as he pulled up to his house and saw Laure's indigo minivan in the driveway, he couldn't help but wish they loved him just a little bit *less*.

Then he hit the top step of his porch, the smell of Laure's homemade spaghetti sauce hit him, and he took it all back.

When he got inside, Laure was in the kitchen, doing what she did best. Their mother was an okay cook, and since Laure and Val had been the oldest, they'd divvied up the chores, and Laure had ended up responsible for dinner more often than not while Val occupied the younger children. Laure, being the classic overachiever she was, had started looking up actual recipes and requesting ingredients from their mother, since she'd worked at a grocery store for most of their lives, and now there wasn't any dish Laure couldn't whip up from scratch in fifteen minutes from the rock-bottom contents of any sibling's refrigerator—with the help of a canvas tote full of spices they'd come to refer to as "Laure's go-bag."

Reg was also in the kitchen, sitting at the already set table and doing something mysterious and purposeful on his laptop. Both of them looked up when he walked in, and Laure gestured him to sit.

"You texted you had to be at the lot at three in the morning," she said, "which is ungodly awful, and since the boys were both at a movie, I figured me and Reg could make you some dinner, Russell and Shaw would have leftovers to eat when they're here, and you could go to bed a little north of ungodly awful and south of 'I'm starving but too tired to eat.'"

Val laughed a little, because his sister charmed him—had charmed him, in fact, since the moment she'd been born. Maybe it was because she was the only girl, and maybe it was because her default mood was purposeful and bright, but he'd always treasured her, even when they were coconspirators in trying to rein in Sal—who had been an unholy terror from day one—and Dean. Dean had really been unfair, Val often thought resentfully. Prock-the-bucolic had come along after Sal, and the whole family had let out a giant sigh of relief, thinking, *Oh, hey, at least the worst is past*! They hadn't counted on Dean and his absolutely genius daredevil brain. Nor on the demonic alliance forged between him and Sal to thwart the two older siblings and their "gross dedication to the rule of law." (Sal, holy heaven. Sal had nearly killed them all.)

"It's appreciated," he said fondly. "Heya, Reg, whatcha doing?"

Reg looked up in a sort of surprised haze, as though he had no idea why anybody would notice *him* of all people. Val tried not to swallow against a tightness in his throat. Damn. Reg had always been the quiet one. Maybe it was because he came right after Dean, who'd been so damned brilliant, and right before Chance, who'd been the glorious sunshine child all families wanted for their youngest, but Reg had always been quiet, the good child, the planner. Once when Reg and Chance had both come down with a terrible fever, their mother had taken both children to the doctor. Chance had two infected ears, which they'd all rather suspected because he'd whimpered inconsolably the night before, but Reg? Reg's ears had been infected, but he'd also had pneumonia and had been well on his way to congestive heart failure.

He hadn't complained once—not *once*—but after he'd been admitted to the hospital, he *had* directed his mother to tell Val to find his school notebook. He'd written something in there he needed Val to see.

It had been his *will*, and he'd been *seven*. Laure had found Val weeping in the younger kids' room, had read the painfully neat penciled printing, and had fallen apart on him. It was one of those memories children didn't tell their parents—or even other children in the family— but Val knew for certain he and Laure had always kept a special eye out on Reg after that. Of a family of rampant extroverts, Reg was the kid who wouldn't speak up for himself, the one who would give away his last toy to his little brother and read a book instead.

Reg may have thought he wasn't noticed, or that he'd been lost in the shadows cast by his little brother's sunshine, but Laure and Val knew who he was, and they would *never* not worry. Val may not have had any children, but he did know what it was to leave your heart absolutely vulnerable to another creature on this earth who might accidentally rip it out, and when his little brother gave him that dreamy, surprised smile, he knew the risk was worth it.

"I'm trying to compute how much those two missing shipments of product were worth," Reg said. He wore wire-frame glasses, and he took them off now and blew on them, then polished them on his microfiber T-shirt like he probably was *not* supposed to be doing. "I think it's… strange. It's very strange that two shipments of such a specialized item would be taken and left to rot. Val, are you sure you *have* to make this run?"

Val regarded his brother thoughtfully. While not the whipcrack Dean was, Reg had a way of thinking ahead, of anticipating what was going to happen. That will he'd written when he'd been seven had come about because Reg had felt ill at school the day before, and had thought that perhaps some planning would be a good idea. He knew Chance wanted his favorite Matchbox car—a truck—but Reg thought it should go to Val because by then he'd been planning to drive one for a living.

"I do," he said. "You know Vinnie and his family. They're depending on me."

Reg nodded. "I'm going to research some other breeding stock Vinnie could use, just in case this goes sour. And I'll email him to have the lab and the genetic testing ready—maybe even research some extras." He shook his head, his brow, which should have been smooth as silk at twenty-six, puckering in concern. "I'm not okay with this. Stay alert, Val. I've got a feeling."

"I've learned to trust your feelings," Val said soberly. "I'll keep my eyes peeled. And definitely pass your ideas on to Vinnie, and to Dean too."

"Why Dean?" Laure asked curiously as she put tossed pasta in a serving bowl. "Reg, can you get the salad from the fridge?"

"Does it have craisins in it?" Val asked, knowing he sounded like a little kid and not caring. Laure really *could* make the ordinary extraordinary. She and Larry had been poor and young—and so happy. They had *not* counted on his stint in the military to earn money for college to cost him his life.

"Go stash that stuff in your arms and come see," Laure teased, and Val darted back to his bedroom to put together a load of laundry for the trip in the morning. By the time he came back out—washed, barefoot, and bearing a basket to put in the washer in the garage—Laure and Reg had the table set completely, and he hurried to start the load before coming to sit down.

Dinner conversation was light and fun. Sal had made sure he had help in June so he could come from Grass Valley, where he ran an art and antique shop, to attend the big family picnic right after Russell's graduation ceremony. Russell had finally chosen a college, and all the siblings had made a commitment to help him pay for it. The kid's grades were good enough, and he'd been one of his high school's best soccer players, so he'd gotten scholarships, but nobody got a free ride anymore.

They talked about Chance studying for his finals, which he took very seriously; Reg's quietly run graphic-arts business, which supplied everything from independent book covers to fully branded logo packs and beyond; and Laure's newest headhunting clients and how she needed to headhunt for her own staff because she *really* needed help.

Somewhere in there, Laure asked him one or two questions about Dean's good buddy and security expert, Rory McCauley.

"He was okay," Val said, remembering the man's self-confident saunter across his parking lot. "Thinks a lot of himself."

"For good reason?" Reg asked, trying hard to keep spaghetti off his chest.

"Oh yeah. Confident and competent—I'm putting money on it. And he does speak well of Dean." Of course, the one way to get the Royals' attention was to praise one of the siblings.

"What about cute?" Reg asked, and Val glanced at him sharply.

"This is not a pleasure cruise," he said, irritated all over again at Rory's smooth assumptions. He let out a breath and tried not to jump down Reg's throat. "Besides, he only wants a hookup. I'm too old for that shit."

"I'm not," Reg said wistfully.

"You're too young," Laure told him with a meaningful look. "And besides, Reg, you're not really built for a one-and-done."

"At this point, I'd settle for a *one*," Reg grumbled, and Val and Laure met sympathetic eyes over the table, because Chance, they suspected, had known at least one boyfriend, but Reg, they were both pretty sure, hadn't had one yet, although he'd been known to quietly pine after a few unavailable men.

"It has to be the right one," Val said. "And thank your lucky stars you're smart enough to not do the revolving door bullshit. Nobody wants to hit forty and realize they're all alone."

And reluctantly he thought of Rory, who was actually older than he was. Had it occurred to Rory that there was more to life than hookups?

Conversation continued on, although Val was left with a wee niggling suspicion about Rory's placement as his shotgun for this trip, and Val finally had to concede defeat and admit he could *not* eat three portions of pasta, as he had when he and Laure had been younger.

But he *might* have room for whipped cream and fruit… for dessert reasons.

When dinner was done, they both chivvied Val to go shower and pack for his trip while they cleaned up. Val bid them good night right when he'd started to yawn, and Laure laughed softly, because it was barely six thirty.

"Be safe," she said after their hug. "Reg and I will do some research and forward it to Dean—he said he'd be near Austin, didn't he?"

"Yeah," Val remembered. "I have no idea what for."

He hugged Reg, who said, "Don't forget pictures of the sky," and Val promised to do that. It was a custom their father had started when he'd taken up trucking with Val as his shotgun, and Chance, Reg, and Dean had missed the two of them when they were on long trips. Val had kept it up, and even though his brothers were all grown, whenever one of them was anywhere but Bakersfield, they all sent each other "somewhere else sky"—even Sal, who had been too old for the game in the first place.

They left, and Val closed the door behind him and toddled off to bed, making sure to turn off his lights and set his alarm nice and loud for Ungodly Awful a.m., as Laure called it. As he closed his eyes in sleep, he remembered the mention of Rory McCauley over dinner again, and chuckled to himself.

Oh yeah. Those assholes had totally sicced McCauley on Val, hoping the two would get together.

Val smiled as he drifted off. God love them all.


RORY MCCAULEY may have been skirting around revealing anything personal when they were at dinner, but apparently he *could* take instructions well. He showed up at the truck lot with two *giant* and *fresh* iced coffees, as well as a bag of chicken-and-waffle sandwiches.

Val had been there for the past hour, powering up the rig, double-checking his hitches and air hoses and generally making sure they could take off and safely hook up the cargo the minute McCauley showed up.

He had to admit that the breakfast sandwiches and sweet iced coffees went a long way to assuaging any doubts Val might have had about the man's company for the next six days. He may not have been ready to *sleep* with the guy, but he was pretty sure they could transport cargo without killing each other.

"Gracias," he said, taking a deep pull on the straw. "Let me show you where to stow your gear."

Val's rig was not a luxury apartment on wheels—and yes, he'd spent some time checking those out and dreaming—but it *was* comfortable. It featured a sleeper that doubled as a couch with storage space underneath, secure cabinets on either end, one for clothes, one for groceries, with a minifridge with lots of water and sodas in addition to several sandwich wraps for the next two days. It also sported net pockets attached to the back of the passenger seat where he stashed his clean laundry. He changed the sheets after every trip—if it was longer than a week or two, he'd stop at a laundromat—and had some cleaner for spills and to generally freshen the place up. Now that he owned the business, he wasn't gone as long as he used to be, but this was still a place where he slept, ate… lived. There was a flat-screen television that folded out from behind the driver's seat, and he had a modest satellite hookup on the roof to guarantee him streaming services so he never missed an episode of his cop shows if he could help it. Generally? The space was clean, neat, and even a little bit colorful, thanks to the brightly colored cartoon-themed curtains, cushion covers, and comforter his mom had sewn to celebrate the day he was able to afford his own rig. There was even a small toilet, which he scrupulously maintained and cleaned, wedged at the foot and slightly behind the bed.

"The passenger cupboard should hold your knapsack," he told Rory after giving the man a hand up into the interior. "You can stow your guns and ordnance under the bed—there's a lockbox for it if you like." He paused. "I mean, I assume you're not going to travel with it over your knees, Wells Fargo pony style."

Rory chuckled. "Nope. The lockbox will be fine. Do you have a security board?"

Val grimaced. "That depends on the load we'll be hooking up from the cattle place. It's going to be small—a twenty-eight-foot trailer, and most of the inside is refrigerator components—but hopefully it's got some alarm technology in the back. Otherwise I've got some soccer chairs under the bed that are going to come in mighty useful for guarding the payload."

"So you say. From what you've described, we're driving straight through."

"Ugh. Man, there's *got* to be some grass-touching and moving the body. I mean, when I was younger, I could do it straight through, but staying in a truck cab for twenty-four hours straight can *break* you. No, that's another reason for a seatmate. This way we can both get some exercise in while never leaving the payload alone." He gave a rather apologetic shrug. "I know that's not the conventional business model. It's why loads like this—don't laugh, I didn't mean the pun— are so important. Providing security for a reasonable-sized payload is a boutique service, but it also lets me pay my drivers enough to take care of themselves while they work. One more lousy hour isn't going to make or break most deliveries, but time to sleep or eat or run around for a minute, or hell, even take a piss that's not in a bottle, can make or break a driver."

Rory nodded. "It probably gets harder and harder to do when your competition is going through drivers like Kleenex."

Val nodded, appreciating the acknowledgment. "Two of my guys signed on with me expecting to be ground into the pavement. While the pay is slightly lower than they were making at the other places, they stay with me because—as one of them says—I don't work them into kidney infections and exploding varicose veins."

"Good for you," Rory told him. Then with a wink, "It's no more than I expected from Dean Royal's big brother, but don't tell him I said that."

"Big head?" Val asked, because he *knew* his little brother.

"Arrogant little shit," Rory confirmed. "I mean *good*, but cocky as hell."

It was Val's turn to chuckle. "That's my boy," he said smugly. "So set up your gear, use the bathroom in the trailer one more time cause it's bigger, and let's be on our way."

"I can do that," Rory said. Then he grinned. "And you're welcome for breakfast."

Val caught his glance and knew he was getting a little back for when Val took care of dinner without asking. "That was kind," he conceded.

"No," Rory said, and his intent was clear. "Not kind. Pure calculation on my part."

Val rolled his eyes and fought off the speeding pulse, because yes, he was pleased that Rory was still trying. "It takes more than chicken and waffles to make me put out, sir."

Rory's laugh was positively filthy. "You haven't tasted the sandwiches yet. For all you know, they're magical sex chicken and waffles, and I'll get my knob waxed on the way."

Val had to swallow against the image, him on his knees in front of Rory's long, rangy body. Or that long, rangy body bent over while Val pounded into it.

Or, well, the other way around.

"No breakfast sandwiches are that good," he said, feigning a confidence he didn't feel. Hell, at this point he was so primed, all he needed was a crude come-on.

"Wait until we're on our way," Rory said mildly, "and tell me then."


TWENTY MINUTES later Val's giant diesel folly (as Sal was fond of calling it) rumbled up Highway 5 to the turnoff to the east where Elite Cattle Company had most of its grazing land, slaughterhouse, and insemination labs. As they pulled off the road, Val tried not to glance around and ponder, but he couldn't help it.

"This place seem… well, un-Elite to you?"

Rory grunted. The grass was green, and the cows were well fed; that wasn't the problem. But the fencing was substandard razor wire, in some places shored up with PVC pipe, and Val didn't know why the cows—the *giant* cows—weren't out wandering the road. The feeding barn appeared dilapidated, the roof sloping in the middle. The hay racks were mostly empty, and the laboratory building they were headed for was a low-slung cinder-block building that didn't look like it could air-condition itself, much less house the refrigerated units of product that should have been loaded into the trailer by now.

"Well, I'd say you were distracting me from how much you liked that sandwich," Rory drawled, "but yeah. I'd have to agree with you."

He glanced around unhappily. "The cows are… well, *fat*. And sort of… weird. Boneless. Like, you know, they were bred without bones in their legs. But healthy. But the facilities… no."

"I was hoping it was a trick of the light," Val muttered, which should have been the reason since dawn was breaking over the horizon, and the gray ambience did serve to make the old outbuildings particularly… grayish.

"Are you sure your friend sent you to the right place?" Rory asked, doubt in his voice. "I mean—"

"Their trailer is rusty," Val muttered in disgust. "Oh Jesus. I'm going to have to be all over this thing in inspection." He cast Rory a sideways glance. "You wouldn't want to do me a favor, would you?"

Rory's return nod held what Dean had told him was twenty years of a solid career in law enforcement. "Let you distract the paper pushers with being picky and shit while I take video?"

Val took his hand off the jouncing wheel of the rig for a moment to touch his finger to his nose. "That would be awesome," he said. "I do not have a good feeling about this."

Rory nodded, and Val wondered if he'd be willing to use some of his resources to look into this operation. Sure, all Val was supposed to do was take the shipment from point A to point B, but given all the trouble they'd had already—and the shady feel of the place—Val was agreeing with Reg and wondering if there was more than bad luck involved in Vinnie's misfortune.

He felt his face go grim and angry as he thought of his friend getting cheated, and next to him, Rory cleared his throat meaningfully.

"You cannot look at these people like that," he said, "or they will think you're suspicious."

"But I *am* suspicious," Val retorted. "Look at this place. I can't believe cows conceive here in a quick fuck against the wall, much less in a test tube with insemination. I can't believe the cows that come out of this place are worth *eating*."

Rory grunted. "I know that." He gestured toward an outbuilding that should have been their dairy, but instead of cows lined up neatly in their stalls, twisted pipes and broken equipment were clearly visible from the road. "There is something *very* hinky about this. But your friend has a lab, didn't you say that?"

"He said it," Val replied. "He needs it to inspect the product, inseminate the embryos, and then implant them in the wombs." He didn't mention the part about Reg looking up independent labs yet, but given the state of this place, he thought it more and more likely one would be needed.

"Romantic," Rory said dryly. "But the point is, *he* can inspect the product, and if there's a problem with it, we can get the USDA involved and the FBI fraud division and all sorts of people who could shut this place down. But all we are—*all* we are—is transport. So let's transport and then take care of whatever it is we're transporting."

Val grunted, because it made sense.

"And the part about me not looking like an asshole?" he muttered.

"You want them to *like* us. Nothing to see here, folks. Just an ignorant trucker and his cowpoke security. For fucks sake, Val, *I* know you're a smart guy, but how hard is it to play friendly and dumb?"

So hard. Rory had no idea how hard it would be. He and his family had spent their *entire lives* living up not only to the name *Royal* but to their ridiculous first names and the super hopeful expectations set on their shoulders by their well-meaning, slightly goofy, and a little out of touch parents. When you were born with a name like Val's, you spent your entire life on the playground proving to the world that book smart was not the only kind of smart, and it didn't matter how brilliant your peers thought *they* were, you were still quicker, tougher, and meaner.

And yes, goddammit, *smarter*.

But as they continued down the rutted dirt road, Val got a good gander at one of the cows behind the barbed wire, and while the cow was fat and glowing with health, there was a sort of… hollowness to the creature, a sort of resignation there, and Val wondered suddenly how much of that cow's meat was genetics and good food, and how much was steroids and sugar.

And suddenly he wanted very much to see if these people were doing right by his friend.

"Nothing to see here, folks," Val said, affecting "dumb country boy" like that's who he was born to be. "Just a dumb trucker, getting his load and not asking no questions, all in a day's work."

"That's my boy," Rory mumbled. "That'll keep us up to our assholes in chicken-and-waffle sandwiches."

Val grunted. "Yeah, I'm still not putting out for one."

Rory's low chuckle was enough to shore up his resolve. "You let me know the secret, son," he said, "and I'll buy a whole whack of it for ya."

And Val wanted to tell this man that all he asked for was a little bit of honesty, some openness, some emotional exchange. It wasn't that Val hadn't *had* one-night stands, but that's not what he was looking for now, and if you didn't go into something as emotional equals, how were you going to make a relationship work?

But he was coming to the trailer lot and could see *his* trailer, landing gear down and ready for him to back into the hitch and lock it, and *now* was not the time.

"Any sex that comes in a paper bag, old man, is not the sex I want to be having," he returned under his breath, and then, very carefully, he went into positioning the cab so all he'd need to do was back the king pin under the jaws to hitch the rusty trailer.

He fixed the brake and left the truck idling before swinging down out of the seat and using the step to the ground. When he got there, he strode back toward the trailer hookup to check things out.

What he saw made him frown.

"That bad?" Rory asked, when he'd walked around to join Val.

"No," Val muttered. "That good. The trailer itself looks like crap, but I'm not HVAC certified. The couplings—the shit *I* could complain about—are in perfect working order. I need to check the manifest to see what I'm signing off on."

"What do you mean?"

Val gave a snort of frustration. "Vinnie insisted on my services. If he didn't specify the condition of the truck, he could be liable if I don't pick up the contents."

Rory let out a low growl. "What are you going to do?"

Val took out his phone. "So happens," he muttered, "I've got a brother for that."

And with that, he started to text Prock.

Goddess bless his brother. Prock lived in Visalia, which meant he could be waiting for them at the nearest rest stop with everything he'd need to keep the refrigeration unit in the back running—including duct tape. Just in case. Just in case this rattletrap of a trailer looked like it wasn't going to do its job.

"Hi, yes," said a pleasant voice coming from the back of the trailer. "Can I help you?"

"I'm Val Royal. I'm here to pick up the delivery for Vinnie Aiello?" Val peered frantically around, trying to find the owner of the voice, and finally a figure appeared from behind the trailer.

A very *lithe*, very *female* figure, Val could see, and he raised his eyebrows as the woman—barely that, maybe twenty-one at the outside—sauntered down the trailer line with her hands in her back pockets and her chest thrust out.

Val raised his eyebrows and then stared the woman in the eyes. "Do you have the contract I need to sign?" he asked, out of patience. God, basic courtesy dictated somebody be out there to greet him from the get-go.

"Uhm, yes," she said, cheeks coloring. She reached into her back pocket and pulled out a tablet, scrolled quickly until she found the right page, and then handed it to him. "I'm, uhm, Violet Cassidy, the, uhm, daughter of the owners."

"I'm Val Royal," he answered, not paying attention to *her* in the least. Scowling, he went back and actually *read* the contract. "And I'm not signing this."

She actually squeaked. "I'm sorry?"

"This contract calls for payment upon pickup. That's not what Vinnie negotiated. He *showed* me the contract. He pays you after the product is delivered and he's had a chance to have his own techs analyze the product and make sure it's viable. And I haven't checked out the refrigeration units in the trailer. For all I know there's a nasty come-stew in there that will bankrupt my friend and cause me to have to burn my clothes. If you'll excuse me, I'm going to at *least* check on what's in the trailer."

Violet Cassidy gasped a little, and Val moved to the back, where Rory had already opened the trailer doors and lowered the gate. After one last check to make sure the landing gear was on the ground and he and Rory weren't going to get dumped on their asses when they walked inside the compartment, Val moved in.

It was supposed to be a walk-in refrigerator with a lockbox freezer filled with cryogenic containers of straws to be used to inseminate the cows. Vinnie had said something about the straws fitting into "guns," and frankly, Val was peacing out of the rest of that conversation. But what Val *did* know was that the sperm had to be either refrigerated *or* frozen. *This* batch was *frozen*—there was no appreciable difference in fertilization rates—and the tanks had to be maintained externally at a certain temperature. Basically, there were a bunch of cryotubes keeping the spermcicles frozen, packed inside a big cold space to help them function.

Val glanced around the refrigerator, which did not seem that cold at *all*, and then checked out the controls on the freezer tanks, which actually *did* register the correct temp. But he could hear the freezer compressor wheezing like an asthmatic goat and wondered how long before the refrigerator went and then the ambient temperature in the back of the trailer got hot enough to kill the freezer no matter how much it wheezed.

"Fuck *me*," Val muttered, and next to him Rory grunted.

"What's the plan, hoss?"

Val shook his head. "I've got my brother headed out to meet us at the rest stop and work on the refrigerator and freezer units, because right now, this will hardly get us to the rest stop, much less across the desert. But my big worry is the contract. I *can't* sign for this, but I don't want to risk Vinnie's business either."

"What does your friend say?" Rory asked.

Val waggled his eyebrows. "Good question," he murmured, pulling out his phone.

Vinnie was already up—probably had been up for quite some time, if Val knew his hardworking friend in another time zone. Quickly, Val outlined the situation over speakerphone, hoping his friend had some suggestions, because he didn't.

Vinnie was by turns despondent and indignant.

"God*dammit,* why would they do something like this?" he snarled. "What in the hell? I've got a thousand head here going into season within a *week,* and this was my business plan for the next year."

"Look," Val said, "did you get Reg's email? He was going to send it last night with some suggestions."

Vinnie blew out a breath. "Yeah," he said. "That kid's smart. But Val—"

He didn't need to finish. It was a lot to do in a short amount of time, but Val had a bad feeling about this. "Vinnie, I'm not saying the product is bad—not yet. But you have the contract that says payment isn't liable until delivery, right?"

"Yessir."

"So doesn't that mean I can sign for it all I want and you don't owe them shit?"

"Yeah, but Val, you take responsibility for the shipment. What if it's already been spoiled?"

"Now see," Val said, "that's what I'm wondering about. If I sign that contract saying I take *possession* of the shipment and clarify *what condition it's in*, can I get the shipment independently assessed? That's what Reg suggested anyway. So before *you* take possession, we get this product tested to see if it's good. And that way if it's bad, you at least aren't out the cost of the shipment to *these* guys."

"But what do I do with the in-season cattle?" Vinnie all but wailed.

"Like my brother said, does it have to be *this* cow jizz? Can't you research some other super stud? You know he'll help you if you ask—he's good at that shit. Because if you can find somebody close to your neck of the woods, you can have that batch run out to you as soon as we get this assessed. I know it's a small window. We get this batch to a facility *near* you for assessment in the next twenty hours, you deal with the fallout, and within the next eight hours, you have another shipment on the way. Can you do that? It'll get you the straws to the ranch in a week, either way."

"Why near Vinnie?" Rory asked.

"Because these people have an impeccable reputation," Vinnie said. "Whoever you are—"

"Rory, my security guy," Val supplied.

"Oh, pleased to meet you. This company has a sterling rep, Rory. And this situation Val just outlined is very not okay, which means I can't trust any of the sources—inspectors, ranches, businesses—in Elite's vicinity to assess the product. There's no way of knowing who's been paid off over there."

"If it's that big," Rory asked, "shouldn't you call in some authorities?"

Vinnie grunted. "You know what? You're right. I'll text you the lab near me that I'll have you drive to, and I'm going to talk to the USDA and have them meet you. Is your HVAC specialist certified? Can he make sure the apparatus is good within two hours after you take possession?"

"You know Prock," Val said without a doubt. "He'll be about half an hour away after we leave this place."

"All right, then," Vinnie muttered. "Okay. We have a plan. It's a shitty plan, and it might still bankrupt me, but it's better than no plan."

"Vinnie, did you have any of these problems with the other shipments?" Val asked suspiciously.

"Nossir. The trailers that were presented with those shipments were in top shape."

Val grunted. "Interesting."

"Why?"

"Because there's… well, there's a girl waiting on us outside."

Vinnie's silence was eloquent. "Well, uhm, Val, you've reassured me for years that girls were not your problem."

"Ha-ha. No, the problem is she's obviously been told to throw her tits at me during this little transaction, and she seems genuinely without a, well, *plan* now that this does not seem to be working."

Another one of those speaking silences, and Val became aware that Rory was *biting his fist* to keep from guffawing out loud.

"Could you maybe pretend it was working?" Vinnie begged. "Look, Val, if you throw a fit *there*, we've got no way to prove they're trying to sabotage the shipment, and I'm out the fee as well as more money if they sue me for backing out on a deal. But if you…. God, couldn't you just *leer*, and make some noises about how we all know your signature doesn't mean anything until this shipment is delivered, and then you can get out of there?"

"I'll keep my phone on to record," Rory said helpfully. "You make sure she knows you're not taking responsibility, merely possession, and I'll send the file to Vinnie and to my son. That way we'll have it in case there need to be legal proceedings."

"Perfect," Vinnie said. "Val, please? Nobody's going to take away your gay card if you smile at the girl and let her think you've been fooled."

"I certainly won't," Rory said, his voice low and rumbly and sexy as hell.

Val glared at Rory, but to Vinnie, who had worked for the last ten years since his uncle had passed to keep the family business *in* the family, he said, "Sure, sure. But if the gay police come and take my card, I'm having them call you," he threatened.

"I'm good for it," Vinnie assured him. "Tell me after you've had Prock shore up the units. I'm going to be hunting for a new stud."

Vinnie hung up, and Rory met Val's eyes with an amused glance of his own.

"Please don't," Val said, mindful that he had to go outside and pretend to flirt with a girl half his age.

"I've got to," Rory said, that wicked glimmer in his eyes that Val was starting to know already.

"Fine. Get it out of your system."

"Aren't I lucky I've already found a new stud of my own," Rory purred, and Val rolled his eyes.

But he also laughed before swinging out of the refrigerator and then the trailer, leaving Rory to lock up and follow him while he went and got his stud on.

Violet, as it turned out, was as inept at flirting as Val.

"So," she said prettily, holding the tablet awkwardly at breast level, "you can put your signature right there, right?" She peered upside down at the signature page and wagged her chin. "Right there."

"Sweetheart," Val said with patience, "you need to put those things away, because you and me need to talk."

Her hands dropped, and she gazed up at him with the saddest anime eyes brimming with tears that he had ever seen.

"But you *need* to sign the contract," she whimpered, and he sighed.

"Let me *look* at it again," he said. "And then we'll talk about why I'm probably not signing it."

He took the tablet from her carefully, not even brushing her fingers, and ignored the warmth and stickiness of sweat on the backside. After some careful studying, he handed the tablet back.

"So," he said, "I cannot guarantee that this product is good. *Look* at this trailer. I can't guarantee that if anything happens to the product between here and Austin it's going to be my fault. I can't assume culpability for shit that I had nothing to do with. My signature on that thing would be a lie, but I'll tell you why you're going to tell the lie that I signed it."

"Why?" she asked.

"Because I'm going to take possession of this trailer whether I sign that contract or not. You can report me for theft or you can tell your bosses I signed the contract and it should be going through any minute now." Some trailers had anti-theft protection that would lock up the brakes as soon as the trailer left the proscribed area, but he was wagering *this* one did not.

"My father said…." Her lower lip trembled. "I'll get into *so* much trouble," she whispered.

"Look, do you work here?" he asked, because she wasn't wearing boots or even the kind of jeans that people worked in. The rips at her knees had been artfully applied, and the striped men's shirt she wore over a lavender tank top had a distinctly feminine cut to it.

She shook her head. "I… I go to college nearby," she said. "My dad called and said he needed a favor if I want him to keep paying my tuition." Her voice dropped. "I… I *really* don't want to go into the family business. My brothers took this place over, and they *promised* I could go into something else."

"What is it you want to do, darlin'?" Rory asked, ignoring the irritated glance Val shot him.

"Environmental science," the girl said, giving the trailer a baleful glare. "But first I've got to have the money to *go.*"

"Okay, then," Val said, blinking. "So whatever's going down here, you have nothing to do with it. Fair. You go to your dad, tell him the contract's in the mail, and I'll be on my way. By the time they figure out I haven't signed a thing—and that even if I *had*, the contract my employer signed is way more legitimate than this ever could be—you are back at school, and everybody here will have a different set of worries. You understand me?"

She nodded and sighed. "It probably wasn't even my dad's idea," she told him dispiritedly. "My brother Robert is *such* an asshole. God. He even picked out this outfit!" She untied the shirt—which now that it wasn't tied above her midriff was *obviously* a woman's dress shirt—and tucked it into her jeans.

"All right, then," Val said. "You hang out here until we're a speck of dust down the driveway and get your big blue eyes all ready. Can you practice for me?"

She batted those eyes at him and said, "Oh my God, I have *no idea* why it's not going through! I swear I saw him push the Sign button, Daddy, I do!"

Val shuddered.

"Bad?" she asked, suddenly that anime forest creature again.

"Nope," he said. "You were really good. Just… just don't make a habit of lying, okay? Something tells me you need to use your powers for good."

She gave him a beleaguered smile. "I have no idea what that means," she said sincerely. "But if you're going to take the truck and not put up a fuss, I can pretend to be a virgin who's never had a beer, and believe me, that's a bigger stretch."

Val tried to keep his eyes from rounding too much and swung into the cab so he could back the king pin into the clamp.

To his surprise, Rory took care of the hoses, running Val through the brake-light checks and pressure checks like a pro, saving Val the trouble of getting in and out of the cab to do it himself. Once the refrigerator doors and the tailgate were closed, Val was on his way, Rory laughing his ass off in the passenger seat.

"Do you mind?" Val asked, annoyed, as they left the property and turned toward the freeway that would take them to meet Val's brother Prock.

"Nope, happy to!" Rory chortled. "Oh my *God*. I can't believe your friend even *asked* you to flirt. You took one look at that tablet on her ta-tas and you were like, 'Okay, fuck this.' It was *precious*."

Val grunted. "I'm not great with bullshit," he said, scowling.

"This is supposed to *surprise* me?" Rory asked, still laughing. "Oh my *God*, that was fabulous. I am now under no illusions about you, Val Royal. Everything I see is everything I get!"

"What's that supposed to mean?" Val grumbled, embarrassed.

Rory must have heard the underlying hurt in his tone because he sat up straight and wiped his eyes. "That means you don't have an ounce of subterfuge in you," he said, his voice suddenly kind. "You can't lie. Apparently it would make your head explode." His voice grew a little rougher then. "Which I guess explains why I got the brush-off the other night."

Val blew out a breath. "It wasn't a brush-off," he defended. "I was busy, I had a busy day planned, and it's not even seven in the morning the day after that. It was more of a caution flag than a brush-off."

Rory cocked his head. "It was a brush-off," he said, not even bothering to sugarcoat it. "You can't lie. It's not in you. So you're not going to have a one-nighter with someone who can't be honest with you. So I didn't talk about myself, and you weren't having any. I get it now."

"So you'll stop hitting on me?" Val asked, not sure what he was hoping for with that question—a yes or a no.

"I was married for five years to a great woman I hooked up with in college. She got pregnant, we married because we were supposed to, and we produced a great kid named Anthony, whom we're both crazy about. And then I confessed that there was a reason Anthony was looking to be an only child, and we agreed to raise him together but live apart. She remarried, I worked a lot, and I haven't had a real long-term relationship since, but I sure have enjoyed the short-term ones I've had."

Val gaped as Rory paused for breath.

"What?" Rory said. "I just spilled my whole life story for you. Are you going to say anything?"

"Why?" Val asked finally, when he could get his brain to function again.

"Why what?"

"Why would you tell me all that?" Because Val's brain was going to be chewing *that* infodump for *hours*.

"Because you want honesty," Rory said with a shrug. "And I still want you."

Val concentrated fiercely on the road, unable to come up with a single response to that.

"Don't worry, kid," Rory said. "You get back to me on that."

"I'm forty years old," Val said after a moment. "I'm hardly a kid."

"Thank God," Rory said with satisfaction. "Anything under thirty-five has me running for the hills." He shuddered. "Just wrong."

Val gave a bark of laughter, but that was it. He was going to have to digest his coffee, his job, and Rory's absolutely bald admissions all at the same time, and Rory was going to have to accept that with the rest of him.

Although points in Rory's favor, he didn't seem to mind that much.

# GIT YER GUN

Prock Royal had "Dad" written all over him. Literally—someone had taken a sharpie to his uniform shirt and informed the entire world that *this* Royal had procreated.

Val was not too stressed to laugh at his brother.

"Nice," he said, eyes crinkling. Rory liked that—Val had been grouchy and intense and serious, but the crinkles at his eyes said that wasn't who he was all the time. And Rory had to admit, if there was a time to go serious, keeping your friend's ass out of the fire was it.

"Which one was it?" Val continued, leading Prock to the trailer. "Riley or Kayley?"

Prock—who had the dark hair and brown eyes that were apparently Royal trademarks, along with high cheekbones and a square jaw— was softer around the edges *and* the middle, but he also had a kind of sweetness in his smile that indicated he lived a *very* contented life.

"Both," he said, quirking his lean mouth. "Riley did the block printing because 'DAD' is the only word she knows, and Kayley did the ones with the heart in the middle in place of the *a*."

Val's chuckle wasn't the sly or coded one Rory had gotten used to. This was a rich, full sound that told Rory a whole lot about how much Val loved his family.

"Well, wait until Charlie gets older. Boys don't write little hearts— they learn how to spell 'asshole.'"

"Sal did," Prock replied mildly. "He would write 'asshole' and put the little heart in the *o*."

Val snorted. "True story," he said to Rory. "I was in charge, Sal got mad at me and tried to tell Mom I was an asshole, and she said, 'You need to treat your brother with love.'"

"So he wrote Val a note," Prock said, picking up the thread. "Dear Val, I love you, even if you are an asshole. And yes, there was a heart in the *a and* the *o*."

Rory laughed outright. "Sounds like a character," he said, grinning.

"He will eat you alive," Val said, and was it Rory's imagination or did his eyes narrow a little, like a man contemplating beating up his beloved little brother if he thought of vamping on Rory?

Or maybe it was wishful thinking.

"He'd try," Rory said mildly, helping Val with the gates in the back. Val led the way up the ramp and unlocked the refrigerator, gesturing for Prock to go in before him.

Prock scowled, took a grim look around the truck, and said, "You got the specs for the product?" in a voice that was completely at odds with the sweet, smiling man who had pulled up in a work van with a purple lion logo proclaiming Royal Treatment HVAC Services.

"Right here," Val said, texting his brother the specs from his phone. "I also found an operator's manual for this unit online, if that will help."

Prock allowed a smile to slip through and rolled his eyes. "Oh my God—ever the big brother. Okay now, I'm going to get to work here." He hefted his box of tools. "Give me an hour to get this in the shape you'll need for crossing into Texas. Your product needs to be colder stat."

"Roger that," Val said, heading for the tail. "Anything you want us to have ready when we're done?"

Prock glanced left and right, like he was telling a secret. "Yeah. Faith has me on this diet? I mean, I *need* it, but I saw a Frosty's Burgers in that town about ten miles away? Can you take the van and get us some lunch?"

Val laughed and held out his hand for the keys.

"I'm gonna leave Rory here, though," Val said. "I want you to have a wingman in case somebody tries to take advantage of the parked trailer. I've got a *really* hinky feeling about this, you understand?"

"Roger that," Rory echoed. "I'll take a double cheese, the works."

Val shook his head. "I'm having a chicken sandwich because, oh my God, you two are making me fat just buying for you."

With that he stalked off, leaving Rory to exchange a smile with Val's brother.

"I don't know what he's so concerned about," Rory said, not able to help himself. "He looks fine."

Prock snorted. "I'm the straight brother," he said. "All I can tell you is that Val's a keeper—smart, dependable, funny, kind. Just hasn't seemed to find a guy who knows what he has."

"Mm," Rory said, lifting an eyebrow. "You are not surprised to know I'm in the market?"

Prock gave a smile that was all teeth. "Lucky guess," he said. "Now if you'll excuse me, I've got to get back to my regular appointments, and I *know* you guys are working on a timeline."

"I'll pull out a soccer chair and make myself comfy in the shade," Rory said. "Holler if you need me."

Rory made his way down the ramp and did that, pulling the chair out from the compartment Val had indicated when he'd been showing Rory around. The back end of the truck was generating heat, since the truck was idling to power the refrigerator fully without taxing the generator reserves, so Rory parked the chair across the way, under a tree and on the sidewalk, his revolver tucked into a pancake holster against his back, just in case.

Once settled he pulled out his phone and proceeded to play a stupid game, allowing his eyes to scan the parking lot every so often while his lizard brain was occupied.

He was not surprised when he saw a battered pickup truck pull up in the spot next to Val's rig.

Casually he stood and wandered toward the rig until he was leaning up against the tailgate, listening to Prock swearing and rattling inside the trailer.

He stood there, close to the F-450 that *still* had no business on the semi side of the rest stop and caught the eye of the passenger who was swinging down the step of the crew cab.

"Heya," the guy said, eyeballing Rory warily and then the trailer. "Me and my friend here were wondering if you could direct us to Bakersfield."

Rory's eyebrows rose. "We are on I-5," he said. "I-5 goes north and it goes south. Bakersfield is south. There are at least six-hundred-and-twelve signs, clearly marked, that tell you how to get there. You should consult one of them."

The guy—midsized, thinning light brown hair, pale blue, almost bulging eyes—searched out his companion. The driver of the crew cab truck was bigger—brawnier, wider, only some of it fat but a lot of it power—with a buzz cut of almost white hair and the same pale blue eyes. Rory was put in mind of the girl—Violet—who had big sky-blue eyes herself, and he wondered if these were the brothers she'd been so afraid of.

"Well, you don't need to be rude about it," said the bigger man, pulling the brim of his greasy red ballcap over his reddened face.

"I am not rude," Rory said, his hand resting on the small of his back. "I am suspicious. You two are in the wrong area of the rest stop, and you are getting awfully familiar with my rig."

"Well, sir," said the younger man, "my brother and I had a trailer of ours hijacked off our property this morning. This one looks an awful lot like ours, and we were just wondering if you had the manifest to prove it's yours."

Rory raised his eyebrows and, without saying anything to indicate there was somebody else in the trailer, raised the tailgate, slammed the doors shut, and pulled the locks down, with his back to the men standing behind him to give them a good view of his gun.

He turned around again and said, "I'll show you the manifest when you approach with an officer of the law," before striding to the cab.

The little one made his move first, a clumsy grab for Rory's arm that Rory countered by grabbing the man's hand and pulling him forward, then raising his knee and bouncing the man's chin off it.

The skinny guy went down, the bigger guy charged forward, and Rory pulled his gun, braced his feet, and stared at the bruiser as he stumbled to a screeching halt.

"You two will stay right there," he said. "And like I said, the next time you approach this rig, it had better be with law enforcement."

With that he swung into the cab, belted himself in, and grateful for the *many* driving classes offered to him when he was in the bureau, backed the rig up smooth as butter.

While he was doing that, he pulled out his phone and hit Val's number.

"Val, hang up with me, call your brother, and explain to him that there were two men, possibly armed, who were threatening to hijack the truck. Then call me back and tell me where the fuck I'm going."

"Fuck, fuck, fuck… go north when you hit the freeway," Val told him. "There's a cut road past the truck stop there that'll get us back south after we find the tracker they probably put on the trailer."

"I'll head there," Rory said. "Call me after you calm Prock down."

"My brother don't scare easy," Val said, grim pride in his voice. "I'll let him know we'll meet him with his van so he can get back to his regularly scheduled life."

NOT ONLY did Prock not scare easy, he also thought on his feet. By the time Rory pulled up behind the truck stop, lowered the ramp, and opened the double doors, Prock had not only fixed the refrigerator well enough to send a blast of cold air *out* of the truck, he'd also located not one but two trackers, one with the cylinders of insemination straws and one outside the refrigerator unit itself.

"The best I can tell," Prock said, "the cylinders have maintained temperature for the last forty-eight hours, so I'm going to say since they were stocked. But the refrigerator that was supposed to maintain the external temp had been tampered with. The compressor was missing a few small, vital parts, and it would have failed by the end of the day."

"So the hope," Val said, "was that either the two guys who approached Rory would get the shipment back or the cryo-cylinders would fail when the ambient temperature got too hot in the back of the truck."

"Yup," Prock said. "That's my best guess. So, well, good job on hiring someone smart enough to get out of that situation immediately, and...." He pursed his lips.

"Good luck getting the shipment to Austin," Val supplied grimly. "I hear you." He held up a bag that was still steaming in the late-morning breeze. "You did good, little brother. I got you onion rings and extra pickles, like you like it."

Prock took the bag and closed his eyes, sticking his face in the top and inhaling. "You're the best," he breathed reverently before closing the bag with regret. "And now, I'm sorry to say, it's probably best we all eat on the road." He paused then. "Val, where were you planning to refuel?"

Val frowned. "Probably when we hit the panhandle. Why?"

"Because that fridge isn't power efficient. I'm going to suggest you fill up when you hit Arizona, and maybe again when you hit the panhandle. I know it *should* be able to get you almost to Austin on a full tank, but...."

"But better safe than sorry. Good advice, little brother. Now bro hug me so we can all take off and you can be safe."

Prock did not seem self-conscious in the least to be pulled into a gruff embrace with Val, and he even kissed his brother's cheek before pulling back and shaking Rory's hand.

"You're a clever man, Mr. McCauley. Keep my brother safe, hear?"

"Will do," Rory said. Then he grinned. "And if you can keep that burger off your shirt, I promise neither one of us will breathe a word."

Prock chuckled before taking his tool chest and his lunch to his van and taking off.

As he pulled away, Val let some of his worry settle back down on his shoulders. "Well, Mr. McCauley, your presence already paid for itself. You ready to see what else is waiting for us down the line?"

"Can't wait," Rory said. "But you gotta tell me the truth."

Val arched an eyebrow at him.

"Did you really get a chicken sandwich after all of that?"

Val snorted. "No, but I did avoid getting the double by a hair."

"I like a man who knows moderation," Rory said sagely, and then they both loaded up again.

Val squared his shoulders behind the wheel and checked his gauges before pulling out of the rest stop. They hadn't gone a mile before Rory felt his first yawn building up behind his ears.

"Goddammit!" he muttered, trying to hide the thing next to his shoulder. "I'm sorry. Those things are catching!"

Val chuckled. "What time did you have to leave this morning? Two? You've been up a while on no sleep, am I right?"

"As have you!" Rory protested, but Val shook his head.

"I wasn't bullshitting when I said I needed to get up early the next morning. I was in bed by seven o'clock last night. Blackout curtains are a wonderful thing."

Rory smiled tiredly. "Well, aren't you smart," he mumbled, and Val gestured with his chin.

"Feel free to cop a sleep in the back. You sleep now, and by the time you wake up, we'll both be ready for a stretch and a jog around the rig, and then you can take over."

Rory bit back another yawn. "Sounds like a plan," he said.

"I'll be listening to my audiobook," Val told him. "Clive Cussler. Let me know if it's too loud."

Rory had expected the sleeping area in the back to be claustrophobic and hot, but he realized it was temperature controlled as soon as he stretched out and saw the dial. Val kept it cool back there, and Rory took the time to kick off his boots and store them in the compartment under the bed, as well as shuck his jeans and sweatshirt before he crawled under the blanket and snuggled right in.

As he lay there, closing his eyes against the light seeping in through the curtains, he could hear the measured tones of a skilled audiobook narrator, and he squinted, peering around the cabin. The engine noise was enough to drown out any conversation or music from the front. Where was the noise coming fr—oh!

He spotted the speaker near the temperature control and saw that it came with a volume and a power switch. He'd raised his hand to turn it off when he felt the sonorousness of the voice, coupled with the rumble of the engine and the hum of the road, all of it proving as soporific in the cool, shaded sleeping cabin as it had been in the sunlit, slightly warmer driving compartment.

He lowered his hand inside the covers and closed his eyes. The voice washed over him, telling him about impossible adventures in faraway lands, and he had a moment of feeling as content on a drive as his son had been as a kid.

He closed his eyes and dreamed of being a pirate on a distant sea, listening to the beat of the waves against the hull of the ship.

THE SQUEAL of the air brakes woke him up, and for a moment he thrashed around, disoriented.

Val's voice came through the speaker.

"We're at a rest stop outside of Phoenix to refuel. Get dressed and join me outside—one of us needs to sit with the truck while it's filling up, and the other can go use the can."

"Food?" Rory asked, his stomach rumbling for breakfast at what looked to be eight at night.

"I've got chicken and lettuce wraps in the cooler if you like," Val said through the intercom. "Or you can go get a heart attack on a plate."

Rory felt the heaviness from burgers so close in a row. Normally he tried to eat smart—something about being in Val's presence, maybe, made him want to flash his cowboy creds.

"Something besides red meat sounds good," he admitted, rolling out of bed.

"Meet me outside while I work the fuel hookup."

"Roger that."

Rory was glad he remembered his sweatshirt as he stepped out of the passenger side of the cab. Arizona was a warm state, generally, but an early spring chill could still bite. He yawned and stretched after he hit the ground and walked up to Val, who was waiting for the fuel pump to switch on.

"Go use the bathroom," Val said, nodding to the large minimart. The station he'd chosen had a side built exclusively for semi trucks, as well as a place to park the thing and maybe switch it off for a while. "There's food inside—actually, a sub shop, so we can get something decent. I want to fill up my coffee mug and use the bathroom for a long, glorious minute or two. You go first and meet me at the parking area, then I'll go."

"Keep your eye out," Rory said, meaning it. "I don't think those two fellas felt much like quitting."

Val grunted. "I agree, and I've been watching out for their pickup truck. I think Proctor did us right by finding those trackers. There are a couple of routes to Austin, and I've taken a few side roads to get here."

"Made good time, though," Rory said, glancing around. Phoenix was off in the distance, like a giant cruise ship against the surrounding dark.

"It's a gift," Val said, shrugging. "My dad told me once that driving was like the ultimate videogame. Once you start feeling traffic patterns in your bones, you know how to fit into them and swim with the tide."

"Too bad your rig is so noticeable," Rory said, glancing at the purple, white, and chrome logo on the side. It was, he'd noticed, the same logo his brother had used as a wrap around his van to advertise his HVAC service company.

Val gave him a tired smile. "Reg came up with it. We all started going into business for ourselves, and Reg—who's a really talented artist and dammit, he should go to school so he could make actual money with that shit—put the logo together so we could all use it."

"What does he do instead?" Rory asked.

"IT," Val said on a grunt of disgust. "He's got a small graphic business on the side, but IT pays the bills. He hates it—lives for the side work. Seriously, we've *all* tried to send him to school, but he insisted we save the money for the baby. It's really spooky. He's the second youngest, but he was old when he was born."

Rory shook his head. "I can't imagine a family with that many kids in it. Seven, right?"

"Yessir." At that moment, the fuel pump clicked, and Val gestured for Rory to go do whatever he needed in the minimart.


RORY MET Val outside with a bag full of mandarin oranges and two chicken subs, no mayo, teriyaki sauce instead. He'd taken a risk, but Val lit up when he heard the menu and asked Rory to put the food inside the cab. He left the engine on idle, and Rory understood that they'd made good enough time to get some stretching and exercise in before they started off again.

Rory was grateful, and as he watched Val jog up toward the minimart, he found himself thinking that Val Royal must be a very good boss.

He also found himself more and more tempted by that stocky, muscular figure, and those quiet, stern smiles. He realized he'd spent seven hours in Val Royal's bed and that sometime soon he'd like to be in there with Val next to him.

He spent their break pacing the line of the semi on the side facing the minimart, his eyes swinging from left to right and back again, his attention focused on people coming out of the minimart and new vehicles coming in, either on the semi side or the standard vehicle side. He was just about wondering when Val would be coming out again when he glanced up at the minimart and stopped short.

Val had obviously emerged from the bathroom into a crowd of four or five other truckers. They had the burly, top-heavy build of men who spent their life on the road using their chest, stomach, and thigh muscles controlling big machinery while not always watching their diets. All the men were standing aggressively, leaning toward Val, and even from this distance Rory could tell the men's expressions weren't pleasant.

Val appeared to be well over it. To Rory's surprise, Val glanced out through the window and shook his head, pointing to the truck emphatically, and Rory read him loud and clear.

*Stay. There. Dammit.*

Rory got it. And he got why. But that didn't stop him from sucking in a breath and grunting when the first guy—built like a Mac truck in human form, with a long grizzled beard and curly brown hair—swung a fist like a jackhammer at Val's head.

Val ducked, and Rory saw the now-familiar black F-450 pull into the gas station and head directly for the semi.

Rory had just enough time to reach behind the driver's seat and pull the shotgun, and he conceded that Val was going to have to deal with his own problems because Rory now had work to do.

# CRAZY BOY

VAL HAD grown up out and proud—his parents, for all their lack of education and high hopes for their children, had also been so damned kind, so damned accepting, that Val hadn't ever really had any doubts that they'd continue to love him.

Of course they had. Ed and Julie Royal were pretty much the best.

But that didn't mean Val hadn't had his share and Laure's share and Sal's share and even Prock's share of schoolyard disputes. He'd known how to throw a punch, and he'd taught Laure and Sal, and Sal had taught Prock and Dean. Dean had taken martial arts, improved on that information, and taught everybody, including Reg and Chance.

If a Royal kid ever came home with a bloody nose, there was always a note from the teacher that said the kid hadn't started it, but the other kid would be out for a few days because the Royals didn't let anybody else finish it.

So Val knew what was waiting for him when he got out of the bathroom, and while he was sort of surprised when he first emerged and saw the gathering of grim-faced assholes around the door, once he'd assessed the body language, body odor, and the lack of hygiene among those surrounding him, he had absolutely no illusions as to where this trainwreck was heading.

But he *was* really curious as to who had set it in motion.

Val glanced around, his gaze cutting to the guy toward the front. The leader of sorts.

"Heya, faggot," the guy snarled, and Val tried not to roll his eyes.

"That's original," he said. "'Cause I'm a gay truck driver. I've never been called a name before. I bet you set your brains on fire you thought of that so fast."

The man gaped for a moment, and there was some uneasy shifting as the men tried to make out whether they had been insulted or not.

Val sucked in his stomach and adjusted his stance, every molecule of physics in his brain devoted to how he was going to set these bodies into motion and get them to stay that way until something uncomfortable stopped them.

"Look," Val said, bouncing on his toes a little. "I know what you guys think is going to happen, and I know what I'm planning to happen. But before we start, I need you to answer me one question."

"Yes, you are a total fag," said the twitchy blond guy next to the bruiser with the grizzled brown hair.

Val gave the guy—he could have been between twenty-five and forty-five, because meth was a bad drug that aged you fast—a grim assessment.

"You should go to rehab," he said kindly. "Your liver is starting to go. You're getting sallow, and your teeth, man, that's just bad."

The twitchy guy's lower lip started to wibble, and Val watched him stutter back, as though the words hurt worse than the fists were about to.

Well. The truth really *was* a weapon.

"But none of that is my question," Val said, pulling his fists up defensively in front of his face. These guys weren't smart, and they weren't fast, but all the guys who weren't twitchy were big enough to level him if one of their punches landed solidly. Val's defensive stance was what would save his bacon. As he squared up, he glanced out the window, wondering if there were more of these assholes waiting to rush in from the wings.

He caught Rory McCauley staring at him from next to the semi, and suddenly Val didn't need his question answered, even though he'd continue to ask it anyway. This whole ambush had nothing to do with Val and everything to do with distracting both men away from the goddamned trailer.

Val pointed at Rory and the truck and mouthed, "Stay there," before returning his attention back to the bulldozer with the grizzled hair and the red ballcap.

"What's your question?" snarled Bulldozer. "We don't got all night."

"You don't," Val conceded. "In fact you're all giving up time on the road to attack somebody who hasn't done a damned thing to you. Who put you up to it? Did someone just get on your channel and stir shit, or was there more?"

There was a frantic meeting of eyes around the circle then, like Val had suddenly produced the magic word, and Val got it.

"There *was* more," he said, starting some subtle footwork. "Somebody offered to *pay* you, right?"

Bulldozer started to circle him then, the rest of them forming a tiny ring in the hallway of the minimart outside the men's restroom.

"What's it to you?" Bulldozer asked. "Not like you're gonna be conscious for it anyway!"

He offered a playful jab, not a real swing, more like a test. *Whatcha gonna do about it?* Val ducked and deflected, not putting all his strength into it because he didn't want them to know how strong he was. Not yet.

"Well," Val breathed, dodging another jab, batting it away from his face with a bit more force, "if I *do* survive, I need to know what to tell the USDA. Because whoever wants you to beat *me* up, is trying to—oop!" He almost didn't duck in time, but he watched as his opponent overbalanced himself working for the big swing. Good.

"Trying to what?" the big man asked, spitting on the floor as intimidation.

"Trying to sabotage my load," Val said. And here it came, the committed punch—powerful but slow. So slow.

Val had time to weave to the side and let his assailant hit the concrete wall behind him with all his force. The sound of knuckles cracking on the wall made everybody gathered there wince a little, and while the leader howled and shook his hand, which was bleeding and probably broken, the twitchy blond guy stepped up and caught Val with a glancing blow on the cheek.

Val took the hit and backed up, giving him a feral grin.

These guys were slow, and they weren't bright, and they were hoping for a reward from two guys Val was pretty sure would bug out when they found Rory there, fully armed.

Twitchy blond guy took another swing, and this one Val blocked and then ducked under and hit the guy's ribs with crushingly hard blows. The man doubled over, winded, and Val caught him with a haymaker under the jaw, dodging away when he went down, and Val was left facing three, his adrenaline up and absolute fury burning in his gut.

The three remaining assailants gave each other uneasy looks, and Val grinned at them, blood dripping from the blow to his cheek and a cut lip. Deliberately he held out his hand and made the universal gesture for "bring it" before lifting his fists in the defensive stance again.

Oh yeah.

Bring it *on*.


VAL STAGGERED out of the minimart, half a bag of ice held on his eye and cheek, and tried not to trip over the unconscious bodies of his assailants as he cleared the door.

What he saw as he drew near the truck made his blood run cold, and he reluctantly dropped the ice bag and reached for the .45 in the pancake holster under his shirt.

Rory twitched an eyebrow his way, shook his head, and kept his shotgun trained on the two guys—Val assumed they were the Cassidy brothers—who were regarding him with sour expressions and hands raised in the air.

Val pulled his .45 anyway and tried not to let his hands shake as he circled around to the side of the brothers, keeping them tracked against the trailer.

"Now," Rory continued, like he'd been in the middle of a speech, "I don't know who you are—"

"The rightful owners of this trailer," snapped the older, bigger guy.

"Mm… no," Rory told him. "I saw the original contracts, and once the trailer left your premises and until it's delivered into the hands of the buyer, it is *our* responsibility. That's not me, that's not my opinion, that is the law."

"Like you would know anything about the law!" the younger guy scoffed. "You're trying to *steal* our trailer!"

"And you're trying to *defraud* the guy who bought the contents," Val snapped, drawing their attention to him. Both of them took sight of the .45 and scowled. "Care to tell us why?"

The pair of them exchanged glances, and then they all heard the sound at once.

The Cassidy brothers broke first, turning and bolting for their truck, but when Val would have given chase, Rory stopped him with a harsh exclamation.

"No! Val, if those cops get here to question us, they'll do the dirty work for those guys—we'll be here all night, and God knows if the refrigeration unit has a whole day in it, even *with* your brother's magic touch."

Val grunted and turned around, grabbing his bag of ice before running toward the cab, his head throbbing in time to every step.

"You get the passenger side," Rory said, hoisting himself up on the driver's side. The truck was still in idle, so Val—who had already seen him drive and park—trusted him some more and ran around the truck, double-checking the back gate as he went.

There was a screwdriver wedged between the two door panels, like somebody had been trying to break in while he and Rory had been otherwise occupied.

*Shit*. What in the *hell* was going on?

Val finally consigned the bag of ice to the parking lot and pulled himself up, conscious of the strain in his shoulders, his neck, and his battered hands, using the handles on the gate, and pulled out the screwdriver, tucking it under the wheel well of the rig next to his while hardly breaking his own stride.

He was settled and Rory was taking the side road out of the gas station, the one that circumvented the main thoroughfare all the police cars were currently coursing down, before the first unit pulled into the lot.

Rory kept driving, nice and steady, as Val gave him directions to a back way toward the one freeway that would get them where they were going while the whole alien spaceship of Phoenix Arizona taunted them with light pollution, restaurants, and a really good time, far beyond their reach.

"Shit…," Val muttered, slouching in his seat as Rory found his cruising speed down a little-used frontage road, kept dark and lonely by a tall embankment blocking off the freeway.

"You said it," Rory responded, and Val felt more than saw the quick once-over as Val leaned his head back against the seat and closed his eyes.

"I am *not* okay with that," Rory said. "You look like shit, by the way."

"What, no praise for fighting like a Trojan?" Val asked, a little bit hurt. "I mean, what's a guy got to do to impress you?"

"You want to impress me?" Rory told him. "Go fetch your first aid kit in the back and sit tight. First pullout I see, you're getting tended to, buddy."

Val grunted, wanting to tell him that he could very well fix his own boo-boos but not exactly sure he *could* tend to the swelling over his eye or the cut leaking blood from his cheek. With a sigh, he hauled himself out of the passenger seat and made his way to the back compartment, sat on the edge of the bed, and pulled the first aid kit out of one of the netted bags strapped to the driver's seat.

He grunted, everything hurting more as he jounced on the bed and unlaced his boots. The plan had been for Rory to drive and him to rest anyway, right? This was just getting ready.

And while he was doing that, he might as well shuck his jeans and fold them on the floor behind the driver's seat, and oh! This pillow on the passenger's side was *right there*, and there was no reason *not* to rest his head on it. The purring of the truck, the dappled shadows of the sodium street lamps overhead layering the darkness with a weak pink light— he'd always loved driving, riding, the rumble of floorboards under him as he was driven through the night.

And God, he was tired. It was, what? Nine o'clock now, after their fateful rest stop? The fight? The two days without sleep prepping? He'd been awake at three that morning, and it was so much his bedtime…. He would shut his eyes for a minute. Wait for Rory to find that pullout. It would be fine.

He woke to the sharp smell of antiseptic and Rory's rough fingers probing his wound.

"Ouch," he mumbled, liking the firmness of Rory's ministrations even as they stung. "You couldn't just let me sleep?"

"Here," Rory said. "Open your eyes."

And then he *held* Val's eye open and shined a penlight in it.

"Ouch!" Val repeated, flailing.

"Stop it!" Rory snapped. "Let me get the other one."

"You suck," Val told him, but he did what Rory told him to because somewhere in his tired brain percolated the thought that there was a very good reason for this.

And then—aha!—there it was.

"I don't have a concussion," he whined. "It's just my bedtime."

There was another cool spray of antiseptic on his cuts and an ice mask over his blackened eye before Rory's hands started dealing with his knuckles.

"I'm sure it is," Rory murmured, "but since I wasn't real keen on you lapsing into a coma in the back of the truck, I'm sure you'll forgive me for checking."

"Whatever," Val grumbled. "Can I go back to sleep now?"

"No," Rory told him gruffly, and Val could see his callused, long-fingered hands over Val's own as he applied antiseptic and bandages, and for a moment there was quiet between them. In fact the air grew a little thicker, and the pain of Val's injuries faded.

"Why not?" Val asked into the suddenly charged darkness. Rory had turned on a lamp affixed to the back of the driver's side headrest, but the recessed area of the bed was still dark.

"Because you scared the shit out of me," Rory confessed softly, smoothing the bandage over with his thumb. "And I'd like to make sure you're okay."

"Not my first fight," Val told him, eyes still on their hands. Rory seemed to be holding Val's fingers less in the name of medical care and more to just… just hold them. To give caresses with rough fingertips and give Val a much-needed sense of connection.

"First fight I've ever seen you in," Rory said, and it wasn't Val's imagination; he was leaning closer in the darkness. "First time I ever took in those odds and actually saw somebody win!"

Val wanted to chuckle like an evil overlord, because yeah, he was proud, but what came out was dryer, softer, almost seductive. "Don't fuck with a Royal asshole," he said, going back on the family pun.

Rory echoed his sound. "That's a shame," he murmured. "I had something like that in mind."

"Yeah, all you want to do is fuck with it," Val grumbled, still disappointed.

"Maybe, maybe not," Rory hedged. He'd pulled out another wipe from Val's kit and was currently getting rid of the blood drips around the bandages, cleaning Val up for show, not for medical necessity. "I never know that sort of thing until afterwards."

Val took a moment to digest this, and it didn't sit well.

"Worst lottery ever," he decided. "Whole reason I don't play anymore."

"Says you!" Rory laughed, but there was a defensive edge to his voice.

"Seriously. Your partner goes into it thinking, 'Hey, I've got a chance!' and after the sex? You're like, 'Sorry, it was great, but it wasn't, you know, *forever* sex, so see you around!' It's like gambling with dick."

Rory winced. "You don't find a lot of men hoping for forever—feels like *any* relationship's a gamble."

"Doesn't have to be forever," Val defended, which was hard because now that the antiseptics were no longer stinging his nose, Rory was starting to smell *good*, like leather and dust and diesel. Val wasn't actually fond of diesel, but it was part of his world, and it gave him comfort. "Doesn't have to be just a night. Sometimes there's the hope there will be lots of nights. Maybe somebody to introduce to your parents. Someone to play with your nieces and nephews. Somebody to hug you when you leave for a job. Not forever on a silver platter. Hope."

Rory rocked back on his heels and surveyed his handiwork before focusing his dark eyes on Val's. "You've got some music in your soul for a man in your profession. Where'd you get that music?"

"Our mother," Val said, smiling slightly. "Made us listen to musical theater. Almost constantly."

"You know the downside of that, right?" Rory asked, smiling slightly.

"Most of it ends sad?" Val supplied. "Yeah, I know. But before the sad part, which, you know, happens to most humans in the course of a lifetime, there's always a bright, shining moment when people are glad to be human. That's why my mom loves it. I guess she gave us that."

Rory grunted. "Can't find fault with that," he said after a moment. "That's... well, I may be able to finish the end of *Les Mis* after all."

Val's laugh was a little goofy—probably tiredness, maybe a little bit of breathlessness. Rory had been crouching so close to him, and his head hurt and his knuckles hurt, and he was very aware that they weren't out of the woods yet. Tomorrow. One more stop to refuel and some backroads and they'd be at the lab, able to make a bona fide delivery to get the product checked out.

It didn't take a genius to see there would be problems, but first they had to get there with the refrigeration unit intact.

As if on instinct, Val's eyes went to the exterior of the cab, where far in the distance he saw a pair of headlights in the rearview.

"You'd better get going," he whispered, and Rory nodded. But before he reached to turn off the light, he feathered a kiss across Val's split lip, and then one on his unbandaged cheek.

"I'll be listening to *Les Mis*," he murmured. "See if I can find those daisies and rainbow sparkles."

"Oh, it'll hurt," Val told him, searching Rory's dark eyes. "The important thing is to see if the hurt is *worth* it."

Rory's mouth twitched up. "I have no doubts," he said, before kissing Val again—just a little bit more firmly—switching off the overhead light, and moving to the front of the cab.

Val allowed himself to nod off this time, and while he was still worried—trouble was still out there—he found it easy to put himself in Rory's capable hands.

# One Day More

Rory's adrenaline was still up after that terrible moment of watching Val take a beating before his own confrontation, so he not only made it through *Les Mis* but also through *Hamilton* and—oh joy!—*Something Rotten*, which did not, indeed, end badly, much to Rory's surprise.

He wondered if he should google "musicals that don't end badly" and then decided probably not—it would probably be a depressingly short list. He took the win and moved on to *Hadestown*, knowing it would suck but by now on a quest for Val's kernel of optimism, of hope in the story. By the time the soundtrack wound down on his Spotify, Rory was, indeed, captured by hope.

As the night forged down and deep through a desert mostly populated by the headlight snake of the freeway, he started to ask himself when he'd lost that hope.

When *had* he started to figure he would be in it for the short term, for the quick and dirty, for the brief liaison, rather than the relationship?

Had it been when his marriage had disintegrated, after he'd admitted to himself—and to his wife—that women, even beautiful, kind, bright women, didn't turn him on as much as the hot guys they were watching on TV?

She'd been horrified at first, then sad.

And then, as he'd continued to be good husband, a good *father*, she'd been accepting.

"It's so hard," she'd confessed to him tearfully. "Rory, I love you."

"I love you too," he'd told her. "Just not the way you need me to. Not the way you deserve."

They'd stayed married for a couple more years after that, to raise Anthony until he hit kindergarten and could deal better with the two homes, and then he and Connie had worked hard to make his world as perfect as possible.

Maybe it had been then, when his nights without Anthony had been his time to explore his sexuality and his nights with Anthony had been no dates allowed?

What about after Anthony had gone on to college?

Was it then? Had he just figured, hey, he was nearing fifty, he was too old for courtship games?

*Wow, Rory. That's cynical. The last person you courted was Connie.*

He'd seen himself living with her forever too. They'd gotten together in college, like you were supposed to, and she'd been so friendly, so much fun. Any other man would have worshipped at her feet.

In fact *Rory* worshipped at her feet, and she'd had him stand up as her bridal attendant in her wedding to a really wonderful man with thinning hair and a potbelly who looked at her like she hung the moon.

Kevin worshipped at her feet too, and Rory loved the guy like a brother for helping to undo the damage Rory's bungling had inflicted on a really great woman. So Connie got *her* happy ever after.

But when had Rory decided he was the lone gunman, wandering into town, solving people's problems, and wandering back to the gun range he ran with Anthony? Had it been his injury? Had *that* made him bitter? He didn't *feel* bitter.

He felt like he'd had his chance for a happy ending, and he'd blown it.

*Even Connie doesn't think you blew it, you moron.*

Hell. Val was going to expect an honest answer, wasn't he? What did Rory have to give him after a night listening to musical theater and searching his own damned soul?

Fear of failure? Weakshit. Total weakshit.

But also—God, was it the truth?

Rory grunted and felt the pressure in his bladder just as he saw the sign for the rest stop. For a moment, he got excited; then he remembered how the Cassidy brothers had shown up everywhere they had.

"Val!" he called back, depressed because he'd hoped to give the man more sleep than this.

Val mumbled something, and Rory saw the control for the intercom to the back.

"Val?" he asked again.

"If you're going to complain about *Hadestown*, blame Virgil," Val mumbled.

"I will not. Ovid could have fixed that shit, but he didn't."

"Fucking Jesus, stop waving your education around like a giant dick," Val complained. "What did you want to ask me?"

"I would like to take a leak, but I would like to not make us a target. Is there a bridge I should piss off of? A turnout? Any ideas?"

Val grunted. "There's a rest stop ahead?" he asked. "Turnberry?"

"That's the one," Rory agreed. "Why?"

"The bathrooms are shut down," Val told him. "You can park there and find a cactus or something. I'll check the back gate. They wedged a screwdriver in there last time."

"Shit! Why didn't you tell me?" Rory felt a little put out. Shouldn't he know everything?

"Because I jammed it in the back of the rig next to us for shits and giggles. With any luck, they're on their way to Dallas instead of Austin, and these fuckers will spend a long time getting nowhere."

"You think it was tracked?" Rory hadn't thought of that, and it was supposed to be his job.

"What do *you* usually do if you find a tool somewhere it's not supposed to be?"

Rory blinked. "Add it to my toolbox," he said.

"Yup. I didn't want their shit in my box. I gave it to the guy next to us. Good luck asking *him* for bull jizz."

Rory chuckled. "Okay, here we are. Do you need to find a cactus too?"

"Yeah, then I can take over—"

"Bullshit. I've got three more hours," Rory told him.

"It's not a contest." Rory could hear the man's mild tone, the tone that said if it *was* a contest, he'd just won.

"It is. I'm winning," Rory told him childishly. "Shut up and look alive. We're pulling in."


True to Val's word, the rest stop was deserted. The rig's lights illuminated what had once been a charming little stop, with picnic tables, two large bathrooms of twelve or so cubicles each, and a couple of changing stations for families or folks who just didn't want to pee with the masses for whatever reason. The bathrooms themselves had been locked, however, and the sidewalks that networked the place were overgrown. A lawn that had once probably been green and lush was overgrown with crabgrass that spidered from clump to clump, spreading like fungus across the cracks in the sidewalk.

Val hadn't been kidding about pissing on a cactus. They'd started to make inroads into the disintegrating landscaping. It would be as easy to hit one than not.

Rory went first as Val was crawling out of the back, and he returned to use a wet wipe on his hands while Val went to do his own business. He returned to where Rory was leaning up against the rig, and for a moment they both paused, looking out into the shadowed landscape. Rory had seen a fox crossing behind the bathrooms and was pretty sure he'd heard an owl—and heaven knew how many snakes were nearby.

While the truck's sidelights were on, Rory had turned off the headlights when he'd set the brakes, and the thing idled in relative quiet while they both closed their eyes, turned their faces to the sky, and took a breath.

To his surprise, Val pulled his phone out of his back pocket and sighted through the camera, aiming above their heads.

Rory looked up and saw the glow of the Milky Way, and off in the distance, tendrils of light from the nearest big city, throwing the cacti into silhouettes. He heard the soft click of the camera, and then another, before Val slid the phone back into his pocket.

"Sky," he said gruffly into the quiet. "It's a tradition. Me and Dad would be hauling, and the little kids asked for pictures of sky. When we're out of town now, even Sal, we take pictures of the sky."

Rory grunted, moved. "I used to bring Anthony stuffed bears from airports," he said, thinking about an entire room full of stuffed bears that Anthony refused to part with, even at twenty-five.

"This is cheaper," Val told him, and Rory watched that lean mouth quirk at the corners. The humor, the sensuality, made Rory shiver.

Rory was suddenly, acutely aware of Val's warm body, shoulder to shoulder with his own, and of the sharp smell of the wipes, as well as the scent of creosote and cactus blooms and dust—and probably owl guano and rattlesnake skin as well.

But mostly Val, his even breathing, his warmth, his strength....

Rory turned first, saw Val, his battered face tilted toward the sky, his eyes closed as Rory got closer to make his move.

Val opened his eyes, peering through the darkness into Rory's. "What?" he asked.

"This," Rory whispered and claimed his mouth.

He started out slowly, palming Val's upper arms, squeezing his biceps as he plundered Val's hard but willing mouth. Val gasped and opened for him, letting him in, and Rory swept inside. For a moment, they were more than two heartbeats underneath a lonely velvet sky. For a moment they grew, expanded, became magnificent, their bodies merging, growing in wonder, becoming part of the world around them as their hearts beat in synchrony.

The kiss ended, and Rory leaned his forehead against Val's, hauling in one breath after another, stunned at the ferocity of his reaction.

To his credit, Val wasn't ready to let the kiss go either, and he continued placing tiny kisses at the corners of Rory's mouth, of his eyes, on his cheeks, while Rory tried to keep himself from shaking.

"That was… that was amazing," he gasped, pulling Val closer. "That… what do I do with that?"

Val gave a humorless snort. "Save it for later," he said grimly. "I'm surprised our two friends didn't sniff the wind and make a beeline for us at this hole in the desert."

Rory's arms tightened around Val's shoulders, and to his relief Val allowed himself to be held, to snuggle, resting his head on Rory's shoulder, where, Rory was starting to realize, he belonged.

"I want later," Rory told him, meaning it with everything in him. His pulse thundered in his throat, in his wrists. His entire body shook with the aftermath of that kiss, and he didn't understand how that could happen.

"You gonna talk to me before later happens?" Val asked suspiciously, and Rory shouldn't have been surprised, yet he was.

He peered down—Val was about three inches shorter than he was, but he didn't look cowed in Rory's arms, only patient. That kiss, he realized, had been 100 percent honest, because Val Royal apparently didn't do it anyway but. Was that why Rory's heart was still thundering in his ears? Why the feel of the man in his arms was so huge? So vital? Because he'd tasted trust, understood that Val Royal wasn't a man to be trifled with? This was a man who could make a small business work in an economy actively trying to kill it. This was a man who could maintain contact with his family, who could balance an ungodly number of siblings and speak fondly of his parents and keep his word to his friends.

Rory got it now. You didn't just fuck and leave a Val Royal. In or out of bed, this man deserved his respect.

Deserved his care.

"Valiant?" Rory hazarded.

"My first name?" Val murmured, stepping back. Rory felt the loss of him keenly, but he was scrambling for purchase here. To have Val Royal was to open himself up, to trust, to believe Val wouldn't let him down. Rory hadn't been able to do that since… since his *wife*, for God's sake, and he was supposed to do it *now* for a man he'd known less than forty-eight hours?

Val met Rory's gaze in the starlight, his lean mouth quirked mildly to let Rory know he wasn't stupid about why Rory would change the subject.

And also, Rory realized, that twist in his mouth was guarding against hurt.

"Your heart," Rory said. "Don't… don't pull away yet." He felt his weakness keenly, but God. He'd never known the stars could be this bright or the darkness could breathe this softly. "Have some faith in me?"

He felt rather than heard Val's sigh, and it was as though his heart started again when Val melted against him.

"It's not a big story," Rory murmured. "No big deaths, no terrible betrayals. Just habit. I came out, split with my wife and realized between my kid and my job it wasn't… you know, a good idea to date. No strange men in the house when I had my kid. No time to date when I didn't. That's all." The words sounded small and cowardly, holding such a good man under the vast crystal sky.

"And you got into the habit," Val murmured, seemingly content in Rory's arms for the moment. "There's no shame in that, McCauley. Ask me how I know."

Rory chuckled rawly and closed his eyes. His skin thrummed with the magic of the man leaning his head against Rory's chest, with the smell of cholla and creosote bushes and desert dust, with the chill of the night sky. "How do you know?" he whispered, wanting to hear more of Val's grumbly voice.

Val had probably opened his mouth to tell him when they heard the far-off rumble of an engine. Probably not their guys, but….

"Don't think about it," Rory said sharply as Val headed for the door. "You've still got three hours of sleep."

"You sleep," Val said, scrambling into the driver's seat before Rory could stop him. "I'm going to be thinking about one helluva kiss."

Rory swore to himself and ran around the rig, pulling up into the cab as Val put the thing in gear.


SINCE VAL had beat him to the cab, Rory took him up on the offer to nap some more. While working operations in the FBI, Rory had learned not to pass up on rest when it was offered, and that particularly went for sleep during his normal circadian rhythms. His hours were more regular now than they were with the bureau—it had been a long time since he'd gone seventy-two hours while chasing down a suspect or closing down an op, and he was pretty sure that Val was used to waking up very early and going to sleep around seven at night.

Hopefully, they should have their cargo delivered to the lab in Austin by seven this night, and… and then what?

Rory knew that the job entailed waiting for a turnaround—wait for the lab results, and if they were favorable, take the longhorn stud in a cattle trailer back to California within the week. But… but what if there was something wrong? It wasn't that Rory was afraid of not getting paid; if nothing else, Val had insurance to make sure his employees would get paid if the clients experienced distress. But what would Val end up doing? He'd made it clear this client was a *friend*, and if he'd learned anything about the man in the last two—wait, *three* days—it was that Val wasn't going to just let his friend twist in the wind if he could do anything about it.

Frankly Rory didn't see himself going back home without Val Royal, and that included if something went heinously wrong with the delivery.

That heartbeat under the desert sky had meant something to him— something important. Rory wanted to see where it would lead, and he couldn't do that if he was the kind of guy to cut and run.

He stretched out in the sleeper cab, his decision made to stick with Val through thick and thin, and he yearned for that moment back. He wanted that conversation. He wanted another kiss. He couldn't remember the last time he'd hungered so much for a might-have-been.

He resolved to do whatever he needed to make the next moment like that the thing of beauty that had been missing from his heart.


HE WOKE up to a scream of real pain, two shots of gunfire, and Val's shouts of fury from outside the idling rig.

# Blood and Destruction

Ugh.

Val stopped to refuel around ten in the morning, a growing sense of urgency pushing him as far as he could reasonably go without risking the fuel needed for the refrigeration generator. He figured he had a decent margin. He could get within five hundred miles of his destination if he pushed the rig until it died (and whoever did that shit should be shot, because it would be a terrible death rattle of a good friend), but he'd made good time through the morning.

This stop was a decent compromise.

He'd been standing on the step in front of the door while the pumps whirred, yawning slightly and thinking he'd take Rory up on the rest of his sleep, when he saw the black F-450 turn into the parking lot.

Anxiously he glanced at the pumps, and they were so close… three-hundred gallons, two-hundred, one….

He'd just unhooked the pump on the passenger side and resealed the tank when the truck squealed into the semi lot, the two guys parking it right in front of the rig, where they'd incur a zillion dollars in fines and maybe even some jail time for endangerment, which is what told Val they were serious.

Knowing how the enemy worked now, he sprinted around the backside of the rig, and sure enough there was one of the men from the night before, eye swollen shut, trying to jimmy the doors with yet another screwdriver, and he saw the shadow of a guy who'd pulled in after the 450 lurking in the shade beyond the parking lot. Apparently these guys traveled in packs and the guys in the F-450 were for distraction.

Val didn't waste any time.

The guy with the screwdriver was standing on the back step, the better to get leverage for what he was trying to do. Val didn't slow down, just changed course, took the guy out at the knees, and kept running as he toppled sideways, howling as he hit.

By the time Val had rounded the back end of the rig and was hauling ass for the front, he saw the smaller of the two guys reach for the handle of the driver's side door to haul himself up.

Val had put the gun in his holster when he'd pulled into the gas station, and he drew it out now and shot two shots overhead toward the desert backing the service station before shouting, "Get your fucking hands off my rig!"

"You stole our load!" screamed the blond guy, but he was standing with his hands shaking over his head.

"And if that was true, you would have sent the cops after us instead of trying to sabotage us yourself. Jesus, you guys, what in the hell is in this refrigerator unit? Some sort of hybrid sperm of an alligator and God?"

Both men gaped at him, and in that breath of quiet, Val heard the distinctive sound of a shotgun being racked.

Rory's voice through the now open driver's side window was laconic and calm.

"Now me," he said as though he'd been part of the conversation all along, "I'd like to see a cross between an alligator and God, but I'm thinking giant gorillas and Martians myself."

Val's adrenaline dump slowed a notch at the sound of Rory's voice, but he was still on high alert.

"Why Martians?" he asked, reaching for the door. Rory leaned forward, and Val grabbed the strap on the side of the seat and hauled himself behind the driver's side while Rory watched his back.

"'Cause," Rory said, head and shoulders still outside the driver's window. "It might explain why these assholes keep trying the same trick. They don't know the ways of our people."

"Check your mirror," Val said quietly. "I left a man down back there and another in the shadows."

Rory's eyes darted, and he started to chuckle. "I do believe you broke the one guy's arm," he said just as quietly before turning his attention to the two men under the shotgun's purview. "Since I don't know who else is back there," he said, "I've got no place to go but forward. To that end, you have to the count of five to get that piece of crap out of my way before I take it out. Your man's got a gun," he said, his voice flinty. "You've got until he gets even with my window."

And then he pulled inside, rolled up the window, and put the truck in gear.

"You sure there was only one guy back there?" he asked.

"Nope," Val said, checking the window on the passenger's side and spotting another guy creeping up with a pistol in his hand.

"Well, their time is up," Rory muttered, and he stood on the clutch and put the rig in gear.

The black truck didn't quite make it out of his damage path. Rory took out the driver's side back quarter panel and sent the thing spinning through the big-rig lot before he pulled onto the highway and started driving like fury.

Val was in the passenger's seat by this time, hanging on to the sissy strap and praying the damned F-450 hadn't done too much damage to his chrome. He was a mite vain about his big royal purple rig; the paint job had been his brother's idea, and he'd worked hard to buy himself a good rig with a top-notch engine and then to pay it off.

He didn't want to have to replace it at this stage of the game.

Rory kept driving, not fast enough to get pulled over, but smoothly enough to make some time in the truck lane, and Val's heart started to slow down a bit.

"Goddammit," Rory muttered.

"What?" Val checked the mirrors again.

"We are not going to have time to get coffee, are we?"

Val chuckled weakly. "Don't make any sudden moves, okay?" he said.

He knew that some rigs had a truly righteous amount of space in the cabin. Val had gone for a more modest sleeper apartment, but he still had a stocked fridge and a microwave. After some noodling about in the back, he reached for the armrest of Rory's bucket seat to flip out the small food tray and the larger cup holder. He set one of those glass bottles of cold vanilla coffee in the cup holder and a heated breakfast burrito on the tray, along with some paper towels, before dodging into the back again and fixing his own breakfast. When he sat in the passenger's seat, he set his iced coffee in the cup holder, the burrito on the tray, and hung a bag of apples from the arm rest in the middle.

"Apples?" Rory asked, not sounding surprised.

"They keep the doctor away," Val said primly. Then he chuckled. "A good crisp apple in the morning—either that or a tart sweet mandarin… anyway, I was raised to appreciate fruit. You're welcome."

"Thank you," Rory said, inclining his head gratefully and taking a gulp of the coffee. "Seriously, I appreciate this."

Val sighed and picked up his own steaming egg burrito. "Well, you're welcome. I appreciate the backup."

Rory grunted. "I wish you didn't need it so damned bad. What in the hell do you think *is* in that refrigeration unit?"

Val sighed, because he'd been gnawing at this too. "I don't think it matters," he said after a moment. "It could be the jizz of a Martian alligator trained to *eat* God's gorillas, and it still wouldn't change one immutable fact."

"What's that?" Rory sounded very interested now.

"That whatever is back there, it is probably *not* what Vinnie paid for."

Rory made a little *oof* sound, but Val wasn't discouraged. It wasn't that he felt like Rory didn't believe him. It was just that Rory was easy to talk to like this, and Val needed someone to bounce his ideas off.

"Why do you think that?" Rory said.

"Well, the obvious," Val told him. "They started out trying to get us to take responsibility for a load they wouldn't let us inspect. When we didn't— and adhered to the original contract of inspecting the load upon delivery— that's when the brothers started following us and trying to get back there."

"Why do you think they keep trying to do that?" Rory asked slowly. Again Val got the feeling he had his own conclusions but wanted to hear what Val thought.

"I think they're trying to sabotage the load," Val said. "And it needs to be done before inspection so they can blame us. They've obviously been in some sort of transport business for a while—they've got contacts. And it's not like the road from Bakersfield to Austin has that many nooks and crannies in it for us to hide. They know we have to make a straight shot if we're going to get the product to the lab before the refrigeration unit conks out. Legal or not, they've got us in a tidy corner. It's on us to get that bull jizz or divine alligator Martian gorilla spunk to the lab where Vinnie arranged to test it, because whatever the lab results, it has to be untampered with or Vinnie loses everything."

Rory nodded, taking another gulp of his coffee. "So do we have enough gas to get us to our target destination?"

"Yeah," Val said, taking a slow, luxurious sip of his own. "And I might even go back and get some more of my sleep in the next hour." He suppressed a yawn. "I'm pretty sure breakfast will make me sleepy."

Rory chuckled. "As it should. You covered a lot of ground this morning."

Val shrugged modestly. "You have no idea what a luxury it is to have a driving partner. Part of me is all proud, going, 'I can do it! I can do it!' but part of me is like, 'Go sleep, you idiot! How often does this happen!'"

Rory's chuckle changed to an outright guffaw. "Well, then, get some sleep while you can, and then we can switch off in a few hours and talk."

"Talk?" Val asked through a full mouth.

"Oh yeah," Rory said. "If it's ten o'clock, I've got a good ten hours to convince you to sleep with me. As soon as you wake up, I see that as my window to shoot for the stars."

Val had to swallow quick or spit out burrito crumbs as he got caught in a laugh. "Oh my *God*, you're arrogant!"

"Nope," Rory said, sounding gratifyingly sober. "Just… determined. Now that I know what I want, I need to convince you that I deserve a shot at it."

Val gave his own soft chuckle. "You think it can be done?" he asked, and while he was doubtful—the man had proved himself competent, brave, and excellent at his job, but that still didn't make him boyfriend material—he did feel like Rory might have earned exactly what he was asking for. An honest conversation. How hard could that be?

"Have some faith in me, Perci*val*."

Val snorted. "I'll have a conversation with you," he said firmly. "But I'm still not telling you my name."

"We'll see," Rory said sagely. "There are all manner of my personal boundaries I am willing to cross to be a candidate for your affections."

Val snorted again before he took another bite of his burrito and swallowed. "Look," he said, "I'd love to listen to more American Musical Theater when I go in the back, but maybe we can scan the CB frequencies for a bit."

"Think we'll pick up anything good?" Rory asked, which just confirmed Val's own opinion. They'd been so busy pushing through their next bit of driving they hadn't used one of the key weapons in any trucker's arsenal to do his job. His communications system.

"Only one way to find out," Val said grimly, and then he yawned. "But let's listen first, because I am going to have to finish my six-to-eight hours here, once my breakfast is all comfy in my stomach."

Briefly, Rory took one hand off the wheel to hold a hand to his chest.

"That is the cutest fucking thing I've ever heard a grown-up say in my life."

Val gave him a disgusted look. "My mother is a wonderful woman," he said. "Just because she's raised me with words that give some comfort is no reason to get all jealous."

Rory chuckled, but Val heard an underlying current that actually surprised him. He *was* jealous. Suddenly Val really *did* wonder about Rory's family, about what he'd grown up with. Maybe it was easy for Val to open up his heart to someone. He'd had breakups before, and even his worst one, right after his unsuccessful stint in junior college, had been met with soup from his mother, trips to the movies from his younger siblings, and a long-haul trip to Seattle with his father.

It was, Val remembered now, the thing that had cemented his career choice, that trip to Seattle.

Val knew he could survive heartbreak. Maybe Rory didn't. Maybe it was *Rory* who needed longer to think about it, or more practice to say it.

Val thought maybe, even if Rory hadn't succeeded by the time they reached Austin, he should give the guy just a little more time. So far, he'd been worth the risk.

THE CB chatter was disquieting in that there was none.

"This is weird," Val muttered, switching channels for the umpteenth time. "I look like tenderized steak. I know I left a mark on more than the asshole with a broken arm back in Santa Fe."

"Is *that* where we were?" Rory asked, only a little surprised. He'd gotten good at finding signs to the freeway, but Val kept to the truck stops outside of town. It all started to blur after a bit.

"Yeah," Val said. "Nice town. Honestly, cold in the winter, and I have to say I'm used to sea-level oxygen, but very rainbow friendly. Great little shops and stuff. I spent three days there once, waiting for a bonded return load in early December. Got a room at a little B and B, went Christmas shopping for the fam. Loved it."

Rory frowned. "Must have been worth it to sacrifice all those deliveries in the busy season."

Val shrugged, and Rory wished he could see the man's expression. "An older couple was moving their staircase from Bakersfield to Santa Fe to install in their daughter's house—apparently Dad had hand carved the thing, and it was for their daughter's custom home. I was supposed to bring a short trailer full of handmade quilts and craft supplies back from a church group to sell at a show in Long Beach. The organizer of the quilt show was in her eighties and had a health scare. It was, you know, the crazy season. My guys all had jobs, I had this one, and everybody was paying premium for deliveries, and, you know, I could have ditched the contract, paid the fees, and left them in the lurch, or I could have hung out, negotiated another contract with a full-sized trailer with some room, and helped the little old ladies out." Rory felt rather than saw his smug little smile. "And get my Christmas shopping done at the same time."

Rory had to laugh. "Buy any of their quilts?" he asked.

"Shh…." Val told him. "My mother thinks I shopped all over Santa Fe for it."

And Rory's little laugh turned into a full-throated guffaw. "You're something, Valatrix Royal."

Val was in the middle of a sip of water, which he promptly spit out. "No, no, no, no, no," he said, wiping his mouth on his shoulder. "Good Lord, where did that come from?"

"Valerie?" Rory asked in a small voice, not wanting Val to kill him in his sleep the next time he went to nap in the cozy little apartment.

"You know, there *is* a way to solve this mystery, don't you?" Val asked, exasperation in his laugh. His voice gentled. "C'mon, McCauley—"

"Rory."

"Okay, fine. You want me to call you Rory, I'll call you Rory. But if you want the whole of my name, I need to know. Why no past boyfriends? Why no vengeful exes—or needy exes or happy exes. I *know* you have a son, and I don't need his personal details, but…." He let out a breath. "You know my sister Laure has two teenaged boys, and Prock's on his third baby. You know Dean and I—and most of my siblings—got our sense of humor from my mom. It's unintentional, but a lot of my family history is on a silver platter for you to see. I-I've had too many 'just passing throughs,' do you understand? I'd rather be alone. If you're going to keep hitting on me, the least you can do is tell me *why* you're just passing through."

Rory let out a breath. "It's… like I said," he started after a moment. "It's such a small story. I knocked up my wife, she had Anthony, and"— his voice softened—"he's the greatest. I mean, I know he's in his twenties, and I shouldn't be all sweet on my kid at this stage, but he's so awesome. Smart and kind, and he actually likes working with me at the gun range, which, you know, I *love*. He got a degree in business, and when we started the thing up, I thought, 'Well, here goes a lot of money into nothing.' But he's making it work and… well, if you ever want to find me when I don't have a security gig, that's where I'll be."

"That's nice," Val said, and the sincerity in his voice did something soft to Rory's soul. It was easy to keep going once Rory heard that sound.

"It really is," Rory said quietly. "And I guess… I like to keep that private. I got in the habit of keeping things close to my vest. I came out right after I applied for Quantico, thinking, you know, I'd never get in. I was a small-town defense attorney, but I'd done some good work and won some shooting contests to be honest, and I guess I had a good reputation. So I couldn't be out at work—not twenty-five years ago— and I definitely couldn't be out when I was taking care of Anthony. And I couldn't ask anybody to share that kind of secrecy. It was bad enough that *I* had to live my life with a toe in the closet. I couldn't ask anybody else to do it. So… what did you call it? 'Just passing throughs'? I got used to those. I'd have them when I was traveling with the bureau, and then back at home taking care of my son, I was a single, celibate dad."

"What about your ex?" Val probed delicately, and Rory could hear that it was delicate.

"She's the greatest," Rory said, wanting to put his hand to his heart but needing to keep both hands on the wheel through a wide curve in the road. "I mean that sincerely. I was her bride's attendant for her second wedding, and her husband is the sweetest guy. Good stepdad to Anthony, worships Connie's shapely little toes. I…." He sighed and went for full honesty. "I'd really love what she's got. I just, I guess I assumed it was all too late for me. I spent my life making Anthony my priority and my career a close second. I never planned for what I'd do if my career ended before I was ready."

"How did you get injured?" Val asked, and Rory grimaced. He couldn't say how he knew this was coming, but he had.

"It was… dumb," he said softly. "My partner and I were doing some basic investigating for another case. I'd just come off a big cartel bust, and I wasn't riding point on this one. The bureau tries not to burn people out. My partner and I were calling people in to be interviewed, doing sort of a gentle probe into our suspected drug dealer's personal life." He shook his head. "And we had recently finished interviewing the drug dealer's nephew. No big deal. The kid looked like he'd been part of the enterprise but was sort of a low-level flunky. We didn't have anything to hold him on, but we did get a lot out of him that he didn't realize he'd given. That sort of thing. So we make our report to the team leader, we're off duty, and we decide to stop for a soda and a candy bar on the way back to the hotel. We walk into the damned Wawa of all places, and the kid is there getting cigarettes. He sees us and…." Rory shook his head, still in disbelief. "I think he was rattled. He'd been questioned. He wasn't sure if he'd said what he oughta. He watched Marty and me walk into *his* safe space, I guess, and just pulled out his gun like this was the Wild West and started shooting." Rory shuddered and kept his concentration on the road and the multi-ton missile he'd be driving if he didn't pay attention for even a moment. "Marty went down first. I managed to make it behind a row of potato chips, but I caught a round in the thigh, which fortunately missed the artery." He shook his head again. "I had to take the kid out—I had to. We were down, he had the gun out, and his common sense had gone right out the window with it. He was shooting at random customers, the clerks. Marty and I needed medical attention, and he wasn't going to let anybody through."

Rory let out a sigh, and that moment came crashing down on him. Allen "Cookie Monster" Giles, in pants hanging down his ass and a Larry Byrd basketball jersey over his white T-shirt, his long yellow hair clumping with sweat, was holding the gun with that inexpert floppy wrist, arcing the barrel all over hell and back while he screamed for people to "Get out of my face!"

Nobody was in his face. Rory had pulled Marty out of his sight, and they were both hunkered behind the chip aisle, and everybody else had found some sort of shelter—including the seven-year-old boy right across from Rory, with limpid brown eyes the size of dinner plates.

He'd looked so much like Anthony, Rory's stomach cramped with it. Rory's gun had been comfortable in his hand, every training exercise, every drill taking over his muscles, taking over his lizard brain, until it was the most natural thing in the world to push himself up and call out, "FBI, drop your weapon!"

And when Allen Giles had turned his gun toward Rory, it had been training that allowed him to fire.

Marty had survived a chest wound, but his fitness had been compromised, and he'd retired to a desk job. He'd lost forty pounds with PT, and he'd always had a good analytical mind, so the move hadn't bothered him too much, but Rory? Rory just couldn't.

He'd loved the day-to-day variation the job had offered, the flying from place to place, the integration of technology and evidence collection and human psychology that came into play with every case.

He'd accrued twenty years—he took his retirement, invested it in the gun club, and Anthony had… well, quit his job in San Francisco and come to live with him in the house Rory had bought about three miles from the range. Rory had gotten his PI's license and kept his gun licenses current, and the combination of the income for his security gigs and what he and Anthony made for giving shooting lessons and running the range with military precision had kept them both well fed and, in Anthony's words, "Not bored stupid."

It had been a good life these last three years, but even Rory had to admit he'd begun to feel the hole left by devoting his younger years to his work and his kid. Anthony had an active—and varied—life dating women and men, and Rory had often thought wistfully about the choices his son had now that he had not.

He'd assumed those choices long gone.

But Val and his stubborn insistence on *not* a "just passing through" was reminding him of what it had felt like to believe those choices were for *him*, and not only for his son.

"Rory?" Even over the noise of the engine and the rattle of the road, Rory could hear the gentleness in Val's voice, and he remembered what he'd been talking about before his mind had leapfrogged.

"I shot him," Rory said, crashing back down to earth.

"That must have been hard," Val told him. "I'm sorry."

Rory grimaced. "Well, I'm not sorry Marty's still alive, or that I am. Or the kid and his mom who were just in there for some road snacks and a soda. It… it was a sucky decision to make, but I'd make it again."

Val grunted. "I'm glad you did," he said.

Rory sent him a sharp glance before returning his attention to the road.

"Why is that?" he asked dryly.

"For one thing, I'm not sure anybody else would have had my back quite so effectively," Val told him. "Except maybe Dean, but if I put Dean in this sort of danger, our parents would *kill* me."

Rory tried to keep his expression neutral, not sure if it was his place to tell Dean's family that Dean often worked violent fugitive task forces, which while not as dangerous as what bomb technicians faced, did have its share of risk.

Val's grim snort told Rory that even if Val's *family* didn't know, Val had probably guessed.

"Don't say a word," Val told him, confirming Rory's suspicions. "We all know he's probably working in a dangerous department and that his load of crap that he's in no real danger on any particular day is particularly pungent and nowhere close to the truth."

"But…," Rory prodded.

"But what *we* don't know, we can't tell Mom and Dad—and that's sort of a tacit agreement the whole family has made so they don't worry."

Rory chuckled. "My God, your family. I remember catching Dean texting on his lunch hour once. The expressions he was making, how excited he got when he scored a point—I don't remember having that much fun with *anybody* besides my own kid."

Val shrugged and then yawned. "Yeah," he said when the yawn had let go. "We're close. We'd die for each other. Which is probably why Laure and Dean risked setting us up together."

"Wait, what?" Rory asked, but Val, chuckling, squeezed his shoulder gently and yawned again.

"I'm gonna take that nap you keep offering," he said. "In the meantime, turn the CB off and keep listening to music. If you really want to turn my key, I'm a sucker for *Jesus Christ, Superstar* and *Into the Woods*."

"You'll listen to *Chicago* and like it," Rory grumbled.

"Indeed I will," Val said and then disappeared into the cabin.

Rory pulled up the soundtrack, but as the opening chords of "All That Jazz" came on, Rory realized that in the course of their conversation, he'd completely forgotten his goal.

And then he realized that the hope of *sleeping* with Val Royal was not as all consumingly important as the role of *being* with the man was becoming.

He remembered that moment of watching Dean text, how animated he'd become, how Dean Royal's flat brown eyes had warmed and crinkled at the corners and how a man who had cut his reputation on being icy and in control had suddenly seemed warm and human and approachable.

Val was all of those things. What would it be like to take a break from his job and find a dry, funny text from Val, inviting Rory to spar with him, goading him to be witty, to poke the man into swiping back.

Their conversation so far had been intriguing, and as much as Rory wanted that powerful, no-nonsense body, he was now hungering as much for Val's *company*.

When this job was done and they were both back in California, Rory wondered what he'd have to do to make "just passing through," turn into "always wanting to see you."

As he started humming along to "All that Jazz," he realized he just might have what it took.

# Razzle Dazzle

Val woke up two hours later feeling like that last tag end of his sleep was enough to boost him for a week. *These* were the times when he wanted a chance to jog around the truck stop, or even hop in the driver's seat and push on until morning.

Except it was now a mere one in the afternoon. Didn't matter. After a yawn and a stretch—and a trip to the tiny travel sink to brush his teeth and rinse the grit out of his eyes—he hit the portajohn and washed his hands. While usually he used bathrooms at truck stops or service stations because keeping those receptacles filled could be a colossal PITA on long trips, he was always secretly amazed that a big-rig cabin really *could* harbor many of the comforts of home.

When he finally emerged and got back in the passenger's seat, he felt charged and ready to go—and only a little aware of his cuts, bruises, and scrapes from the multiple fracases he'd managed to survive the night before.

He belted himself in and took a look around, the wide green plains declaring them well outside of Austin city limits and still under the blazing blue dome of Texas.

Still, he was surprised when he saw the sign for Waco.

"You went out of your way," he said, curious.

"I saw one too many black trucks," Rory told him sourly. "I've got Ford 450s on the brain now, and considering we're in *Texas* and *everybody* needs a crew cab and towing capacity, I gotta tell you, I'm starting to feel twitchy."

"Still didn't lose any time," Val said, pleased. "In fact, I think we'll be there two hours early."

"Great," Rory said, still sounding sour. "I've got to piss like a racehorse—and afterwards, I want to have a little talk about whether or not you think these assholes will be waiting for us."

"Oh, they'll definitely be waiting for us," Val said grimly. "It's why I called the USDA—and Dean. I'm going to check with both of them here while you hit that little button on the tablet there…." Val had set up a map tablet on his dashboard—not that he always got signal—but the refresh button was set permanently on "find a truck stop bathroom near me" because sometimes there wasn't a road shoulder that would hold a big rig, and sometimes a big boy needed a big bathroom.

Rory did that and grunted. "Five miles," he said, sounding relieved. "I can make five miles. Do you think *you* can make five miles?"

Val frowned, puzzled. "Well, yeah. I used the little boy's bucket in the water closet. That's what it's for."

"I don't mean until you have to *pee*," Rory said, laughing at what sounded like a joke only he knew. "I mean is anything bad going to happen to you? Are you going to step outside and be surrounded by wasps?"

"Wasps?" Val gaped.

"Are you going to fall into a hole?"

"Probably not—"

"Flies? Boils? Time travel back to the Civil War? Look, man, I'm up for anything. But you got to let me know."

"I am *not* getting teleported to the Civil War," Val told him. "What in the actual hell?"

"No—no, you can't make light of this," Rory insisted, and Val noted that they'd clicked down a mile toward the rest stop and thought that might be a good thing. Rory was acting *very* odd, and while delusions of time travel had never plagued *Val* when he really had to pee, you never knew with some people.

"Light of what?" Val asked, laughing. "Your UTI delusions?"

"No, goddammit, I've got a point here!"

Val stared at him. "Okay, okay. What's the point?"

"I was driving here, freaking out about black trucks, wondering what you'd taste like—"

"Nungh." Val had to swallow. He hadn't been ready for that. "Like kissing?" he asked, feeling small and young when he was forty goddamned years old!

"Like your come down my throat, if you must know," Rory snapped, and Val clunked his head back against the head rest. He'd been trying so hard not to think about sex and Rory McCauley.

"This?" he asked gruffly. "This is what you're thinking about as you drive my rig?"

"Not at first," Rory admitted. "At first I was thinking about *Chicago*. Then I was thinking about *Into the Woods*. Then I was thinking about the movie version of *Into the Woods*, and then I was thinking about Chris Pine, who looks nothing like you, but suddenly all I could hear was you, singing 'Agony,' and I thought, 'I'd like to see him rip open his shirt in agony for my touch. That would be fun,' and then I remembered the last two days. If you were in the movie, you would have fallen off the waterfall. If you were on the stage, you would have fallen off onto the floor. When we finally get rid of this load and get a nice hotel, my treat, and a bath and a steak, I am going to fall asleep with you in my arms and wake up screaming, 'Oh my God, Val, somebody's going to beat you!'"

By this point, Val was laughing so hard he couldn't breathe.

"Oh my God," he whooped. "Oh my God. Rory, we've got one mile to the rest stop, man. Just hold on. For Christ's sake, hold on—the minute your eyeballs stop floating, I promise you, sanity will return."

"You say that," Rory muttered, shifting gears as the offramp came into sight. "You say my sanity will return, but I just spent a long time in my own head, convincing myself to let you in, telling myself that a grown-up relationship could not possibly be worse than living alone and watching middle age charge at me like a slow train, thinking about what might have been."

Val caught his breath and allowed his laughter to taper off. "Aw, man, don't think of it like that. My whole life I've been looking forward to… to what my parents have! And trust me, it's not glamorous. Their idea of a rockin' good time is taking each other's blood pressure and scratching each other's backs. For date night, they research good salt-free recipes and go shopping for them. It's… it's *insane* how boring they are."

Rory's sourness eased along with Val's guffaws. "Then why do you want it so bad?" he asked, coasting into the parking lot and scanning for any suspicious Ford 450s—or maybe that was just Val, catching his paranoia.

"Because they do," Val said, his smile wistful. "They just… amuse each other is all. They look forward to the grocery store because it's an opportunity to talk. They like scratching each other's backs because it means they get to touch. They take bets on who has the BP closest to the target zone. Once I stopped fooling around, relationships started looking like opportunities—you know, to have someone in my life I looked forward to being with as much as they did."

Rory grunted and brought the rig into the nearest angled space in the rather crowded lot. After it was positioned—and Val was full of admiration for his confidence, because not everybody could drive a rig and Val really *was* lucky Rory had been taught—Rory set the thing in idle and squirmed while he pinned Val with a glare.

"What are you saying?" he asked, his voice a little thready with discomfort.

"I'm saying middle age doesn't have to suck if you've got a partner to—"

"Suck you?" Rory quipped grimly.

"Get the hell out of my truck," Val told him. "Take ten, run some laps, and come back and let me do the same. Holy Jesus, you try to talk to a guy—"

Rory grinned at him. "God, you're easy." Then he opened the door and slid out, leaving Val to check the mirrors and back-end cameras like an automaton, because Rory wasn't the only one spying bad guys around every corner.

Ten minutes later, Rory came trotting back to the truck, and Val glared at him sourly and made a motion with his finger, indicating Rory should do some laps before Val forgave him. Rory laughed and saluted, and Val's shoulders relaxed, knowing the other man was on the job.

He wondered at that, how he could trust Rory McCauley so quickly, know the man had his back—but he had no doubts. Maybe it was because the night before, when he'd been about to engage his opponents in the minimart, Rory had trusted *him*. Don't leave the haul alone. It had become their mantra with this gig. And as ridiculous as it seemed to have to risk his life and his rig and his business for a dying refrigerator full of bull semen, Rory seemed to grasp the importance like Val did. It wasn't only about the *haul*, it was about the people—Vinnie's family, his employees, his wife, his kids, his stock—who were counting on the haul arriving when it did. The more Val was on the road with this one, the more he was sure Reg had been absolutely on target and there was something amok with the payload. The first two loads gone awry had pretty much put him and Vinnie on alert. They'd been warned. And Val had no doubt now that the Cassidy brothers were the ones responsible; just like he had no doubt that they were the ones in the F-450.

Of course the *big* question was *why*—and it was a question Val planned to get right on just as soon as Vinnie's investment was secure. Whether that meant the product was usable or not was not on his agenda.

It was that it hadn't gone bad on *his* watch. So far he'd done absolutely everything to ensure that if there was anything wonky about those straws of cow spunk, neither he nor his client were liable. If this load of spunk was really a load of crap, Vinnie could recoup his funds, and Val would not have lost the shipment. But he had to be in a position of being able to prove that when they arrived at the lab to test it.

Funny, his folks had been hoping for doctors or lawyers or professors. Hence the extravagant and improbable names. Val had not been happy during his two years of junior college, and he'd taken to his blue-collar business like a duck to water, but apparently a little bit of lawyering had seeped through.

It was like he could finally see the point.

Val watched as Rory made a circle of the truck, the engine's idling a comforting rumble that had sung him to sleep more often than he could count. Before he fell into that comfort, he picked up his cell and called Dean.

"Where you at?" Dean asked crisply, picking up before the ring was even done.

"Just cleared Waco," Val told him. "Rory's doing truck laps at a rest stop, and I'm doing my own in ten, then it's straight through to the lab. Checking to see what's up?"

Dean grunted. "Well, thanks to your info—and Reg's research—we have confirmation that your two troublemakers are the Cassidy brothers, and the USDA has shared some disturbing bits of history. You ready?"

"Hit me with it," Val said, watching as Rory rounded the truck and went for another lap.

"First take a look at the pictures I'm texting you."

Val's phone buzzed and he got another gander at the two guys who had been harassing Rory the night before—and who had tried to ambush them at the rest stop.

"There's our scumbags," he said with satisfaction, and after reading the details that came with the mugshots, "Rob and John Cassidy I take it?"

"Yes indeedy. Oldest children of their father, James, who built up Elite Cattle from three heifers and a bottle of jizz nearly thirty years ago. Here's his pic, back before old age and bad habits hit him hard."

The man in the picture had small eyes in a flatly planed, craggy face, and Val frowned as he contrasted it with the next pic Dean had sent, in which the man was older, frail, his big frame clothed in baggy skin and baggier clothes as he leaned on a cane and towed oxygen behind him.

"Bummer," he muttered. "Remind me to watch my sodium."

"Yeah—steak night is suddenly not quite as attractive."

Val frowned. "Steak night?"

"Yes. One night I eat steak, one night pork, two nights chicken, one night fast food, and two nights vegetarian. I can trade off chicken or pork nights, *never* add fast food, and fried tempura *never* counts as vegetarian."

Dear God. Val's little brother. "What about fish or sushi?" Val asked in spite of himself. "Where do those fit in?"

"Hmm… it depends. Fried food gets lumped into fast food, but the omega-3 fatty acids are essential for—"

"Stop, Dean. Just stop. You are making me tired. Let's just make a promise to never take up smoking and scotch as a hobby and I think we'll be okay."

"Sure." Obviously Dean felt as though his health would fall to shit if he so much as ate a chocolate bar, but since he wasn't raiding Val's refrigerator, Val might not disown him.

"Anyway, James Cassidy's health falls downhill—"

"Goes. It goes downhill," Dean corrected.

"I'm going to throttle you through the phone waves," Val muttered. "For fuck's sake, let me finish a thought."

"Hey, you're the one who interrupted me. You didn't need directions to my diet—"

"Yeah, yeah, yeah—I hear you. Let's focus, okay?" Val wondered if Dean ever remembered all the times Val had stepped forward to take out the kids who'd tortured his little brother through grade school. Times like this when every word out of Val's mouth felt dissected and pureed through Dean's analytical brain made him doubt it very much.

"Sooo," Dean said, drawing the word out, "James Cassidy's health falls downhill, and his two sons take over. On paper Elite Cattle Company is still the thriving business it's always been. But…." His voice dropped, and Val could picture Dean sitting at his computer, scrolling through figures. "Yes. There we go. So Elite Cattle Company continues to thrive, but there are… glitches."

"There usually are," Val said, unsurprised.

"So Elder Cassidy's first stroke was four years ago…." Dean was *definitely* scanning figures as he spoke. "The company toddled along with steadily decreasing profits, and then—oh!"

"What?" Val watched as Rory made a third lap around the truck, smiling a little because the man wasn't slow, even in boots. His long rangy frame moved easily, and Val could see some of the stiffness working its way out of his backside and thighs as he went. The man sure was a joy to watch.

"They had—well, it's called an *industrial accident*, but apparently there was a coolant failure in one of their stock houses."

"They lost meat?" Val asked absently. *Such* a joy to watch.

"They lost *stock*," Dean said, sounding shocked and appalled at the same time. "Remember how hot it gets? Well, most places have shade and water and covered barns, but this breed is apparently really delicate. They *had* a cooled barn, and the AC broke, and...."

"Oh God," Val muttered, his attention finally wrenched away from Rory McCauley's ass by the awfulness that implied. "How many head of cattle did they lose?"

"It says here one hundred fifty." Dean sounded suspicious.

"Did they get an insurance payout?" Val asked. He'd seen the cattle around the place. They looked good and healthy, he'd thought. And plentiful.

"They did," Dean mumbled. "And a *really* sizable one at that. I mean, I realize these cows are supposed to produce, you know, meat of the gods, but this is...."

"What?" Val prompted, scanning for Rory again. And there he was, doing what would probably be a final lap.

"Didn't you say you're transporting bull jizz?"

Val almost groaned. "Yes, bull semen is my payload." He paused. "It's in the trailer I'm hauling," he amended.

Dean snorted. "I'll take that for what it's worth," he said. "But no—there should be seminal samples from their prize bull, Ambassador, in your shipment. That's the bull that's listed as their primary stud."

"Okay, yeah," Val said. "Although, you know, if Mom and Dad had eight—"

"Oh God, don't get me started," Dean muttered. "We're just lucky Laure and Prock didn't get in on the naming thing. The horror. Anyway, Ambassador is listed as their stud. It's his jizz you should be carting around. There's only one problem."

"What's that?" Val asked, motioning for Rory to come in so he could have his shot at the urinal.

"Well, while Ambassador isn't mentioned as a casualty of the facility breakdown, there are three head of cattle here that were worth—collectively—as much as the other one hundred fifty that died."

"Oh my God," Val said in recognition. "They didn't just lose their *cattle*, they lost their *studs.*"

"Yeah," Dean muttered. "Probably."

"But there were young cattle on that property," Val said. "I saw calf pens *with calves* in the distance. Who's their stud if Ambassador was lost in the accident?"

"That there is the hundred-thousand-dollar question." Dean was quiet for a moment. "You know, there are rules against inbreeding cattle. Did any of those cattle look… I don't know. Deformed?"

"Yeah, Dean. Every fucking cow on that property looked deformed. But I checked on it—that's just what those things look like."

"Great," Dean muttered. "I'm only saying, maybe that's what they're trying to hide."

Val grunted. "This is the third shipment. The other two were stolen en route. I mean, *two* shipments of bull jizz. It was probably these two guys."

"The insurance paid for both of them?" Dean asked.

"Yes, but Vinnie had already filed his business plan. Even if the Cassidys got paid for their junk by the insurance, *Vinnie* needs this product or his business plan is void. He needs proof that there is something hinky here so he can *not* pay the Cassidy family and give that money to somebody else for a different stud, and so the insurance companies can maybe reimburse him for his other losses. That's why he hired me. To ensure the delivery. But since we're being chased by the Cassidy brothers, I've got to assume they were behind the other two thefts and were trying a different tack on this one. Not out-and-out theft, but sabotage. When that didn't work—"

"Out-and-out theft is fine," Dean supplied grimly. "So yes, your plan to get to the lab and get what's in the back of your trailer tested and verified—or tested and determined to be lacking—is a good one. But here's the fun part."

"Uh-oh."

"We need the video from your truck cameras to make a case against them."

"Oh my God."

"Yeah, I know. It's either that or video from some other creditable source. And until we get video of them actively trying to sabotage the shipment, I can't get men to guard you *or* the people at the lab while the comparisons are made."

"Oh. My. *God.*"

"And we've got a line on your boys, and their F-450 is coming off another highway, but they're as close to the lab as you are."

"Are you fucking kidding me?" Val asked. Next to him the door opened, and Val thought longingly of using a bathroom that was more than half an inch wider than he was.

"I am not," Dean said. "But… but give me a minute. I'll call you back in ten minutes. Could you do me a favor and stay where you are?"

Val brightened. "Oh boy, *can* I!" he said.

Dean grunted and hung up.

"What?" Rory asked.

"Oh, I've got ten minutes of what to catch you up on," Val said. "But first I'm going to go use the bathroom, and then I'm going to take my own jog around the truck, and then we're going to talk plans. What do you think?"

Rory scowled. "That was your brother on the phone?"

"Yeah."

"Dean?"

"Yeah."

"And he's the one cooking up the plan."

"Yeah."

The scowl deepened. "You do know your brother's cray-cray, right? Like, he's only been able to keep one partner for the last five years crazy."

"They have a decent clearance rate," Val defended, like he'd been defending Dean his entire life.

"Oh, they have an *amazing* clearance rate," Rory snapped. "But that doesn't stop people from calling Dean and Marcus the craziness twins."

Val chuckled. "Really?"

"Yes, really—"

"That's awesome. I'm going to bait him with that the next time he calls. And if I don't hurry, that's going to be while I'm on the pot, and that's embarrassing. Watch my back, partner—"

Rory leaned forward, grabbed Val by the front of the shirt, and hauled him in for a kiss. A hard, good kiss that hit all of Val's corners and his spots and left him panting and a little confused when Rory let go of his shirt.

"Wha—"

"You have been battered and beaten in the last two days, and I am really starting to get attached to you. I'm starting to *reevaluate* because of you. I'm starting to have *dreams*. So you think long and hard before you listen to your batshit crazy little brother and follow him off the cliffs of hell, okay?"

Val knew his grin was stupid but couldn't help it. "You'll follow me anyway, won't you?"

"Shut up," Rory growled.

"That's all right. I'm worth it." And with that, Val slid out of the driver's seat and went jogging for the rest stop.

His entire body tingled. Dean called as he was shaking off his arousal, and they were still discussing the plan when he clambered up into the cab of the rig.

Rory was munching on one of the chicken wraps Val had packed in the dark hours the day before, eyebrows raised like he was pleasantly surprised.

"Curry," Val said, holding his hand over his phone. "Helps me cut down on the salt."

Rory laughed a little, and Val went back to listening to Dean.

He signed off five minutes later feeling a little reckless, a little bloodthirsty, a little like kicking ass.

"What?" Rory asked suspiciously. "What is that expression on your face?"

"Hold on to the chicken strap," Val said, curling his upper lip in a snarl of excitement. "It's gonna get real interesting."

# The End of the Day

Two hours later Rory was buzzing along in a refrigerator truck the size of a U-Haul, muttering to himself, "This is so stupid. *So* stupid. So dumb. I can't believe those assholes talked me into this. This. Is. Insane."

Oh, it was. It was nuts. But it made a twisted amount of sense.

Dean had done most of the prearrangement, which just proved he was one of the coldest, most organized motherfuckers Rory had ever worked with. Rory had to admit that he and Val were a much better fit. There was something *visceral* about Val. He was smart, and a planner, and he'd cold-bloodedly put his client's and company's needs ahead of his own. But then he'd taken out five meatheads in a minimart with only a black eye and a busted lip and cheek to pay for it. Apparently the thing Val Royal had in spades was the ability to back his word up with actions.

Rory approved.

And now it was his turn.

Dean had taken care of the two refrigerator trucks and the notary to witness shifting part of the load to each truck—backed up, of course, by the cameras Val had hooked up on the back end. Prock's work on the refrigerator unit in the big-rig trailer held up, and the interior had been a frosty zero degrees Fahrenheit to back up the smaller self-contained units inside. Every gauge had been triple checked—there should have been no heat degradation of the product *at all* in their rather epic twenty-three-hour drive from Bakersfield to Austin, detours and all.

Now all that remained was getting proof that something was wrong with the sample before the Cassidy brothers forced Val's rig off the road.

Val was the one who was bonded to the job—*he* was responsible for getting the payload to the lab, where Vinnie was waiting to take possession and submit the cannisters for testing. While having backups, Dean and Rory, get there with samples that would hold up in court, the contract Vinnie and Val had signed was very particular: Vinnie had to be there, and there had to be video verification.

But that didn't mean they couldn't use a little bit of distraction and theater to make that happen.

The tablet on the dash rang with Val's number and then Dean's, and while Rory understood why they'd need to communicate with phones, there was a reason CBs were still favored by truckers—the ease and clarity were better.

They just really didn't need anybody listening in on their convo.

"I'm here," Rory told them when the line connected. "You see any bogeys?"

"I got two on my ass," Val said. "Our buddies in the F-450 and one of the big rigs I saw when we were getting fuel in Arizona. They're both right up my sphincter, so I'm going slower. How about you two?"

"I got nobody," Dean said. "My ass is pristine. Not a dingleberry in sight. McCauley?"

Rory checked his mirror and grimaced. "I see two of those assholes from Arizona, one on my ass and one on my front, but I don't know if they know it's me yet. Everybody stay on the line so we see if this gets better or worse."

"Great," Dean muttered. "That's gonna be damned boring."

Val gave an absolutely evil laugh, and Rory heard the first notes of "End of the Day" first.

"Oh *hell* no," Dean protested, and Val started to belt out the lyrics at the top of his lungs.

And what was Rory supposed to do, leave him hanging?

For the rest of his life, he'd remember the next twenty years, erm, minutes as though orchestrated by the writers of *Les Mis*—oh, there was gonna be hell to pay, indeed.

Val, Rory, and Dean were each taking a different route toward the lab, which was in a big industrial complex on the outskirts of Manor, itself about an hour outside of Austin. Manor was close enough to the intersection of two major freeways and a sizable intersecting road for there to *be* more than one route. Rory and Val were on the two major freeways, and Dean was on the intersecting road about ready to take surface streets to the complex, so it was logical that he didn't have any "dingleberries," as he put it.

Since Dean was their most unimpeachable witness for delivery, they figured it was important for him to get there first, unnoticed, so the product could be well on its way to being tested before Val and Rory—and their shadows—arrived.

So it didn't surprise him to hear Dean's interjection of, "Guys, I'm here. The lab is ready for us with their first bay door open."

Rory was going to say, "I'm ten minutes out," when suddenly, over the phone, they could hear the rat-tat-tat of something that sounded like fireworks, but oh shit, oh shit, oh shit—

"*Fuck*!" Dean shouted. "Guys, there's an ambush. An F-450 and two 150s in the back bay. Them good ole boys got guns. I'm pulling out! You know what to do!"

And with that Dean's call ended, leaving Rory feeling cold and angry—and sure Val was going out of his mind.

"Okay, then," Rory said. "I'm ten minutes out of location B. Val?"

"I'm passing location A on Dean's ass," Val said tensely. "I've got everybody's attention, and yeah, these good ole boys got little meth-boy popguns like he said."

"Little guns, big guns—" Rory began, but Val wasn't stupid.

"It's the bullets that kill ya," Val told him. "Get your ass to the B site, Rory. Me and Dean, we're gonna run a family pit maneuver here and see if we can't get some more backup now that Dean's got confirmation that there's active hostility to getting the payload to its source. I gotta call the USDA to see what's up. You...." Val trailed off, sounding uncharacteristically hesitant even in the middle of the sudden-stop audible he was calling.

"This old boy knows how to keep lead out of his ass," Rory told him. Then, soberly, "Watch your own ass, Val." They'd planned for this, yes—Val and Dean heading for the first agreed-upon location. But however the Cassidy brothers got their info, it did *not* extend to the hurried conversation Dean, Val, and Rory had held while splitting the load between the rig and two smaller refrigerated units, when they'd engaged the services of another lab, just in case, and plotted a way for Rory to get there.

But that didn't mean Rory wasn't going to be listening, heart in his throat, until he knew those assholes with the guns were far away from two guys he *at least* regarded as friends.

"First I gotta get rid of these fuckers on Dean's tail," Val muttered tersely. "Signing off."

Rory checked his online map and glanced up, almost swerving off the road as a torn-off bumper from the shoulder came loose in the wash of the rig in front of him. God*dammit*. Sure enough, the pickup in front and to the left of him was slowing down, and the rig behind him was speeding up. They were on a freeway with civilians but—oh thank *fuck*.

The guy in the SUV coming up in Rory's blind spot suddenly veered right, probably having gotten a flat from some of the same debris Rory had barely missed. Rory braked hard and, spotting his hole in traffic, swerved to his left. The SUV skewed in front of Rory's pursuer, and the two of them skidded off road in a swirl of dust while the rig in front of Rory charged down the dead man's strip, bumping haphazardly as the driver strove to stop the heaving hunk of metal without jackknifing the trailer from the rig.

This branch of the highway stretched three lanes in either direction, with the exit just a mile away. Rory saw traffic starting to slow down as the debris marked its damage path through the speeding cars, and caught his breath. The only way—*only* way—the people on Val and Dean's six gave up their chase was if *somebody* got to the lab and got the product tested first.

As the red lights of slowing traffic began to pop up on the horizon like warning lights on a computer console, Rory took a deep breath and stepped on the gas.


VAL SWORE and used his considerable body strength to keep the rig on the road. They were ostensibly in a commercial area, although traffic was thin and mostly traveling fast and light, which was good. Val had no idea how to keep civilians safe in this situation.

The PIT maneuver had been developed to hamstring high-speed chases in congested areas. One vehicle—in this case Dean, who was being pursued—would slow down enough to hamper the instigator's room to evade. Then another vehicle, one with some *heft*, would tag the backside of the instigator's ride—in this case, the Cassidys' F-450—hard enough to spin it sideways and then box the speedsters in.

This looked *great* on television, when the biggest hurtling projectile was an SUV. Driving a big rig in a PIT maneuver was a good way of cooking up cream-of-adversary roadkill soup and a manslaughter charge, not to mention endangering Val's little brother in a big way.

But Dean was bitching on the phone for Val to man up and do it already, and Val thought that no jury on the planet would convict him.

"You had better be in good enough shape to take care of the guys with the guns on my ass," Val snapped. "If your rig goes over and you get shot in the face, our parents will never forgive me."

"Oh please," Dean retorted, his voice the teeniest bit breathless. "You've been their favorite since your first baby scowl. We're totally clear for the next mile, Val. *Now, goddammit, now!*"

Val tapped the gas—even a love tap in a big rig took considerable strength, and a spurt of speed took a good long runway. This wasn't a matchbox car; this was thirty-five tons of machinery, including the moderate load in the back, and it did not start on a whim or stop on a dime, and if Val was aiming it at this F-450, he goddamned well better mean it.

He watched as the little guy in the passenger seat stuck his arm out the window, holding a pistol. It could have been a .45, but from this distance it looked like a peashooter. Val's blood ran cold nonetheless because the bastard was aiming that thing *at his little brother*.

Val *stood* on the gas, engaging his entire body and core as he steered the thing, aiming at the already demolished back quarter panel and a little sick with the knowledge that he was about to take out a $100,000 truck for $60,000 of bull jizz.

But then, he wasn't the one who had made that decision, was he?

Over the still open line, he heard the sound of firecrackers through a windstorm, and heard his brother swear.

"Dean? Are you hit?"

"No, but I think we're gonna lose our deposit on this truck!"

"Be ready!" he cried. In his rearview, he could see the two other trucks they'd picked up as Dean had sailed past the lab's loading dock, and he grunted. If he was going to take those assholes out, there was really only one way to do this, and Dean was right—he was going to have to do it now.

5-4-3-2—

*Kreeeeeeeeesh!*

Unlike the little push they'd given this truck when Rory'd been pulling away from the pumps, this was two great big machines traveling at sixty miles an hour. The crackling crunch of the chrome front of his rig taking out the steel and fiberglass of the F-450 actually felt *worse* than the jarring to the rig. Standing on the rig brake *and* the trailer brake while wrenching the wheel sideways pretty much ripped every muscle in Val's core, chest, arms, and back, but by God the damned rig *turned* when he told it to, and in a moment he was perpendicular to the road, the trailer rocking in desperate, earth-wallowing heaves as it tried to jackknife and topple to the ground.

"*No!*" Val screamed, every muscle in his body dedicated to the machinery that would keep his rig upright.

*Eerk—BAM—eerk—BAM!* The sounds of the stressed metal alternating with the crash of the rig when its wheels rocked off the ground and then came booming back echoed in Val's stomach. No. No. No, goddammit, *no!* He couldn't afford to let his rig topple, he couldn't afford to let his rig topple—

The sound of the two trucks in pursuit crashing into the trailer and tearing through the metal—even the reinforced refrigeration on the side—drowned out his scream of frustration as the trailer pin tore from the rig clamp and knocked the whole works off the back of his truck and into the massive ditch on the side of the road.

The rig itself gave one last rock and a crash of the wheels to the ground that snapped his teeth shut and then shuddered to a halt. As Val shook like a leaf, he watched his little brother, semiautomatic weapon in hand, stride across the road and aim the thing at the two brothers, who were still wiping blood off their foreheads and trying to remember their own names.

Val didn't even want to see about the henchmen who had ripped apart the trailer and driven their F-450s into the ditch.

In the back of his ringing ears, he heard Rory shouting. "Val! Val! You there?"

"Sort of," he panted, turning his engine to idle in case it would be needed to move the vehicle. Although this stretch of road wasn't busy, he knew that there was a small, steady backup of traffic on either side of the wreckage.

He was still staring, still dazed, when Rory's voice came over their makeshift intercom. "It's over, Val. I got the fridge truck into the loading bay. The lab's got the samples now. Whoever's after you, you can tell them it won't do no good."

"Fucking. Awesome." He took a deep breath and grabbed the phone from the rest in the console. "I'll be back on in five."

Val laughed helplessly to himself before tearing his still-screaming muscles reaching behind his seat for his own gun. He slid shakily to the ground before taking a breath to steady his legs and striding up next to his brother.

"USDA's coming," he told Dean.

"So's the FBI, ATF, and DEA," Dean replied sourly. "I don't care if they should be involved or not. I damned near called the U.S. Marines."

Val was about to retort that they'd probably need the Army Corps of Engineers to sort out the mess they'd just made on this little highway when the two Cassidy brothers emerged woozily from the dented front of the mangled 450.

"Don't matter," the bigger one—Robert—panted happily. "We won. That fuckin' jizz ain't never gonna land."

Val and Dean met eyes and started to chuckle.

"What?" Robert demanded, and next to him his smaller, younger brother demanded the same thing.

"What? What's so funny?"

"Jizz is in the lab right now, boys," Val drawled. "You want to tell us what they're going to find?"

The two men closed their eyes and groaned, and in the background Val heard the wail of sirens through the massive ache in his head as he settled himself down for a long, long wait.

RORY HAD to admit it to himself—if Vinnie didn't have "dedicated family man" written all over him, he would have been a smidge jealous of how loyal the guy was to Rory's Val.

Or, well, Val Royal.

Val's "old high school buddy" had shown up as Rory had been chafing in the lobby of the laboratory, a midsized, quietly handsome man with brown eyes in a tanned face, worn jeans and a neat if frayed button-down shirt, cowboy boots, and graying brown hair cut military neat.

None of that really impressed Rory, though. What *did* impress him was that while Vinnie's entire livelihood, his family ranch, his stock, his ambitions for the future—*all* of that—hung in the balance, his first question was about Val and Dean.

"How are they?" he asked anxiously, and Rory shrugged.

"There was a ruckus," he owned. "Our boys are sorting it out with the authorities, and the authorities are sorting it out with their superiors, and somebody is towing all the goddamned trucks."

Vinnie appeared stricken. "Val's rig?" he asked. "My God, that thing is his *child*."

Rory nodded and worked hard at keeping his posture against the wall languid and relaxed. "Yup. He says it needs to be checked out, but it was running on its own power when they drove it off. Can't say the same thing for the *trailer*, which means his brother is going to be in-fucking-sufferable that this entire plan came together."

Vinnie relaxed too, a faint smile on his face. "Dean? Yeah. They were like that when Val and I were in high school. We'd bring home our homework, and Dean would wander in—he couldn't have been more than six—and look at Val's trig or physics and go, 'Why aren't you doing it that way?'" Vinnie chuckled. "Used to make Val apeshit, but he'd listen, and then he'd do what his little brother said and *both* our grades would improve." Vinnie lifted a shoulder. "And then Val would get me to cut class so we could scare the crap out of the second graders who kept beating up the six-year-old who had been promoted to their class."

Rory smiled a little. "I knew Dean in the bureau. Could see right then them kids were tight."

Vinnie sighed and sank into one of the lobby chairs. Rory had already tried one. His legs were too long, but Vinnie fit nicely. "Their mom's the best, though. Fridays...." He chuckled again. "We'd stop by on Fridays—practically every kid in the neighborhood. Their mom worked at the local grocery store, and on Fridays they'd clear stock from the shelves. Val's mom would collect the cookie and chip packages that were going to get thrown out and bring them home and put them on the kitchen table. It was a free-for-all, except Val and Laure and Sal were absolutely ruthless about making sure nobody got sloppy or mean. But it was snack time for sure." He sighed a little. "Kids would help her do dishes and confess their deepest secrets. She had a way of making us see our parents as people, not tyrants. Of giving tips. You know, like, 'Hey, maybe wait until your dad has a chance to take off his shoes and read the paper for a bit before telling him there's one more thing he has to worry about.' And sometimes if the parents really *were* being awful, she'd intervene. She had a basement room with a couple of old couches, and I know more than one kid spent time down there because going home was dangerous. She'd call aunties or grandparents—or the state, if she was really worried—and make sure the kids were safe." He shook his head again. "Best woman in the world."

"Wow," Rory said, blinking eyes that were suddenly burning. "That explains a lot about that family."

"Val's the best," Vinnie confirmed. "It's why I asked him for help. He…." Vinnie took one of those breaths that told Rory he wasn't unmoved by how much hinged on the mysterious processes going on in the sterile portions of the lab right then. "He was the one person I could count on."

At that moment one of the technicians, dressed in a Tyvek bunny suit, emerged from the back of the building. "Mr. Aiello?"

"Yes, ma'am?" Vinnie stood up.

"We have some… concerning results from the samples your friend brought in. I understand the USDA inspector is coming to consult on this matter. Would you like to wait for him before we discuss—"

At that moment the door blew open and a sixtyish woman wearing a navy pantsuit and an emerald scarf blew in, with three younger men bearing briefcases and tablets in her wake.

"Mr. Aiello?" she said. "I'm Inspector Denise Glen. Have the results come in?"

Vinnie nodded, and the two of them started toward one of the consulting rooms in the back. Vinnie glanced at Rory and gestured him to join them. "Come on, Mr. McCauley. Val's gonna want to know what all the fuss was about."

Rory grinned and decided he could probably learn to love Vinnie Aiello just like Val did. "Wouldn't miss it," he said and joined Vinnie and all the suits to go see what the McGuffin actually looked like.

VAL SAT on the edge of the ER gurney and resisted the urge to lay back against it. He'd done that once when the doc had checked him out, and he now knew it for the trap it was.

"How you doing?" Dean asked perkily from his place on the visitor's chair.

"I hate you," Val said. "Why are we here?"

"Because you were part of an eighty-ton train wreck, and I want you assessed for soft tissue damage," Dean said. "I had my own checkup. Now stop being a baby."

Val barely refrained from whining. "This bed hurts me more than some painkillers and some sleep," he growled, and the look he got from his little brother was truly sympathetic.

"Yeah, that's why the doc is prescribing you some megadose muscle relaxers and giving you a week before you can drive again. Dude, that thing you did with the rig was truly impressive, and some torn stomach and neck muscles are nothing to joke about."

Val grunted. "Well, it's hard to joke about them when they're screaming in my ear," he admitted.

Holy God did he hurt. Everything hurt. Neck, back, head, stomach, ribs, thighs—upper and lower—head. Had he mentioned his head in that last list? It felt like he needed to mention his head again because *that* felt like a big meaty painful balloon.

Augh!

"Do I have a concussion?" he asked, trying to determine if that had been gone over. "It feels like I have a concussion."

"Yes, you do," Dean told him mildly, glancing up from his phone. "And the fact that I had to repeat it means you have a worse concussion than you let on when you got out of the truck."

Val groaned. "We arrested the bad guys, right?"

"Yessir, we did," Dean replied. "And the FBI would like to commend you on your driving, Mr. Royal. I told them I'd pass that on."

"Fuck you," Val muttered. "Did we ever figure out what this was about?"

"Sure we did" came a voice from the doorway. "Now scoot on over on that bed, son. I've got a story to tell."

Something—the painkillers, the muscle relaxants, *something*—must have kicked in right then, because Val could swear he felt everything in his body melt a little bit closer to normal.

"Rory," he said, aware he was near to crying. "God, man, so good to see you. How's Vinnie?"

"Up to his eyeballs in insurance paperwork and Feds," Rory said, and true to his word, he scooched right next to Val on the edge of the ER gurney before draping an arm around Val's shoulders.

Val couldn't help it. He dissolved, slumping against Rory's strong body and going limp with the comfort.

"Tell us the story," he mumbled. "Just know I've got a concussion, and I might not remember it all."

Did he imagine that kiss on the crown of his head, or was that real? Didn't matter, it continued to make things better in Val-land, and that was all he cared about.

"So," Rory said, his voice rumbling his shoulder under Val's cheek, "like you two guessed, this goes back to when the AC died in their stock building, killing off a hundred and fifty head of their top breeders, Ambassador among them."

"Bummer," Val conceded. That much loss of stock—and so horribly—wasn't to be wished on his greatest enemy, including the guys who'd tried to kill the three of them.

"Yeah, well, it would have been the whole herd, because all of Ambassador's baby-makers were in a freezer in the same unit. It was a massive loss, and from what the USDA lady told me, it was apparently chalked up to human error. The AC had been getting weaker for years. The old man had told his sons to replace it, but the boys had racked up gambling debts, and they decided to pay those off instead."

"Fuckers," Val murmured, but without heat. It was hard to be mad, even at idiots like Rob and John Cassidy, when Rory's arm was around his back and his head had *finally* stopped hurting.

"They're the worst," Rory agreed. "But they did find a way to keep the herd from dying out. Unfortunately, it was illegal and involved cow incest."

"Oh hell!" Val protested. "You were the perfect man, and then you said 'cow incest.'"

Dean—Val's stoic, number-crunching little brother—*snickered*.

"Sad but true," Rory agreed. "In this case, it was on a grand scale. One of Ambassador's progeny had been retained as another breeding stud. He hadn't yet been shown or rated, but the brothers were desperate. They needed refrigerators full of prize-winning bull semen, and they needed it stat, so they collected and inseminated and fudged the records and said it was Ambassador's spunk. Which would have been *great*, except...."

"Genetic abnormalities?" Dean asked, because Val's little brother was smart that way.

"Bingo." Rory touched his nose with his finger. "It's almost like you belong to an organization known for its investigative skills."

"You taught me everything I know," Dean replied flatly. "So all of the new bull's—"

"Dorito," Rory said, amusement lacing his voice. "Because apparently the creature is as dumb as. And also he's orange."

"So Dorito's progeny start cropping up with... what?" Dean cocked his head, and Val was suffused with a wave of affection for his little brother. So smart. So lonely. Too bad. He was a funny little bastard, but sometimes it seemed like only the Royals knew.

"Well, technically it's called BLAD," Rory said. "Don't ask me what it stands for, but essentially it means sick cattle and cows that miscarry more often. So the Elite Cattle Company's herd goes, in the span of two years, from a thriving business to a tragic mess."

"But all the cows *we* saw were normal," Val remembered. Reluctantly he sat up a little, but he wasn't sad when Rory put pressure on his far shoulder.

"Stop that," he murmured. "Lean on me. I like it."

Well, fine.

"And all the animals we saw *were* normal," Rory continued. "Because they made a deal to give half their best breeders for the services of another stud, which helped to revitalize their herd. But the brothers— who aren't that bright—are getting offers for Ambassador's sperm, because as you recall, they *fudged the paperwork* to get Dorito's spunk passed off as Ambassador's so they could inseminate their own herd. Ambassador was a great stud, and he was still on the USDA registry as alive and making babies."

Val *had* to sit up now, but this time it was with excitement.

"They sold it," he said, getting it. "They're gamblers. They sold that shipment and then stole it. The other guy got insurance, they got the money for selling the shipment, win/win."

"It was," Rory agreed. "And it was a scam they pulled off three more times—once in Wyoming, once in Canada, and once in California—"

"They spread it out," Dean said cannily. "So word wouldn't get around."

Rory nodded. "Indeed they did. And then came Vinnie. Vinnie's business plan was by far the most ambitious—they figured one big score, right?"

"But Vinnie kept trying to buy the same spunk," Val said. "And theft twice was fishy enough."

"This time, it had to be something else," Rory said. "So they tried to sabotage the freight container after you signed off on it. But you were too smart, and for that matter so was Vinnie. So they had to try to either sabotage the container on the road—"

"Or once we decided to get it tested, to intercept it before it got to the lab," Val finished off, the whole thing clicking into place.

"What's bothering me is how they knew," Rory muttered. "We were using telephones, not CBs. How'd they intercept our plans?"

"That would be my office," Vinnie said, stepping into the cubicle and making it officially crowded. "It turns out one of the brothers plays blackjack online with one of the secretaries' husbands. You kept me posted on every move, Val, and she was tapped into all my communications. She's being held pending charges right now."

"Oh my God," Val mumbled. "I am so relieved. I was seriously wondering if they were psychic or something, because those bastards were *everywhere*."

"I know it," Vinnie said, shaking his head. "I have to tell you, the extra lab reservation that Dean made was a thing of genius. By the time I knew where Rory was going, the whole thing was over but the shouting."

"No shouting," Val practically whimpered, and Vinnie put a gentle hand on his knee and squeezed.

"Don't worry, I'm only here for a minute, and then I'm stealing Dean and taking him to my place for a steak dinner and a good bed to sleep in before his flight back to Sacramento tomorrow morning." Dean worked at the field office in Roseville.

"I don't get a steak dinner?" Val whined.

"You," said the doctor, who had entered on Vinnie's heels, "get a short hop to a nice hotel. Mr. McCauley here promised he could get you comfortable accommodations not too far from the hospital, with someone who would keep an eye on you for the night."

"Oh thank God," Val muttered. "This fuckin' gurney here, doc—this can't be good for me."

"It's not," the doctor—their age, with thick blond hair and gentle blue eyes—said with a wry smile. "Which is why we're setting you free to sleep and eat with supervision, and then after you come back tomorrow at one for a checkup, you are free to drive the hour to Mr. Aiello's ranch and rest for the week required before you drive your rig back to California."

Val was going to protest. He was good at it. He knew how to whine and bitch and complain until he got his way. But he glanced at Rory, who smiled at him with hope, and suddenly he saw this for what it was.

An opportunity he might not get in the midst of his ordinary life.

"Sure," he said, watching Rory's face relax. "Who *can't* use a week's worth of R and R. Vinnie's place has a *pool*."

"And a Jacuzzi," Vinnie added. "And a cook and a housekeeper and a patio with a mister. It'll be like a hotel, but you'll get to say hi to the wife and kids, who will only be there long enough to delight you and not enough to cramp your style."

"That's a guarantee I don't think you can make," Val kidded, and Vinnie shrugged.

"They're going to Florida in two days for spring break. I'm joining them before you two leave. I think I can about put a gold seal on that."

Val's mouth fell open in surprise—and gratitude—and then the doctor shooed everybody out while he made one last check and the process of leaving the hospital began.

# You Better Shape Up

Rory managed the best hotel he could find between the hospital and Austin, and since it was billed as a resort for those who wanted to escape "the pressures of the city," it wasn't bad.

Val maintained a clenched-teeth quiet during the drive there, and Rory recognized a man dealing with pain. Dean had gathered their essentials from the rig before it had been towed, and Rory shouldered both knapsacks and his rifle case. The fact that Val let Rory lead the way and open the door for him was indication enough that driving a rig through a metal hurricane was not as easy as Val had probably made it look.

"Oh," Val said, stopping just inside the doorway. "A king-size bed?"

Rory snorted. "Don't get your panties in a bunch," he said. "I don't hit on injured men."

"Pity," Val told him and then proceeded to limp into the room, his back held like fragile glass.

"Don't get comfy," Rory said. "In fact, get naked." He dumped their stuff, such as it was, on a handy padded bench and set his rifle case carefully in the corner. "I'm gonna go make sure this place has the one damned thing I asked for, okay?"

"Sure," Val muttered, and he was still trying doggedly to lift the hem of his T-shirt up over his head when Rory returned from the bathroom.

"Is that water I hear?" Val asked, and Rory stood in front of him to gently take his T-shirt hem and lift it with care over his shoulders, around his elbows, and over his head.

Oh, his boy was bruised—some of them were already coming out—and Rory grimaced as he dropped the shirt on the floor.

"It is. Don't worry, automatic shutoff." The hotel bubble bath smelled like lemon and sage, and it wafted into the main suite. "Here, I'm gonna get familiar, don't—"

"I know, I know. My panties remain unbunched."

Rory chuckled. "As long as they remain off long enough to get you into the Jacuzzi tub."

Val let out a sound of decadent longing that probably hurt his already abused stomach muscles. "Really?" he asked pitifully.

"Really really," Rory told him.

"Is it big enough for two?" Val said, trying a coy look from under his eyebrows, but the wince he gave for craning his neck said everything Rory needed to hear.

"Not tonight it isn't," Rory said softly. He'd brought a towel in, and now he wrapped it around Val's waist, trying not to linger. Flat stomach, strong thighs, an ass that should have been squishy but wasn't? All a go.

Rory had never wanted anybody more, and the fact that he was being gentle and chivalrous made him feel as close as he'd ever been to a real lover and not a one-night stand.

"I'm—ouch—trying not to be mad at that," Val muttered. "God, we were only in the car for half an hour. Why is this—gah!" He'd made it to the bathroom and was trying to put a toe in the tub.

"C'mon, big guy," Rory cajoled. "Here, there's a step. Let me help you… there we go…."

"Whoamygod…." Val groaned as he sat on the bench of the tub and leaned against the sloped back. "This is… holy wow… if it was a teeny bit hotter…?"

"Nope." Rory slapped his hand away from the spigot control. "Remember that concussion? No steaming hot bath, just happy, happy lukewarm."

"Fine." Val sighed. "This feels too good to complain. Wow, did you know what you were doing."

"My son had one of these installed in our place when I was injured," Rory told him. "And that was when I decided that his teenaged years be damned, I was leaving him in my will."

Val smiled in sympathy. "Rough?"

"Nothing dramatic," Rory confessed. "He was a moody little bastard. Basic kid shit. Trying to make his mom and me feel bad about the broken home, that sort of thing. But you know, we've all got our shit times growing up. It's why we celebrate milestones like high school and college education, you know?"

While he was talking, he leaned against the counter to take off his boots and put them in the closet. After shucking his socks, he rolled up his jeans to the knees and perched on the edge of the tub, resting his feet on the bench.

To his surprise and everlasting joy, Val wrapped his hand around Rory's calf under the water and just… touched, smoothed his palm and broad fingers over the curve of the muscle.

"Nice," Rory murmured.

"You're easy to touch," Val told him.

"Well, maybe next time we do a room like this, I can join you," Rory said wistfully. He was pretty sure Val was going to need help out, and he wouldn't be great at that if they were both naked and slippery— no matter how much the image tantalized him.

Val squeezed his calf. "That reminds me," he said, brought back to his more practical self by the warm water. "I…." He bit his lip and turned his head. "I mean, *technically* your contract is up, you know. You were contracted to get the load here and then to take one of Vinnie's breeders back to Elite Cattle Company. Since they're eyeballs deep in fraud and attempted murder charges, that contract's void. I mean, I'm stuck here until I can drive the rig and the rig is cleared, but…." He cleared his throat, his hand dropping away from its exploration of Rory's skin.

"But what?" Rory prodded.

"You… you earned your fee. You're, uhm, free to go. If you want to."

It was the way he wasn't looking Rory in the eye that saved Rory from heartbreak—that and the "If you want to."

"What if I don't want to?" Rory asked, keeping his voice low.

"I… I'd love you to stay," Val said after a moment, turning carefully to look Rory in the eye. "We could go hang out at Vinnie's place—which is like an oasis in the desert, it's so pretty. They've got a Jacuzzi too, you know. And, well, Vinnie said the whole family would be gone in two days. He's got a whole guest wing, but, you know." The water was too tepid for heat to be making Val Royal's cheeks that red, and Rory decided to save him the trouble.

"If you put your hand back on my leg," he drawled, "I would consider it a pleasure to go visit your friend Vinnie with you." He bent and captured Val's wet hand in his own, pulling it gently higher, until it was on the inside of his knee. "In fact," he said softly, "I may have called my son to tell him I won't be back for another two weeks. Just, you know, in case we think of something to do to kill the time."

Val laughed softly. "Like maybe take our time driving from Austin to Bakersfield?"

"Oh my God, three days at the least!" Rory laughed. "That was some epic time we made."

Val gave him a shy smile. "That could be its own country song," he said.

"You know," Rory said, "since country music is *my* jam, I bet I could find a song that would fit the bill."

He left the bathroom for a few minutes after that to order food and then came back to bundle Val up in one of the plush robes and set him up in the bed—clean, dry, and completely relaxed—in time for room service to bring up some passable steaks.

Val ate about half of his before setting it aside and stretching out on top of the comforter, obviously doing a mini-pilates routine of stretching and releasing the muscle groups in his body. "That was great," he murmured. "But seriously—I would bet Vinnie's got a four-star meal ready for us tomorrow night. You haven't had steak until you've had one of Vinnie's."

"I can't wait," Rory told him. He kept the television on low for a while, Val dozing lightly while Rory ran gentle fingers through his hair.

It was not a kind of evening Rory had ever spent with a man, and he was starting to see the kind of future Val had envisioned when he'd said he was ready to settle down.

As Rory turned off the lights and the television—and set his phone to wake Val up in a couple hours to make sure the concussion wasn't getting worse—he gazed out over the skyline of Austin from the hotel room window and wondered what kind of vast horizons he could experience in the arms of a man like Val Royal.

It was at least worth a little vacation time and some travel to find out.

People often underestimated Texas; the state was nearly three times the size of the UK alone. So while Rory grew up in the panhandle, around Lubbock, driving around Austin was a whole new thing. After Val got his head checked out—and was told to come back in a week to both get cleared for driving and recover his rig—he gave Rory directions to the Arboretum, where they found a menswear store and made some quick purchases.

"This is probably a good idea," Val said through a yawn. "Sam, Vinnie's wife, is doing the whole shebang tonight. Vinnie's been asking me about steak and—"

"Raw. Still mooing. Opinionated," Rory said promptly.

"So I've noticed." Val laughed as they neared the SUV. He was moving stiffly again, and Rory made note of the time. Another painkiller, he figured, and probably the extra muscle relaxant too. "I told him that. So, you know. We get there in an hour—"

"You go rest," Rory prompted.

Val nodded, conceding. "I go rest," he admitted. "And then we meet for dinner afterward. Tomorrow it's us and Vinnie, and you know…." He waggled his eyebrows.

"Four days in a stranger's house," Rory said, hitting the Beep button. "I get it."

Val snorted softly and set his clothes in the back of the rented SUV. "You really don't," he said, yawning. "But you will."

An hour later, as they drove through acres and acres of cattle country, Rory had a dawning epiphany.

"Wait a minute," he said, feeling dumb. "We've been passing the same spread for the last half hour, haven't we?"

"Yup," Val mumbled. He'd taken his meds and slept soundly, head tucked against his wadded-up sweatshirt.

"Is this… *Vinnie's* spread?"

"Mm-hmm…," Val said. He squinted blearily around and added, "In about a mile there's going to be a really dramatic lacework arch with Vinnie's logo done in wrought iron. Turn there and keep driving until you see the cow's palace." He giggled to himself a little and fell back asleep.

So Rory was *starting* to get it when he saw the "really dramatic arch"—which must have been twelve feet high and had an elaborate logo version of "Conti & Sons" done in wrought iron over an arching rainbow of warped brass. The whole arch was supported by marble Grecian columns, and it was big enough to fit two big rigs side by side.

And the road, which had been a rough and pothole-filled county road as they'd roared through cattle land, suddenly became newly paved and smooth as glass.

"Damn," Rory said, *thinking* he got it.

And then he saw the "palace" and "it" hit him square in the solar plexus.

"*Oolf….*," he breathed, taking in a modern two-story stucco fortress, surrounded by beech trees that shaded every window. There appeared to be an entire copse of them on the other side of the house, and as the driveway wound to the west, taking them to a parking area designed to host dinner parties attended by people who commuted by limousine, Rory remembered hearing something about a pool and a Jacuzzi at "his place" and realized that the trees were probably some sort of landscaping in the back to separate the homestead from the rest of the rolling green acreage in the immediate vicinity.

The size and the scope of the place was breathtaking. He'd seen hotels smaller than Vinnie's home, but he'd never seen any more luxurious.

"You went to school with this guy?" Rory wondered out loud.

"This was the other side of the family," Val said. "You see how it says, 'Conti and Sons'?"

"Yeah?"

"Vinnie's mom was the one named Conti, and neither of her brothers wanted the ranch. She married poor, they lived modestly in Bakersfield, but he visited his grandfather and uncles here. He…." Val smiled. "He really loved it. His wife, Sam, is from money. I mean, *lots* of money. But Vinnie brought her to our house first, you know, to meet my folks? She was so classy. Remembered everybody's names, helped with the dishes, played cards with my folks after dessert. Vinnie took me outside and told me he'd needed to see how she treated us—'cause let me tell you, my parents' place is a pile of rubble after seven kids on my folks' salaries—so he'd know if she was really as kind as she seemed. She's the one who told him he was smart enough to run this place. I think it's all he ever wanted."

"God, Val, your family. They sound like Hallmark movie people."

Val snorted. "Hallmark wouldn't let my mother on the set. That woman… I mean *truckers* are supposed to swear."

Rory laughed and grabbed their stuff. He locked his rifle in the back under some blankets to keep it from getting too hot in the steamy sunshine of spring. There were children in this house, and he didn't know the rules, and while most people in Texas liked to brag about being able to shoot, he was a guest here.

Then he and Val made their way to the front door, and Rory had never felt so small in his life.


A FEW HOURS later, after he and Val were given their own room where Val had rested while Vinnie gave him a tour of the house and grounds, Rory couldn't remember the last time he'd *laughed* so much in his life.

The house was as lovely inside as it was out.

There was a grand dining room and ballroom in the east wing of the house, but the west wing was a *home*. The floors were tiled, with soft colorful rugs underfoot in the bedrooms, and the whole house seemed to be rooted in the concepts of passive air-conditioning—although there was plenty of *active* air-conditioning should they need it—as well as airy spaces and peace.

The floors were dark, the alcoves were shaded, the painted walls were eggshell with accent walls in terra-cotta and forest green. The great family room, complete with *giant*-screen TV, was surrounded by a wraparound window with an equally wraparound *shutter* that could be remotely closed partially—to block out the sun if it was too bright—or completely, to help the AC do its job if the outside temps got too brutal. The back of the wing opened onto a patio, and while there was a smaller *inside* dining room nearer to the kitchen, Rory was led to believe the patio was, while the weather held, the heart of the house. Shaded with mini palms, strategically placed in planters wherever the sunlight came in too strong, as well as a remote-controlled portico, the patio had a floor of polished stone, surprisingly comfortable alfresco dining furniture, and a separate space for a "living room" of sorts, with lounging furniture and even a sound system. The Jacuzzi and pool were, as Rory suspected, a little farther off from the patio and shaded in beech trees, as well as surrounded by a safety fence that also enclosed changing rooms and a gazebo.

The place was a cool, shady oasis. There was even a fountain between the dining area and the lounging area, and Rory was once again reminded of a resort hotel.

The elegance was breathtaking, but so was the welcome, and it was the welcome that shone through during dinner.

Rory and Val both dressed, and Rory was glad. The girls—all three of them, aged nine, eleven, and thirteen—were dressed in cool sundresses, and even the youngest had sweet little sandals and adorably painted toenails. (Apparently that had been something they'd done that day, and Rory was one of the first admirers of the delicate shell pink.) Sam—who had heavy wheat-blond hair pulled into an updo, wide gray eyes, and an adorable cheerleader nose—wore a simple white sheath dress and a sapphire pendant.

Vinnie was dressed much like Rory and Val, although Val had apparently visited often enough for Vinnie to notice Val's new clothes.

"For us?" he asked, giving Val the once-over. "Not necessary, my friend."

Val grinned wickedly. "*Very* necessary since my one good outfit is still in the back of the rig." He winked at Sam, who was smiling at him as well. "And of course very worth the effort, Sam. It's always such a pleasure to be here."

"Stop talking sweet," she said, taking a sip of her wine, "and tell me all the gossip. And I mean *all.* Is Laure dating? I called her last week and nagged her, but I don't think she took me seriously."

Val shook his head. "Naw. Sam, she's so busy with her business and her boys. They're driving her to distraction."

"Has the youngest heard about college yet?" she asked anxiously. "I know we were all crossing our fingers."

Val nodded. "Yup. He got into his first choice, UCLA."

Sam actually clapped. "And she didn't tell me?" she squealed. "I'll kill her!"

Val shrugged modestly. "I think I'm the only sibling she's told," he admitted. "We were getting the finances squared away before we started bragging about the kid. His financial aid package only goes so far."

Vinnie's eyes—an average brown on the surface, but deep and thoughtful when you'd been in his presence a bit—darkened. "Val, I told you—"

Val waved. "We got it covered, Vin. You've got no worries. I'm doing good, Sal's doing *great*, and Dean's been putting away money too. It's like Chance. The kid had the will and the drive, and the family made sure it happened."

"How's he doing?" Sam asked. She glanced at Rory. "Chance was just a baby when I first met Val's family, and Laure had just gotten married—she had Russell less than a year later. I don't *have* any siblings of my own, so I babysat the *hell* out of those kids, and Shaw when he came along two years later."

"What about Reg?" Rory asked, pleased that he remembered the kids *and* their order.

Sam grimaced. "Reg is supernaturally old and wise, and he was at four, but sure. I 'baby' sat him." She punctuated the word with finger quotes. "I loved that kid, but I always had the feeling he was humoring me. I'd say, 'Okay, Reg, time for bed,' and he'd say, 'I've brushed my teeth, washed my face, and put on my pajamas. I just need help getting Chance changed.'" She shuddered. "And Chance would give me his hand and say, 'PJs!' I mean, Chance needed me. Both boys still love me. We're still close, but I'm saying, Reg raised himself." She wrinkled her nose. "And as for Chance, I may be like his aunt, and I guess you don't tell your aunt about how your second year of college is going."

"He's okay," Val said. He snorted softly. "He had a helluva crush on Dean's partner—"

"Marcus?" Sam asked. "He was cute."

Val rolled his eyes. "Did he hit on you? Because I get the impression he hit on everybody *but* Chance."

Sam's laughter was sweet, like chimes, and young. "See, when Dean brought him *here*, the only person he could talk about was Chance."

Val eyed her in horror. "Chance is a *baby*."

"Of course he is," she said smugly. "Which would explain why Marcus didn't hit on him."

Rory nodded. It had been the same reason he hadn't hit on Dean— too young. But also not quite right. Apparently Rory liked his Royal well-seasoned.

Val shook his head, about to say something, and then he winced. They were lingering over their plates, anticipating dessert, and Sam was the one who said, "Val, darling, go to bed. I'll have dessert brought to your room."

Val straightened and winced again. They could all see the moment when he conceded.

"Fine," he said, and Rory stood to guide him up. "Thank you," he said graciously, and Rory could tell it was rough to be gracious because he obviously hated to be weak. "Rory, please stay. Yes, I know Vinnie and Sam and the kids will tell you all my bad traits, but you know, if you can deal with me after that, I think we're good."

The girls all protested, and he bent to kiss every cheek on his way out, including Sam's. After he was gone and the staff had come in to clear the table and set down dessert, there was a brief awkward silence.

"Mom," said the oldest, "after dessert, can we go watch some TV in the family room?"

"Of course, Bella-love," Sam told her affectionately. "Not too late. We're leaving early, and I'm going to be by in an hour or so to make sure everybody's packed."

After the girls had left—chattering excitedly about Disney World—Rory polished off the rest of his to-die-for chocolate mousse and smiled up at his hosts expectantly.

"Is this the part where I get grilled about my intentions?" he asked dryly.

Vinnie seemed so unassuming, but his laughter was as rich as the place he called home. "Val's a big boy," he said. "And you obviously like him fine if you stuck with him this long. We just want to get to know you. Warn you a little, maybe, about what you're getting yourself into regarding the family."

Rory snorted. "They are tighter than the rust-welded tire bolt on a 1982 Toyota? Yeah. That much I figured."

They both laughed, and Sam shook her head. "They are tight," she said. "And there are personality pitfalls and traps like with any other family. You may have already figured that Val and Dean butt heads a lot."

"Are they the most alike?" Rory hazarded.

Sam put her finger on her nose. "Bingo. Laure is the peacekeeper and the pulse of the siblings. You've met her?"

"Spoken with," Rory confirmed. "She's a nice lady."

Sam sighed. "The family project is to find her a good man. Not because she needs one, mind you, but because she deserves someone good in her life. Bet you can't guess the catch there."

She looked at him expectantly, and Rory put together what he knew about Laure Royal, who had two teenaged sons, had married young and been widowed far too soon. The woman who had called him with the job offer, saying Dean had given her headhunting service his name, had been warm and quick-witted, and Rory thought about what it took to own a business all your own in this world, particularly one you built from the ground up.

"No man is good enough for her," he hazarded. "And all the ones good enough are gay and candidates for her brothers."

"Give the man a cigar!" Vinnie crowed.

Sam wrinkled her nose. "Ew," she complained, gazing at her husband with pleading in her eyes.

"That he will only smoke outside, an acre away from the premises," Vinnie filled in dutifully.

"I love you," she sang. "But yes, there you go. You've passed Royal Family Dynamics 101. Are you ready for the advanced course?"

Rory cocked his head. "Will it tell me what 'Val' is short for?"

Vinnie and Sam met eyes and smirked. "Nope," they said, obviously enjoying being in the know.

Rory gave them a narrow-eyed glance. "Well, then," he said grandly, "I guess I'd rather find out from Val himself."

They laughed, and Vinnie offered him more wine—which he accepted.

"You pass," Vinnie said. "Now tell me some more about that epic drive from Bakersfield. I haven't wanted to press Val because he's still recovering, but…." Vinnie made "gimme" motions with his fingers, and Rory laughed before launching into the epic ballad of "The Race Up Bull-Jizz Mountain."

By the time he made it back to the darkened bedroom, he was loose from some *very* good wine, and he'd decided he liked Val's friends almost as much as he liked Val Royal himself.

His efforts to be quiet obviously failed, because as he was hanging up his new slacks and sport coat, Val mumbled sleepily from the bed.

"Did you enjoy yourself?"

"I did," Rory said, sliding out of the crisp white shirt. There was a laundry hamper in the corner of the room, and he asked a stupid question. "Do they have, uhm—"

"Staff that will launder that and starch it and hang it back in your closet if you hang it on the door?" Val asked. "Yes. And before you feel guilty, I'm pretty sure they've put half the young people in the small town nearby through college with their generous salaries. Did I mention she's from money?"

"I gotta say," Rory said, doing as instructed with his shirt and throwing the T-shirt in the hamper so he could climb in next to Val as bare as possible, "money isn't usually as sweet as Sam Conti—"

"Aiello," Val corrected. "Remember? The whole last name thing. Whatever. Sam Buchannan Aiello is pure class, but Vinnie's her soulmate, so he's not bad either."

Rory chuckled and slid under the covers with Val, hiding from the air-conditioning under the thin cloud-soft quilt. "I can tell you this much," he mumbled, lining himself up with Val's back and molding himself gingerly along the line of it.

"What's that?" Val asked. "And tighter. I'm all medicated and relaxed, and you feel really good."

"They sure do love you and your family."

Val chuckled. "Yeah. Yeah, they do. Gotta tell you, between my mom and dad and Vinnie and Sam, I've got a lot of good relationships to show me what to shoot for."

Rory's eyes were heavy, which was probably the only reason that didn't scare him silly.

"What makes you think I'm a good bet?" he asked, lost and enchanted in Val's body already, the low-key thrum of arousal purring in his stomach with every rasp of skin on skin.

"You've had my back from the moment we met," Val said before bucking gently backward. "And my God, you turn my key."

Rory chuckled like he was supposed to, but underneath the rumble in his chest was the unspoken knowledge that staying here, under Val's friends' roof, in Val's bed like a lover—that was a commitment of sorts. Val's family would know about this. Val's parents. Whether Rory was ready or not, this was going to be a real relationship, the kind in which Val would expect Rory to pony up.

The thought should have scared him—scared him shitless.

And in the end, he was so scared he closed his eyes and held Val closer and fell fast asleep.

# There's a Million Things
# We Haven't Done

Val plowed through the clean, cool water under a sky of blazing azure, the soft shush of the trees overhead letting him know that there was a breeze to help cut the humidity and heat. He'd set his phone up, playing *Hamilton*, and he knew that one well enough that even when his head was under the water, the music kept his body moving smoothly in time.

Ye gods, he loved to swim. As impractical as the tiny pool at his house had seemed to be, it had paid for itself because he managed to do laps a couple times a week. His stays at Vinnie's house were almost always punctuated by a daily workout in the much bigger pool, and although Vinnie had left that morning, this day was no exception.

His back, neck, and chest were finally relaxing on their own, his bruises colorful but no longer aching when untouched—or unmedicated. His head felt *miles* better, and while his freestyle was nowhere near his best time, the feeling of being in the water and using those muscles gently was enough to make him nearly weep with relief.

Five whole days.

Vinnie had negotiated with him to use the pool and the house for an extra night. The nearby town was small and picturesque, Vinnie had stables not far away, and Val and Rory were welcome to saddle up the recommended horses and ride, and of course Vinnie knew Val's weakness was the pool.

"Aw, Vinnie, you don't have to do all this—"

Vinnie shook his head. "Val, it was close. If we'd had to forfeit to the insurance company, we might have lost all this. I insist. Alejandro's our chief of staff, and he'll be bored shitless unless you use him, and he hates that. Makes him feel useless. He's used to working his ass off, so throw him a bone besides laundry, will you?"

Val rolled his eyes, although Alejandro was pretty much the gold standard for having a domestic assistant who could help you completely organize your life.

"I just don't want to take advantage."

Vinnie cocked his head. "C'mon, Val. It could be a honeymoon, or it could be a torrid affair. The point is I want to see you happy. You've been searching for a match, somebody who could deal with your business, deal with your family. Rory seems like he could do both. Take some time to figure it out, okay?"

Val groaned. They were having this conversation on the patio, where they'd met for breakfast, just the two of them. Rory was running—apparently something he usually did in much greater distances than around a semi rig, to keep his leg limber—and it was Val's first unmedicated chance to talk to his friend.

"He might not work out," Val confessed. "I mean, I am *really* excited to see, but—"

Vinnie laughed shortly. "Val, on any given day even the best relationships could turn on a dime. Say the wrong thing, make the wrong decision, poof!" He made his fingers wiggle. "There goes all your good intentions and good deeds for twenty years, down the hole. You know why they don't?"

Val's eyes were huge. "No, and now I really need to!"

"Because two people who care about each other have already decided they won't let that fucking happen. This is your time to hammer out terms. What are your makes, what are your breaks. Can you decide not to let that fucking happen." Vinnie stood and squeezed Val's shoulder. "Now I've got to go so I can join the girls. I know you'll be gone by the time we get back, but remember—Alejandro is my spy, and he'll tell me if you used my hospitality like it's meant to be used, okay?"

Val stood and they did the bro-hug thing. "Thanks," he said, conceding at last. "It's kind."

"Well, we're not square by a long shot. Have fun."

And with that, Vinnie left down the hallway, waving to Rory as Rory came in from the front.

"He leaving?" Rory asked, sitting down at the table in a sweaty huff and pouring himself a big glass of orange juice.

"Yeah. Car's packed and everything. We just wanted to connect first."

"Hmm…," Rory said thoughtfully. "It's not fair, you know. You've got five brothers by birth, and then you went and found yourself another one. Some of us don't even have one."

Val cocked his head. "You never really did tell me about your family. You said your folks were dead, but that's about all I know."

Rory blew out a breath. "What's to know? My dad split early. We found out he'd died when I was about twenty. Mama was sick by then, so I didn't tell her. She was under no illusions."

"What was she like?" Val asked, suddenly hungry for the knowledge. "Your mom?"

Rory looked like he'd balk at first, and while Val was getting a picture as to why Rory might want to keep such things close to his heart, Val was on the verge of risking… *everything* on this man. Suddenly the woman who had raised Rory McCauley, with his sardonic sense of humor and the devil in his smile, was of paramount importance to Val.

"C'mon, Rory," Val said, and he found he was pleading. "You turned out okay. What was she like?"

Rory snorted. "If I turned out okay it's because she was the best," he said, and his voice was wistful. "I'm just… if you must know, I'm embarrassed. Anthony was such a great kid. God, he really was. And I was…." He swallowed. "I was a horrible teenager," he confessed. "And horrible teenagers are not kind to their mothers."

Val eyed him with compassion. "Everybody's a horrible teenager," he said. "I used to fight with Dean like a pit bull fought a kitten. I mean, the kid is twelve years my junior—"

"I've worked with Dean," Rory said dryly. "I'm pretty sure he gave as good as he got, even at six. And he's so much like you. It was inevitable. But that's sibling stuff." He let out a short bark of laughter. "I don't have one, but I understand that goes with the territory. This was…." He shook his head, and for a moment Val despaired. He was never going to open up. Rory was always going to keep a part of him far away from his heart, far away from Val, and Val would never really know him.

"I was *ashamed* of her," he said after a minute. "She was a waitress in a diner, and I was ashamed of her. I used to have to go to the diner after school to do my homework, you know? And one day there was a bank robbery in town, and Mama saw it go down. So the FBI shows up, because it was one of a series of them, and I am in the back stall, doing my homework, drinking all the free fountain soda I could stomach, and trying to crawl backward through the wall with my buttcheeks alone. It seemed like every time she opened her mouth, she let loose something else that the guys in the suits didn't understand. Not her deep Texas drawl, not the way she said y'all, not when she said 'britches'—every word made me want to fucking disappear."

Val heard it: The deep shame, the self-hatred for being a prick as only a middle schooler could be. He sat and listened, wondering if Rory had *ever* told this story.

"So the FBI guys are… well, gentle. They're kind. Thinking about it now, I'm pretty sure my mother was shook-up, you know? She saw guys with guns right across the street, and she'd been afraid for her life. But the feds were sweet to her, and she told her story and offered them free drinks, and the guy in charge stood up and said, 'Now Miss Evie, you sit down here a spell and let me get the coffee.' And Mama says, 'Could you get my boy a slice of pie? He always has one after school.' And somehow, that seems like the *biggest* indignity, you know? But he got my mother coffee and stared down her horrible boss who might have fired her otherwise, because he *was* an ass, and then came to my booth and set the pie in front of me and bent down and…." Rory choked on a laugh. "He whispered, 'Your mother is an angel, you ungrateful little shit. You treat that woman right and show her some respect.'"

Val grinned at him, surprised, and Rory nodded.

"Yessir, that lawman pretty much scared me straight." He snorted. "Well, as much as he could anyway. But… but that scary-looking guy in the ugly suit thought my mom was *something*, and… and I realized when I grew up I wanted to be just like him."

Val took in that story with some even breaths, his eyes on Rory's rough-hewn features. He could see that squirmy adolescent kid in the back of the booth, could see him respond to a little bit of tough-love parenting from a stranger with squared shoulders and a lifted chin.

See the sadness that, for a moment, he hadn't appreciated the woman who'd raised him.

"Did you ever see him again?" Val asked.

Rory shook his head. "It's a big bureau, and I didn't make it in until maybe fifteen years later. But it sure did give me something to shoot for. In my behavior too. It was like I needed a man—just one goddamned man—to teach me how to talk to my mother like she was a queen. It's funny how much we take that for granted."

Val nodded. "Yeah. Maybe because there were so many of us kids—and maybe because my parents worked as a team, backing each other up—but my folks managed to effectively drill respect into us. Kindness. I came out, and they loved me, and twenty-five years ago that wasn't something you took for granted. And of course, I paved the way." He chuckled. "My dad actually kept forgetting Prock was straight. I remember him saying, 'But Dad, I like girls! I won't *have* a husband like all the others!' and Dad literally doing a double take."

Rory chuckled. "I'm madly jealous, you know," he admitted. "You may have figured that out."

Val nodded thoughtfully, and when he opened his mouth, what he said surprised even him.

"My parents were supposed to go to New York for their honeymoon," he began. "But they were so poor everything went wrong. They took a bus for one thing, so it was more time in the bus than actually on the East Coast, and they rented a car when they got there, but they rented a shitty car that died on them before they'd even cleared Newark. They ended up, by mischance and a terminal misunderstanding of how the New Jersey turnpike system works, in Princeton, New Jersey, and instead of going to the Statue of Liberty, they spent an entire day touring the campus. Now they'd both wanted an education, but Mom had been taking care of younger kids, and Dad had been working on cars since he was sixteen, and that opportunity sort of flew right by. But they spent that day on a college campus, just young enough to be mistaken for students in their best jeans and sneakers, and they got this idea."

Rory blinked at him, eyes growing wide, and Val shrugged rather sheepishly.

"Yeah. They wanted their kids—and even then, I think, Mom was already pregnant with me, and they were planning on a *bunch* of us, and God love 'em, that's what they had—to shoot for the stars. They wanted their kids to grow up to be lawyers and doctors and to go to school, and they'd had a chance to look at graduation announcements and fliers on campus. By the time they left Princeton, they knew exactly how to let us know that we could be anything we wanted."

"Oh no," Rory said, half in horror, Val reckoned, and half in admiration.

"Oh yes," Val told him. "Valedictorian, Laureate, Salutatorian, Proctor, Dean, Registrar and Chancellor. I'm Valedictorian Princeton Royal, and if you ever meet my parents—"

"I will respect the hell out of them," Rory said softly. "Because their son Val is a fine man."

Val smiled at him and stood, bending down to kiss his cheek. "I'm going to go swim," he said, thinking about moving his body cleanly, about his muscles being loose and cool and relaxed.

About touching Rory's heat like that and taking it inside.

"Want me to join you?"

"Rinse off first," Val said. This time, he kissed Rory's mouth. "And maybe wait for me to dry off after the shower."

Rory deepened the kiss, sweeping his tongue inside and dominating Val's mouth before Val pulled away, his breathing a little unsteady.

"And maybe not," Rory said, his own voice gruff. "Maybe I can't wait."

"I'm worth the wait, Rory. Trust me."

And with that he left the table to put on his board shorts and gather a change of clothes for after the shower. And maybe some personal toiletries as well.

He'd used the pool house before. There was a shower and an airy, shaded lounge with big fans, and today there wouldn't be a soul around to know what was going on in there.

He shivered with anticipation as he wandered across the green, turning his face to that stunning sky and enjoying the breeze sweeping down from the mountains in the east.


RIGHT AS his muscles started to protest, as his breathing got a little bit labored, a shadow darkened the end of the pool as he finished his lap. He pulled himself to the edge and grinned up at Rory, who was squatting in the perfect position to block the sun.

"You about done yet?"

Rory was freshly showered, and while he was wearing comfortable clothes—cargo shorts and a madras over a tee—he didn't look ready for the pool.

"I was just thinking about the shower," Val said. "Are you going somewhere?"

"I was thinking about visiting the town after lunch," Rory said. "If you want to. Frankly, I was bored, and the big house was creeping me out." He grinned. "Save me, Val, save me from having to watch TV on a perfectly gorgeous day!"

Val chuckled and moved to the stairs to accept the offered towel. "All right, then," he said. "I'll be out in five." He shivered a bit, the breeze taking a bite after the hour in the water. "Maybe ten. Gotta warm up."

"Take your time," Rory told him, and for no reason at all, Val felt his skin heat.

Maybe they'd taken all the time that had been needed?

The thought was exciting enough to fight the chill.

HIS BODY temp had just begun to normalize, and he was turning the tap off when he felt a gust of fresh air in the humid bathroom. When he opened the frosted door of the spacious cubicle, Rory was there, holding a bath sheet, looking at him with wicked eyes.

"Couldn't wait?" Val murmured. He went to take the bath sheet from him, but Rory spread the thing between his arms and gestured with his chin.

"Let me pamper you a little," he said, bashful enough to be charming. "I understand this is supposed to be a big deal."

"Of course it's a big deal," Val said, stepping into his arms. "It was a big deal when you swaggered across my parking lot, took my shit, and then hit on me."

Rory closed his eyes as he wrapped the towel around Val's body and gathered him in. "You said no," he rumbled, and Val licked a drop of moisture off the column of his throat.

"I didn't want one and done," he said.

"I've never been seduced via danger before," Rory told him, lifting his chin, showing off his clean-shaven throat and obviously begging for the attention.

"It apparently worked." Val sucked gently at the join of his neck, and Rory made a halfhearted attempt to dry his hair before dropping the towel and massaging his scalp through the wet strands.

"You're killing me here," Rory moaned, and Val reached up slightly and tugged on his earlobe with his teeth. "I had a plan, Val Royal. I was gonna—oh God. That's a weakness."

Val breathed out slightly through his nose and stepped back enough to let the bath sheet fall to the floor. Rory had left his shoes outside the changing pavilion, so when Val unbuckled his cargo shorts and shoved down, shorts, belt, boxers, and all fell to the cool tiles at their bare feet. Then Rory pulled away enough to yank off his shirts, and then he captured Val's face between his palms and kissed him.

Val fell into the kiss, allowing Rory to back them across the bathroom to the open door to the pavilion.

The pavilion itself was an airy space, with blinds open to allow the breeze through, ceiling fans of dark teakwood working steadily on, and billowy white curtains, as well as sturdy rattan couches and lounge chairs.

And a bed in the corner, with soft linen bedsheets and a pale blue, light-as-a-feather quilt and plump, decadent pillows. Val knew for a certain that the girls had been known to go down for naps there when they'd had too much sun and were ready for a rest, and he also knew—because Vinnie wasn't shy—that the bed had seen harder use.

And now, the well-laundered quilt was pulled back, revealing a towel laid flat over the sheets, a small bottle of lubricant... and a prescription bottle?

Rory had swung about and was ready to lay Val back on the sheets when Val stopped.

"The bottle?" he asked, eyes crinkling because he was pretty sure he knew what it was.

"PrEP," Rory said, looking disgruntled and the faintest bit embarrassed. "So, you know—I mean, I brought condoms—"

"I haven't done this since my last test," Val told him. "About two years ago. You want proof?" God, this was a mood breaker. It's why he'd used to buy condoms, to avoid this discussion.

"No," Rory whispered, reaching behind Val and repositioning all of the items. "Your word is good."

"Thank God." Val lay back against the pillows, and Rory climbed in bed next to him.

The kiss resumed, and Val lost himself in it, the cool air moving over his body, Rory's flesh heating him to unbearable heights.

Rory's hand on his cock was almost a surprise, because it was raw and earthy and grounding, and Val gasped, arching into his touch.

"One more bit of housekeeping," Rory murmured, moving his head down to suck in Val's nipple as he stroked.

"Now?" Val moaned. "Housekeeping—oh God—harder?"

"No, not harder," Rory taunted, before licking his sensitized nipple again. "I'm topping, right?"

"First," Val breathed.

Rory actually *let go* of Val's cock. Val grunted and reached down, wrapping Rory's fingers around him again.

"Don't panic, cowboy," Val whispered. "Just make love to me now, and we'll figure the rest out later."

Rory's stroke resumed, followed quickly by Rory's hot mouth, the delirious pressure of his palate, his tongue, his fist, driving Val to distraction.

"You gonna," Val panted, "get around to topping soon—ah! God!"

Rory had slicked his fingers and used them now to slide in past Val's entrance, to fiddle, to play, to stretch. Val planted his feet wide apart, forcing Rory to wriggle between his legs and go to work, one hand stroking, the other hand stretching, and his mouth laving and sucking, while Val buried his hands in that thick shaggy hair and lost his mind.

"Rory!" he gasped. "Gonna—"

"Come," Rory hissed, his breath dusting the wet, sensitized head of Val's cock.

Val cried out softly, thrusting hard down Rory's throat, and he spurt and spurt and—augh! All the stimulus disappeared, and Rory rushed up his body, his greased cock at Val's entrance, knocking softly to come in.

"Please," Val begged, past pride or dignity. Oh Lord, the things this man's touch were doing to his body. He'd forgotten what a man's hands and mouth felt like, but this was bigger somehow. Oh God, had he ever known?

Rory pushed slowly inside, then pulled out, then pushed in again, and Val groaned in completion when he was all the way seated.

"Like a fencepost," Val panted.

Rory chuckled, the sound strained, and started to thrust. "Complaining?"

"God no—bring it on."

Rory might have chuckled again, but he didn't have enough breath to make it resonate. He was thrusting now, his eyes closed tight, his head thrown back. Val wanted to see his face, and he squinted through the sweat running into his eyes to see a look of utter concentration, utter abandonment, so lost in the moment that Val smiled and gave himself over to the euphoria of the act. Every thrust made him shudder, every withdrawal made him cry out, all of it building, building, building—

"Oh God, Rory," he begged. "Come. Please—oh—" Rory pegged Val's gland again, hard, and he lost all cohesion, flew apart, blossomed into a soft needing thing, lost in the fog of submission and orgasm, until Rory cried out and hammered into him, rutting as he came.

For a few moments, Val was awash in the breeze, the white curtains, the lazily spinning ceiling fans, and Rory's harsh breaths in his ear.

Finally Rory said, "My God."

"Yeah," Val whispered happily.

"That was… wow."

"Worth the wait?" Val teased.

Rory's knowing brown eyes were wide and bright as they took in Val's face. "God, you're beautiful, all fucked out and not giving a shit."

Val chuckled and squeezed Rory's cock, still wedged solidly inside him. Rory groaned softly, and Val felt him grow the teeniest bit harder.

"Who says I'm fucked out, old man," he taunted, and Rory grunted, pushing up to his elbows again, body still covering Val's.

"I'll show you old," he growled, and Val moaned ecstatically as Rory began round two.


THE FIVE days weren't enough, Val thought later, but they would have to do.

All those plans for activities Vinnie had laid out for them like summer camp, but in the end, they really did spend most of the time in bed. They did make it to town for a day, but after Val topped Rory on their second night, they both agreed that maybe the horseback ride was out.

Rory was unexpectedly nervous that night, and Val would forever remember the little crinkle of his brow as he came out of the bathroom, showered and fresh and a little defensive.

"So, uhm, how do you want to do this?" Rory asked, almost growling, and Val stared at him.

"You've never, uh, bottomed before?"

"Of course I have," Rory snapped. Then he looked away. "But usually that was with one-night stands, and I just bent over and let them go at it."

Val stared at him. "If you bend over like a mare in season to 'just let me go at it,' I am walking out of here," he said frankly. Then he came up behind Rory, still wearing the cargo shorts and button-down he'd worn to dinner on the patio, and began to kiss Rory's bare shoulder. "Just let it happen," he murmured, feeling Rory's taut muscles start to relax. "Believe it or not, I know what I'm doing."

Rory gave a rough chuckle as Val kissed his way down Rory's vertebrae. Val squatted behind him, and Rory fell forward, hands on the bed.

Val grabbed the bottle of lube he'd put in his pocket before he discarded his clothes and set it within easy reach before he leaned forward against Rory's backside, rubbing his back, his flanks, his thighs, with a gliding touch and gentleness in his palms and fingers. His fingers drifted along the scar on Rory's thigh, and when Rory tried to hide that, Val whispered, "Don't."

"Unsightly," Rory said with emphasis.

Val kissed it and said, "Proof that you lived," before standing up and resuming the full-body caress.

Rory hummed and fell to his elbows, obviously enjoying himself, and Val leaned forward to lick his ear. "Like this?" he asked.

"Feels best," Rory admitted softly.

"Not face-to-face?" Val asked, making sure.

"Later." Rory moaned softly as Val's hand drifted down and he feathered a touch along Rory's crease, his hole, down under his balls. "Oh wow… I'm starting to really want this," he confessed, so Val did it again, his lips traveling along Rory's shoulder, his neck, even his shoulder blades, while his hand wandered, drifted, dipped—

"Ah!" Rory sighed, and Val could see his upper thighs shaking.

Val grabbed the lubricant this time, and when he slid a finger into Rory's waiting chamber, Rory's sound—the quaking, needy, breathy, begging *aahhhh* of it, made Val's cock swell and tingle in reaction.

He slicked the head of his own cock and got in position. "Ready?"

Rory buried his face in the mattress and begged.

Fucking Rory McCauley was like riding a bull, Val would decide later. Rory's strong body bucked against his, insisting on more, demanding pleasure, and Val answered with hard thrusts, the slap of their flesh filling the bedroom, filling his senses, pounding through his blood.

Val gripped hard at Rory's lean hips, and when Rory dropped his hand to stroke himself, Val shivered in anticipation.

"God yes," he grunted. "Do it. Stroke it. God, Rory, I want to feel you—"

Rory cried out, spurting against the sheets, and Val kept pounding against the hard clench of Rory's ass on his cock. Rory groaned, falling forward face down, and his hand kept its wild rhythm on his cock as he writhed in orgasm. Val kept fucking, kept fucking, kept—

He buried his roar of climax against Rory's back, and Rory howled into the sheets as they both stuttered to completion, shudders of come racking their bodies, clenching and releasing them as they rode the wave to comedown.

This time, as they lay side by side staring at another lazily spinning ceiling fan, Rory gasped, legs spread apart, knees bent slightly, as he dripped Val's spend from his body to the towel underneath his hips.

"Wow," he said, as Val dragged his fingertips across Rory's sensitive nipples again.

"Wow what?" Val was pretty replete—well, mostly replete. Desire for the man next to him dogged him, like an itch he couldn't scratch or a thirst he couldn't quench. He pinched Rory's nipple to see what he'd do next, and Rory gasped some more.

Val felt his cock quicken in response.

"I'm usually done after something like that," Rory confessed before dragging his own fingers to his steadily rousing cock.

Val gave him a sultry look. "Want to see how done I'm *not*?" he asked, shifting on the bed so he was between Rory's bent knees.

Rory moaned and spread his thighs wider, so wanton, so deliciously *slutty*, that Val's itch was suddenly a fiery burn in his belly.

"Yeah," Rory sighed, as Val moved down to take his long, thick "fencepost" into his mouth for the first time. It still tasted like come from his previous orgasm, and Val sucked it hard, cleaning him off.

This time was slower and harder. This time was face-to-face. This time, as Val's orgasm almost turned him inside out, seeking to spill his ejaculate in Rory's ass, Val thought, *It's got to be done, doesn't it?*

Even as he slid to the side, exhausted and—oh please, for just a little while?—replete, he heard a mocking echo in his head.

*Does it?*

And when they woke in the morning, this time Rory was pushing his way insistently into Val's ass, and Val had his first inkling that no. Maybe it wasn't ever going to *be* done, and that's when he knew his worry with Vinnie had barely touched the surface.

As he buried his face in the pillow and begged for Rory to pillage him, he realized that the worst thing wouldn't be "What if it didn't work out?"

The worst thing would be "What if it *did,* and we have to change our lives, and neither one of us can."

He'd managed to table the fear before he climaxed that morning, but deep in his heart he knew it would resurface.

Five days. They had five days to get the first of it out of their systems so maybe they could talk like grown-ups on the way home.

AT FIRST, Val could admit it, he was too thrilled to get his truck back to worry overmuch about talking like a grown-up. God, he'd missed driving. Maybe it was the power of being the biggest guy on the road, and maybe it was the way the world was wide open and bursting with promise as he drove.

Maybe it was that the rig was all his—bought and paid for—and he'd earned the right to drive her, and he knew he was good at it.

Maybe it was all of it, plus another dazzling April day in Texas, with three days driving and a good man by his side, but whatever it was, Val couldn't force himself to be the grown-up, to have the grown-up conversation or force discomfort between the two of them as they rode.

Dammit, they were having too much fun!

Rory's company hadn't gotten any worse after the harrowing conclusion of their epic chase or their interlude at Vinnie's. And Rory was less guarded now. He spoke openly about his son, from Anthony leaping off the high dive when he was only five—much to his father's terror—to the boy leaving the house without his mother's knowledge to go search for an ailing cat. He'd been twelve at the time, and they'd found him, cross-legged under a hedge, singing to the poor thing as it passed.

"Augh!" Val said, clutching his chest with one hand as he drove. "Hard to get mad at him for that!"

"I *know*!" Rory admitted. "Me and his mom were like, 'Welp.'"

Val countered with a story of his nephews and the escaped hamster that ate the stuffing out of their mother's recliner before meeting a terrible end, and how he and Sal—an interior decorator—and Prock had spent an entire weekend and all their extra pay fixing the recliner and going to find a replacement for poor Hamtaro. When they'd finished, they'd produced a super-recliner with extra-comfortable stain-resistant fabric, working heating elements in the back, neck, and thighs, and a vibrating function.

Rory was full-on belly laughing before Val was done. "Did you all just not… you know, *stop*? I mean, that's a *lot*."

Val shook his head. "Laure—you've met her on the phone, right?"

"Oh yeah," Rory said. "Pretty levelheaded."

"Yeah, but she'd just squished a hamster and yelled at her kids, and she was trying to start her business because her late husband's military pension was not doing it. When *that* sibling calls you up a crying mess, you go in and *fix it*."

"I guess you do," Rory said, and there was a note in his voice that had Val risking a sideways glance.

"What?" Val asked.

"I love that your family goes to the wall for each other. It was just me and Mama, and that was lonely."

Val *hmm*ed, because he'd already resolved not to risk the rapport, the drive, the good feeling with anything too deep.

"No, no," Rory said, "out with it. I can see you had a shaft of insight…."

The innuendo in his voice made Val laugh, but he'd ridden Rory enough about being open; he knew Rory wouldn't let it rest.

"Yeah, fine, you caught me," Val said at last. "Maybe it's why you assumed you had to be alone for so long. Because as far as you could see, that's how the world worked. You tried to have a family, but you weren't cut out for *that* kind of family, and nobody told you that a different kind was an option."

Rory grunted, and Val could sense him struggling for words.

"No, don't say anything now," he told him. "Just chew on that. Tell me more about your kid *now*—I mean, he do anything that knocks your socks off?"

"Got his degree in business to help me run the gun range," Rory said.

"Damn, that's pretty impressive," Val replied. "You like working with him?"

"I do," Rory said, sounding incredibly satisfied with that part of his life. "He's smart—I mean, he's a smart*ass*, but he's also damned competent. It's sort of terrifying, really. I taught him to shoot at sixteen, and I was *so* scared. But he took it seriously. Every damned minute of it. I thought I was going to have to shoot up a favorite toy or something. There's whole articles written up on how to show a young person how serious a thing a gun is."

"That's…." Val was horrified, but then, his dad had shown *them* when they were eighteen. "God, it didn't come to that?"

"No," Rory said. "No—he just, I don't know. Showed up. Kids are like that, I think. They're crazy little bastards sometimes, rocketing around in their own heads, and you think, 'Is this going to be that dreamy kid who couldn't remember where he put his wallet every day for a month, or is this gonna be the kid who took care of the geriatric cat every day for a year?' And the rock-solid kid, the steady kid who took things seriously and knew you didn't fuck around with firearms— *that's* the kid who showed up." Rory paused for a thoughtful moment. "I think… I think if he hadn't, I would have put the firearms away and maybe taught him later. I gave him that damned stuffed cat when me and Connie split so he wouldn't miss me quite as much. It meant something to us. I don't think I could have lived with making him tear it apart with ordnance."

"I think that's a solid way to parent," Val said. "No matter *what* the shooting magazines say."

Rory grunted. "There's some crazies in the business. I try to run a solid place without any of that weird prepper crap going on, but…."

"I'm very aware of where we live," Val said dryly. "My folks keep making noise about moving to Oregon for retirement, but Dad keeps working for *us* and not retiring, and I think it would break Mom's heart to move away from the grandkids. It's…." He sighed.

"What?"

"My dad was a long-haul trucker for a while. In fact he got me my first job when it became clear two years of junior college were about all I could stand. I took the idea and ran with it and bought out the old bastard who owned who *we* worked for and tried to make it a better business. But one of the things I loved about it—still love, in fact— is that I can go anywhere, in the country at least, and still come back home."

"What about when you're ready to get out of it?" Rory asked.

"I figure in five, maybe ten years, I sell the company off. I've had it appraised, done some investing—it should keep me fat and happy until I'm a ripe old age. Then Europe, Africa, Thailand, here I come."

Rory whistled. "Wow. Didn't see that coming."

"Don't *you* want to travel?" Val asked, a little disappointed. "That was the one thing I really missed about not being rich and having all the scholarships. Chance is going to Croatia for an archeology dig so he can study ancient civilizations. I mean, it's not anything I could have done—requires way more focus in the classroom than I ever had—but God, does that sound cool."

"I'd love to," Rory said, sounding surprised. "I just… I don't know. It never sounded fun alone."

"Well, if you were with me, we wouldn't have to *be* alone," Val said. "See how that works?"

There was a long silence, and then Rory said, in a funny kind of choked voice, "You do make me think about the future different, Val Royal."

Val preened. "Well, there's some bennies to being a grown-up after all, Rory McCauley."

"I'm beginning to see that."


THE FIRST night, Val found them a decent motel—not a hotel with all the amenities, but something off the highway with good beds and a restaurant nearby that understood vegetables were for eating too. Lots of truckers used it because it was within walking distance of a diesel station, so the place catered to its base. The outside may have looked simple, but if a trucker was going to stay there instead of their rig, its beds, carpet, bathrooms, all needed to be *pristine* and comfortable, in the way a home was comfortable, otherwise why fork out the money?

He and Rory thought the bed was exactly what was needed, and the night they spent there was acrobatic and, well, loud.

Rory left an extra twenty for the maid, and they slipped away at dawn.

The next night, they were in the vasty nothingness (as Val called it, because he'd always been a fan of *Firefly)*, and after eating their dinner standing up, Rory had gathered their trash and stashed it in the receptacle in the rig and then kissed Val under the stars.

They'd had to go slow and gentle that night, because they were big men and the bed in the rig wasn't that big, but the quiet around them, the spice and hot dust of the desert, the wild spray of the stars above them, made it a slow and gentle sort of night.

The last day, Rory drove, pushing them toward Bakersfield, where they arrived at Val's truck lot at eleven at night.

Val sighed as Rory parked the rig in its slot, and the force of what he wanted for the two of them crashed down on his shoulders.

"I bet you got lots to catch up on," Rory said, blowing out a breath.

"Yeah," Val agreed. "But I don't need to be at the office until noon."

Rory's mouth quirked up. "I could probably leave about then and go clean up my own business," he said. Then he sobered. "At the very least, I desperately want another night."

Val studied him. "If you spend another night," he said honestly, "I'm just gonna ask for more."

Rory's eyes searched his face. "No harm in asking," he said. "I might do the same."

It wasn't a promise of marriage or a forever vow, but it was enough for Val to clean out the fridge and the trash and grab his dirty clothes and linens so he could drive them both to his little house, and he could let Rory in.

VAL HAD his little "check the house" rituals. Shaw and Russell had done a standup job on plant and fish duty—and they'd even left some stuff in the fridge for breakfast, lunch, and dinner the next day. He ran a check on the pool, with the lights on in the back, with Rory over his shoulder.

"Nice," Rory said softly. "I may have to use that sometime."

"It's small," Val said, remembering the glories of Vinnie's Olympic length beauty, but Rory just slipped his arm around Val's waist and kissed his temple.

"It's a good size," he said. "The kids leave it okay?"

Val walked out to the little whiteboard he kept next to the locked enclosure. "They did a treatment yesterday afternoon," he said. "And they had two friends over, and I've got their phone numbers." He chuckled. "I did not ask for their phone numbers, but you know. Good kids."

"Yup." Val turned his head in the gentle cool of the spring night air and saw Rory, closer than he needed to be, his eyes glowing in the ambient light from the pool itself. "What?"

"I really want to hold you tonight. You got any chores before we both jump in the pool and then turn in?"

Val gave him a brilliant smile. "How'd you know about jumping in the pool?" He'd been longing to do it, but he hated to put Rory off on their last night.

"It's a guess," Rory said. He took a step back and yawned and stretched. "How about I fetch my board shorts from my bag and let you run around and do your thing. I know what it's like to be gone. I'll hop in while you make sure your washer and dryer didn't migrate and there's no blond girls sleeping in your bed."

Val snuck in a kiss before dodging away. "She can find somewhere else to sleep. I'm the only bear allowed."

Rory was still chuckling as they suited actions to words.

Val ran around and misted his window succulents, making sure they were getting enough sun. He checked his tank of neon tetras to see if it needed cleaning. (He had a giant bottom feeder in there that seemed to regard the whole world with fishy malevolence but still kept the tank in good shape, as did his tiny snails.) In good weather—anything less than eighty degrees like tonight—he would run around, open all his windows, and turn on the house fan in the roof to cool things down.

Then he did a load of laundry, checked the fridge—this time to make a list—so he knew what he'd need to get in the morning, and usually he took a shower of a length directly in proportion to how long he'd spent on the road since his last one. This time, he grabbed his board shorts and joined Rory in the pool.

They only swam for half an hour. Long enough for them to do some laps, to stretch some muscles, to shake off the rattles of the road. Then they dried off, shivering a little, and Val hung up his board shorts in the bathroom before slipping into a warm shower.

Rory shucked his own shorts off and hung them next to Val's before he slid into the shower behind him and wrapped those long arms around his shoulders.

Together they quietly washed away the sweat and the grime that came with being on the road, but they could not seem to wash away the melancholy of parting.

Rory topped—he was more comfortable that way, and Val didn't care, not really, as long as they were joined—but it wasn't the actual fucking that carried him over. It was the broken cry Rory gave with his final thrust and the way he cupped Val's face in his hands even as he threw his head back and came.

When it was over, and the moving air in the house had cooled their sweat enough to pull Val's summer blanket over them, Val turned toward him in the darkness and asked the inevitable question.

"And then what happens?"

Rory turned toward him and smiled. "And then they both went to work for a week and a half because they left some shit hanging, and I've got a security gig this weekend, and I need to see how my son is doing."

"And then—"

"And then we make plans for that weekend," Rory said evenly. "And we text in between. And we call. And we—"

Val kissed him quickly, then pulled back, his eyes closing. "Hope. We hope and work to make it so," he said. "That's all I needed to hear."

The next morning he cooked them eggs for breakfast, and they sat at the table and scrolled their phones, making the occasional comment, as though they'd been eating breakfast like that for years. When Val dropped Rory off at his pickup truck, they didn't kiss—because that would be asking for trouble at a lot filled with truckers—but Rory opened the door and grabbed his rifle case and his bag and said, "If you don't hear from me, text. This ain't a game of who wants it more, Val, I swear."

"I want it more," Val told him, not batting an eye.

"I'm starting to doubt it," Rory said, his grim smile showing the challenge had been accepted. "Talk more soon."


A MONTH LATER, Val was thinking they'd call it a draw.

They'd texted—he'd seen pictures of Anthony, who was a stunningly handsome young man, not quite as tall as his father but with an easy smile and a fond look for his dad behind the camera. In return, Val sent pictures of Prock and his kids, including baby Charlie, who was, Val could admit it, the apple of his eye, and Laure and her two sons, both of whom were taller than Val (and he was still mad about that).

There had been one visit, a weekend, torrid and exhausting and delirious, when Val had tossed moderation to the wind and survived on takeout and sex and could have sworn he lost weight and improved his wind.

He couldn't stop craving Rory's skin, his smile, his smell.

He'd made a couple of hauls in that time and had missed Rory riding shotgun, their chatter, his laconic wit—he'd even started listening to classic country, because Rory kept insisting he was missing out.

Rory had taken to humming musical theater when Val called, to prove he still listened. Val knew he was biased. He'd been hunting for a person, a companion, a friend and a lover, before his family had conspired to put Rory McCauley in his life, but now that Rory was in, Val was *all* in.

He wasn't sure how to tell Rory that, though. Rory *had* a life. He *was* busy. He'd done a couple of security gigs in the past month, one of them quite exciting, for a local celebrity. He and Anthony had been busy vetting a new manager for their shooting range—from what Val understood, they were quite extensive, right down to traveling to LA to talk to former employers. Rory was absolutely adamant that they not get somebody irresponsible or offensive or dangerous. He was all about education, moderation, and de-escalation, and he needed his employees to follow suit.

So when Rory sent him a picture of Rory, Anthony, and—of all people—Violet Cassidy, who had turned out to be a levelheaded young woman not usually inclined to throw her breasts at people, and who had been taught to shoot by her father when she was sixteen years old, he could only laugh at the weirdness of life that she had turned out to be the perfect person for the manager job.

*She looks much happier here than she did trying to seduce me*, he texted back. *How'd she end up at your doorstep?*

*Coincidence*, Rory sent back. *She needed a job that would pay tuition, because that wasn't bullshit, and she's been certified and permitted for pretty much every gun we own and lease to shoot. When she recognized me, she shook my hand and said, "You've seen the worst of me, so I get it. I'm sorry for wasting your time."*

Val blinked. *Well, I think the real Violet was a pretty frank young woman—that I wouldn't want to mess with.*

*My impression too. I told her to sit a spell, have a cup of coffee, and talk. Anthony took her around, and she didn't flirt once. Neither did he. And she knows her shit. I got a good feeling about her.*

*It's good to see a picture of you and Anthony*, Val texted, because he loved comparing them, seeing which features the son got from the father. He figured if he'd been straight, he would have had kids of his own now, and while that wasn't in the cards, he did love happy families.

*When do I see the folks*? Rory texted back, and that startled Val into remembering something he'd been meaning to bring up.

*We've got a big family barbecue the weekend after this one*, Val told him.

*Want me to wait to visit you then*? Rory asked.

Val stared at the text, surprised. *That's tough*, he replied. *See you in three days or see you in a week and a half but introduce you to family.* He paused. *I'll take seeing you in three days. Family can wait. I miss you now.*

God, he really did. It wasn't even so much the sex—although his whole body was reminding him that his last drought had been a couple of years, and his entire sex drive had gotten finely tuned during that time with Rory. He was, in fact, *hungry* for more, his body thirsting for the smell of Rory's skin like this entire part of California usually thirsted for water.

*You think I won't show*, Rory accused, and Val dialed the phone right there.

"You would too," he said without preamble. "Do you think after all we've been through I wouldn't trust your word?"

"Well, then, why not wait?"

As they texted and talked, Val was doing one of his twice-daily passes around the yard, checking on the rigs he housed there, making sure the drivers were doing what they should, when they should. He knew it was a little bit fussy, but he'd headed off more problems at the pass by being out and about and available for questions than a thousand security guards or supervising foremen could do without him. At Rory's words he stopped and ducked behind a trailer for some faux privacy.

"Because I'm horny," he said, pressed enough for time to be brutally honest. "I want you. I miss you. Yes, I want the whole commitment thing, but I am excited enough about having fun to want to have some first."

Rory's voice went from offended to sultry. "So I'm dessert as well as dinner," he asked.

"And you're also quite a snack," Val told him, borrowing some of his brother Sal's slang. He lowered his voice. "The last two weeks did not go as quickly as I thought it would."

He liked his life, dammit. He loved his job, loved his drivers, and loved his family. But at night when he closed his eyes, he missed the sound of Rory's breathing. In the morning he missed those companionable moments, both of them scrolling their messages, talking briefly, drinking coffee.

The things he'd wanted a man in his life *for* were missing when Rory wasn't there.

"Same," Rory said softly. "Maybe I can do both?"

"Could you?" Val had never felt so pathetically grateful. "Because boy, that was a rough decision. Man, I would *really* love for you to meet my parents. Is that sad? That's sad, isn't it. I'm supposed to be a grown man. But Dean and Laure told them, and now Mom's on me for not taking selfies, and—"

"Aw, son," Rory drawled, "if Mama were alive I already would have dragged you to coffee."

Val's chest warmed. "That's quite a compliment," he said, proud.

"Well I miss you too. Yeah. I'll be at your place Saturday morning and leave Monday, and—"

"Bring Anthony," Val blurted. "The next weekend. When you meet my parents."

"Really?" Rory sounded surprised.

"Yeah, really. It'll be big and noisy, and my folks have a bigger pool than mine and a big lawn, and we're not in the middle of a drought, so it'll be a little bit green. I mean…." He suddenly felt awkward. And young. "It's only fair."

"I'll ask him," Rory said. "I… that makes me happy you'd ask."

God, Val hadn't felt this giddy in ages. "So you're coming Saturday?"

"Yeah. In the morning."

Val had never once envied his flamboyant brother Sal—but suddenly he wished he could twirl. "Yay," he said. He was grinning and couldn't seem to stop.

"I'll call you tonight," Rory said. "Around eight?"

"I should be home," Val told him, and then they rung off.

And then he texted Laure that he was bringing company for the picnic.


RORY HELD the Glock 34 as naturally as he held his cowboy hat when he was inside. He sighted the target, let out a breath, and squeezed the trigger as it left his body. The report was dulled by his soundproofed headphones, and he set the gun down, muzzle forward, as he pressed the button to pull the paper target back toward him so he could see it.

"Jesus, Dad," Anthony said with disgust. "You suck."

Rory scowled at his son. "Perfect bullseye," he said.

Anthony took the target from his hands and thrust his finger through the last hole Rory had put in the thing. "Three inches to the left. You always hit dead center. Always. What's wrong?"

Rory shifted from foot to foot and then turned to unload and clean the Glock before putting it back in its case. He'd waited all day for some shooting time for himself, and while Anthony hadn't caught them, he'd seen that the last shot hadn't been the only one that hadn't gone where he'd aimed. He won contests with this gun, dammit. He was *an expert marksman*. "A little bit off" was not good enough.

When he'd closed the case, he turned toward his son, who had thrown the target away and moved to the next booth to disassemble his own gun. Anthony's target had looked a lot like Rory's—but then while Anthony enjoyed shooting, he wasn't particularly competitive about *anything*.

"You gonna tell me?" Anthony asked when they both had their gun cases in their hands and were heading for the walk-in safe tucked into the side of the long cinder-block corridors that were the range.

"It's dumb," Rory muttered, feeling about twelve. He'd seen Anthony have conundrums like this when *he* was dating. Most recently when he'd been seeing a corrections student at CSU Stanislaus. The young woman had been trying to decide between staying in central California after she got her degree or transferring to a law school—that had accepted her—and changing her life goal from law enforcement to the law, period. Anthony had debated with *himself* as to whether to urge her on to bigger and better things or beg her to stay and make a go of it with him.

In the end, they'd said goodbye, and while Rory was proud of his son, on the one hand, for doing the mature, grown-up thing, on the other hand he wanted his son to have the kind of love he'd fight for. Rory had never had that, until now, and he thought Anthony deserved it.

And that was the thought, right there, that let him share what was bothering him.

"I figured I'd go to Val's this weekend," he said as they both clipped their personal weapons into place in the specially designed safe. Anthony pulled out the tablet and the scanner, handing the scanner to his father so Rory could take a quick inventory of all the weapons that had been pulled that day to lease and then cleaned and replaced into the safe. It was four—they'd closed up a little early because it was slow and they had no appointments.

"Sounds great," Anthony told him. "Violet and I have the weekend, and you don't have any security gigs. Why's that got you all off-target?"

Rory kept scanning. "Well, next weekend is his big family picnic thing. He wants me to come to that too—you're invited."

"Most excellent!" Anthony chirped. "Again, why's that a problem?"

Rory finished the last of the inventory and nodded to Anthony, who closed out the day in the tablet.

"I don't know. I'm excited about both things, really. I just don't want to leave you alone, and what if he ODs on my company? I mean, two visits in a row might send him fleeing for the hills, and—"

"I'm twenty-five," Anthony said bluntly, and Rory followed him out of the small safe area and through the now-darkened range. Together they shut off the lights and locked up, then headed for Rory's pickup, which was the last vehicle in the parking lot.

"Yeah, but it's not fair, you doing all the work at the range, and—"

"Dad, do you like this guy?" Anthony asked.

"Yes." Rory had no doubts on that one.

"Do you love him?"

Rory gaped. "Well, I hadn't thought about—" He stopped himself because *of course* he had, and after Val's insistence that he face his thoughts and his feelings, he didn't feel right about lying.

"Bullshit," Anthony muttered. "I call bullshit. Pop, we've got Violet—and I insisted on hiring her for a reason. You've got two good managers, and your shooting lessons can all be scheduled on one day a week. Stop fucking around, man. Don't let this thing die because you didn't want to fight for it!"

Rory knew his mouth was opening and closing like a fish, and he wanted to say, "But what about Lisa!" He didn't because mentioning the one that got away felt like fighting dirty.

But Anthony gave him a bleak look and said, "I know what I'm talking about, don't I?"

Rory nodded dumbly, and Anthony held out his hand for the car keys. Rory handed them over, not sure when his son had gotten to be the grown-up in the family, and Anthony muttered, "Get in. You've got shit to do tonight."

"Like what?" Rory asked, finally finding his tongue.

Anthony shot him a look like he was the dumbest asshole on the planet, started the truck, and drove toward their home.

LATER THAT evening, Val bustled out of his truck with a bag of groceries in one hand and his work knapsack over his shoulder so he could hold the phone with the other hand. He wished he hadn't done that thing with the phone, because Laure hadn't left him alone since.

"He knows how big our family is?" Laure asked for the fifty-dozenth time.

"He's met half of us, including you," Val replied for the fifty-dozenth-and-first. "Laure, why is this a problem?"

"I don't want to scare him off!" she said, and that would have really startled him, but his attention was arrested by the figure lounging on the swing in the shadows of his porch.

"Highly doubtful," Val said, happiness clawing through his shock. "He's here."

"What?" She sounded as surprised as he was.

"He's here. Laure, I'll call you back."

He hit End Call and slid the phone into his pocket. He carried his shit up the porch steps because that seemed the thing to do, and came to a stop in front of Rory as he pushed himself up to stand.

"You're here," he said, stating the obvious.

"A surprise to me too," Rory said.

"For a while," Val said, noting the full suitcase and the rifle case on the porch next to the swing.

"Also true." Rory nodded. "If that's okay."

"Oh it is." Val's eyes were going to pop out of his head. "Where's your truck?"

Rory frowned sulkily. "Would you believe my kid has it? Little asshole. We got home from the range, and he packed my bag, grabbed my rifle case from the closet, threw them in the truck while my jaw was still on the floor, and told me to get in."

Val's eyebrows shot up. "Were you… uhm…."

"Being a pain in the ass, according to him," Rory said, still apparently baffled. "Look, all I did was ask him if he thought seeing you two weekends in a row would send you screaming, and suddenly we're heading to Bakersfield. Something about if he'd known I was this stupid he would have lived with his mother. I don't know. I am honestly still boggled."

Val found his lips were disobeying his command to stay firm. His grin popped out again and warmth that had nothing to do with the warm May day flooded through him.

"You're insufferable without me?" he said. "Did I read that right?"

Rory scowled. "I couldn't make up my mind," he protested. "See you this weekend or wait and meet your family. I wanted both, but that seemed a little—"

Val kissed him, hard enough to dissolve his toes. Rory gave a helpless little whimper and opened his mouth, melting into Val's arms with unadulterated need.

"Forward?" Val whispered, pulling back from the kiss.

Rory nodded and rested his forehead on Val's. "I missed you," he confessed nakedly. "Anthony read me the riot act on the way over. Said I could contract my security gigs from here as well as our place, said the whole reason he spent the last month finding Violet was so I could leave the gun range to him." Rory swallowed and added bitterly, "It's like the little shit won't even miss me."

"I don't think that's true," Val said, wondering if Rory didn't recognize family machinations because Anthony and Rory's ex-wife had been Rory's only family for so long. "I think maybe he knows what I know."

"What's that?" Rory asked, and he looked lost enough for Val not to tease him with this.

"That you're finally ready to settle down," Val said, hoping. Please. Please let Rory not fight this. God, seeing him here, on his porch, when Val had been thinking about him all day—it felt so damned right.

But Rory didn't shrug it off or shake his head or push away. "You just feel so damned good." He sighed and melted into Val's arms some more.

Val held him, closing his eyes and smiling to himself. "So," he asked. "Am I going to meet Anthony?"

"You have to," Rory grumbled. "He dropped me off here and told me he was on his way to fetch dinner, and then he was going to come back and hammer out a custody agreement."

Val snickered. He couldn't help it. "I'm sure he gets the smartassery from his mother's side."

Rory rolled his eyes. "Don't feed me bullshit now, son. I just bared my heart to you."

Which made Val sober. "I love you, Rory McCauley. Let's get busy on that rest-of-our-life thing, okay?"

Rory bit his lip, so uncharacteristically uncertain that Val's heart stuttered. "I love you too, Valedictorian Princeton Royal. And I promise, nobody will ever hear your full name from me."

"I believe your promises, Rory," Val said. "Let's get you moved in."

ANTHONY GOT back as Val was clearing out drawers for Rory to use, and Val heard father and son bickering in the kitchen. He left his task with a stack of clothes to put in the guest room closet and then made his way to the source of the good smells being sorted and dealt on his kitchen table.

"All I'm saying," Rory railed as Val entered, "is that it was rude not to give the man a little warning."

Anthony opened up a cupboard and handed his father three plates. "Matching dishes, Pop. He's got matching dishes. This man is ready to nest—I don't think you caught him too off guard."

"The flatware also matches," Val said, leaning against the frame separating the kitchen table from the living room. "And there is artwork in the hallways and wallpaper accents in the bedrooms. Hell, there's even rugs in the bathroom, but some of that is my sister's doing, because she likes to think she can keep six brothers civilized, and some of that is my younger brother's doing, because he's an interior decorator who thinks he can run our lives if he can coordinate our art with our carpet with our furniture."

Rory's son looked even more like Rory in person than he did in his picture. He turned to Val and extended his hand. "God, it's good to meet you."

"Back atcha," Val said, shaking firmly. "Your father is so damned proud of you it's almost revolting. But not quite. You dumped him on my porch, so I can forgive you for being perfect."

Anthony cackled. "Yup!" he crowed. "Did I call it or did I call it! Now what else do we need on the table?"

"Beer, milk, or OJ?" Val asked, rummaging through the fridge. "Ooh—I've got some sodas here too."

"Milk," Anthony said. "Unless I can crash on your couch tonight. I was either going to take Dad's truck and then have him get it sometime next week or have a friend who's driving out our way pick me up. It's your call."

"I've got a guest room," Val said. "I think your dad would really love to have his truck."

"*His dad* is standing right here!" Rory complained. "When did you two form the coalition to take over my life?"

Anthony gave his father a fond glance. "Dad," he said, with the condescension only a grown son could have for his wayward parent, "you've done a great island impersonation my whole life. And you've been an absolutely stellar father. But I'm grown, and so are you. You get to have somebody good." He smiled at Val. "You're good. I heard the story of your run to Austin about six hundred times now—it gets better every time."

Val preened for a second. "C'mon, Rory, you sit down. Anthony and I will set the table. We'll know you've accepted your fate when you start giving us shit again."

"Oh bullshit," Rory retorted. "*You* sit down. We're the ones who invaded your house. Let us at least feed you for your trouble."

The bickering started again, but the table got set, and when they finally sat down to some of the best Thai food Val had ever tasted, Val could feel it in his bones.

They were going to be a damned fine family.

# AT THE END OF THE DAY

"I CAN HEAR you thinking," Val murmured. "Go back to sleep."

"Would it be dumb to say I'm excited?" Rory asked, scanning the now-familiar interior of their room, the edge of the gold-and-blue blackout curtains where the early morning sun of June was starting to peek through. It had been a week and a half since Anthony had packed up his shit and dumped him off on Val's doorstep, and Rory hadn't regretted his son's bossiness once.

Rory had worked a gig in the past week, and the commute hadn't been much longer from Val's than it had been from the little house that he'd shared with Anthony. And between his truck and Anthony's, they'd moved most of his clothes and possessions into Val's place a little at a time.

Some stuff—a lot of it, actually—got to stay in the little house outside the city limits, but Rory and Anthony had kept the place nice and pretty current, so it was a young man's home as well as a… well, not so young man's home too. And Rory got to see Val almost every day.

In fact, the day after Rory had arrived, Val had needed to go on a two-day haul. Rory had come with him, and the road, the company, even the sex in the sleeper unit, hadn't palled one damned bit.

Just that easy, Rory could see himself simply… staying. Just staying here. Being with this one man, waking up next to him, loving him… oh yes.

Most assuredly loving him.

Loving him for the rest of his days.

But Anthony's impatience had jumped the gun a little. Rory was *supposed* to meet the family first, but Val assured him that the big family picnic at his folks' house would be the place to do it. When Val had extended the invite to Anthony, the boy's response had been, well, predictably whimsical.

"One of those big family reunion things?" he'd asked. "Like you see in the movies? Dad said this was a pretty big deal—are you sure your folks wouldn't mind?"

Val's snort was starting to sound as familiar as Rory's own breathing. "My folks?" He rolled his eyes. "Anthony, you don't understand. My mom had seven kids the regular way and spent my formative years trying to adopt the neighborhood. She's got five grandchildren by birth, and she'll swear you're the—" He paused to count on his fingers. "—I don't know, the twelfth? I lose track after Vinnie's girls, but Laure's best friend has kids, and Sal's bestie from the sixth grade too. There's kids everywhere. It's terrifying."

"What about your dad?" Anthony asked, and Rory listened closely because while Val obviously thought the world of him, he seemed to be a little quieter than Val's mom.

"Dad'll love you," Val reassured him. "The thing about Dad is he just sort of assumes Mom'll be adopting the world. So, like, the first time I brought Vinnie home, Vinnie was having a fight with his parents, and, well, his own dad had a temper. So I'm about to quietly ask Dad if I can invite Vinnie to stay the night, and Dad goes, 'I gotcha set up in the basement, Vin. You can stay there as long as you need to.' And I didn't know this until later, but Dad apparently visited Vinnie's mom the next morning and helped get Vinnie's dad out of the picture. All quiet. No big deal. Just my father being a hero, you know?"

"I get grandparents?" Anthony asked excitedly. "At twenty-five? That is *amazing*. Thanks, stepdaddy Val—you give the *best* presents!"

Val had grimaced. "You're welcome to them, as long as you never call me stepdaddy again."

Anthony thought about it and nodded. "Yeah. Yeah. Dad's boyfriend is better. You do give good presents, though. I'm almost as excited as Dad!"

So excited, in fact, that he'd spent the night in Val's guest bedroom, the better to get an early start on Val's portion of the picnic prep. Apparently Val's specialty was potato salad—five pounds of it—and snickerdoodles, which Anthony had baked the day before.

It was fun to watch his son get so invested—so *excited*—about the new family in Rory's life, but Rory… well, there were things he just couldn't do with his adult son in the room next door.

"No," Val admitted now, in the dark. "It's not dumb to be excited. I'll be real. We all still gather during Christmas Eve. Christmas Day is for other families or kids or what have you, although Mom still has a sort of open-house-slash-brunch. But Christmas Eve is fried chicken and potatoes and green beans, and we all bring our favorite stuff to add to it. Prock's wife makes the most *amazing* German cabbage. It's absolutely filthy for you, but we all love it so."

Rory chuckled lightly. "So you're… I don't know. A family." He paused. "And I didn't know that about Vinnie and your dad." He thought about how Vinnie hadn't said a word. "Does Vinnie ever come to the summer picnic?"

"Every other year—the off years like this one, they have a similar thing with Sam's family, but the girls swear they like my parents better." He sounded smug—but then, he really did have the goods there. "So it's okay to be excited. But don't be worried. They're going to love you."

"I'm… I don't know. Kind of old," Rory admitted, because yeah. Almost fifty. It was a little old to be "Hey Mom, here's my boyfriend!"

"Shh…," Val whispered. "Don't tell my parents this, but I'm going to be *forty-one* this year. And I am *not* a virgin."

Rory shook his head. "Shut up," he muttered.

"Sure I will. But my boyfriend has to close his eyes and go to sleep, since he says we can't have sex."

Rory shuddered, just *thinking* about Anthony in the room next door. "No sex," he confirmed.

Val laughed softly. "I love you, Rory. It'll be fine."

"I love you too, Val. It had better be."

His eyelids finally felt heavy, and he managed another two hours of sleep.


THE DRIVE to Val's parents' was only about half an hour, with Anthony in the back of Val's extra cab, asking questions the whole way. Val seemed… bemused, and a little flattered, Rory thought, as though he'd never realized his family could be such a big deal to other people. But to Rory and his son, they were, and that made him happy.

When they finally pulled up to the stretch of property, Rory was impressed. The backyard was a solid acre or two, and there was a wide strip of stubble field next to it where it appeared everybody else had parked. The ranch-style house itself was smaller than Rory had assumed—seven kids was a lot—but it couldn't have more than five bedrooms, tops, and that was if one of the rooms was closet sized, like a den or something. But it was a cheery yellow with white trim, and the front yard was ablaze with planted irises and tended rose bushes, rock follies and glorious stained glass lawn ornaments that welcomed people with a whole rainbow of whimsy.

Val led them around the side of the house to the back, where, on a concrete apron that extended from the porch, two big picnic tables sat, laden with food and about to become heavier, given what Rory and Anthony were carrying. Between the two tables an older woman, likely in her midsixties, was fussing with the covers on the food. She had a ponytail of blond-gray hair and wore a batik sundress over what was probably a swimsuit, and when she caught the movement at the corner of the house, she glanced up and smiled, waving wildly at Val, who waved back, a fond expression on his face.

"Ed!" she called. "Eddie, they're here! Val brought them. Hot damn, the old one's cute. Come meet the new boyfriend!"

Anthony's snort of amusement only made Rory blush harder.

"Are you ready?" Val asked softly. "She's going to hug. You ready, Anthony—"

But the warning was too late. Julie Royal, all five feet, five inches of her, was running across the grass in a tornado of rainbow batik excitement.

Val got the hug first, of course, because his mother loved him, but in a moment it was Rory's turn. Val Royal's mother was wiry and strong, and she hugged him harder than he ever thought possible, and just when she let go, Val's father, who was not much bigger than she was, stood there with a hearty handshake and an ear-to-ear grin. His ears stuck out the teeniest bit, and he had a bare, bony face that made his expression of joy seem ever so important.

And the look on Val's face as he introduced them was so proud.

There was a whole group of people there: a pretty, strong-faced woman with a lustrous fall of dark brown hair that Rory assumed was Laure; a thin, angular version of Val with a wicked glint in his eye and a determined swish that must be Sal. He already knew Prock and Dean, but he could spot the youngest Royal, tan and lithe and permanently bemused, and knew he was Chance. At Chance's elbow was a slender young man wearing a pair of wire-framed glasses, blonder than the others but still with the unmistakable Royal chin and jaw, who was probably Reg.

Like that, Rory fell in, through the invisible barrier of newcomer into the giant pool of family with Val Royal at his side, and the last of his lone wolf fell away, leaving him with a new pack.

The siblings gathered around and introduced themselves—Rory felt pretty smug to realize he'd been correct, but he was still surprised when Dean came to sort of corral him from the herd to take him aside.

"Your eyes are glazing over," Dean said dryly.

"Your family," Rory said, shaking his head. His eyes searched out his son, who was standing with Chance, Reg, and a couple of young men with the unfinished look of teenagers whom he seemed to remember as Laure's sons, Russell and Shaw. Anthony was embattled in a fierce game of horseshoes in a flat area to the side of the pool, and Rory noted a sideways look he gave toward Reg.

He knew that look. It was almost predatory, although Anthony was usually the one being chased.

"Hmm…," Dean murmured. "You saw that too?"

"Think your parents will mind?" Rory asked, wondering if he'd have to go have a *very* awkward conversation.

"No." Dean shrugged. "He's not hitting on Chance—who always gets the attention. It's nice to see somebody notice Reg. I didn't realize he was gay, though. That's a surprise."

Rory realized how much he and Dean *hadn't* spoken about themselves. Val was different. He'd known it from the first moment the man had gone off talking about the importance of bull jizz.

"Bi," he replied mildly. "I shall be… very interested… to see what happens next."

Dean Royal gave a sudden, brilliant grin. "See? Family watching—it's our favorite sport. You'll fit right in. I'm going to go play the winner in that game. If I don't beat Chance into the ground, that kid's gonna get a big head."

He wandered off, and Val pulled up beside him. "Taste this," he said, and shoved a morsel of chicken into Rory's mouth.

Rory almost swooned. "Holy God," he muttered. "I've never been horny for chicken before."

"Laure's new recipe for marinade," Val confirmed. He handed Rory a drink of water from a bottle on the table next to him and then pulled another morsel from the small paper plate in his hand. "Now taste this."

This was pork, and if it came closer to giving Rory a taste orgasm, that might have been because the chicken was foreplay.

"You're going to ruin me for other food!" he complained when the spots had cleared from his eyes.

"Sure, sure," Val said. "Now which one did you think was better?"

"That's asking me to choose between testicles," Rory complained, and Val's shout of laughter made heads turn their way. Then Rory realized that Sal—who was tall and angular and arrestingly pretty, was standing next to Laure looking fierce and competitive. "Oh no," he added, getting it.

"Oh yes," Val told him, scowling back at his siblings.

"They're having a contest."

"I'm supposed to be the deciding vote."

Rory looked at Val's plate, which was empty, only two small, discrete saucy spots left. "I need more samples to help you decide."

Val gave him a look of triumph. "And now it's on *you*!" he crowed. "Sal! Laure! Rory says he can decide if he can get a bigger sample."

Val disappeared, and Laure and Sal advanced, each of them with a full piece of meat on a plate, and Rory wanted to laugh because of all the problems he could have imagined having this day, *this* moment was not one of them.

He had to declare a draw, but after asking both the siblings about their recipes, he hoped he managed not to wound any feelings. And he *did* get a sense of Sal's bitchy humor and Laure's hard-nosed, practical mothering. By the time Sal got called to the horseshoe pit and Laure went to help her mother chop tomatoes for yet another salad, Rory was completely caught up in Val's quest to find both of his siblings a good man.

He watched Dean surreptitiously check his phone, his back turned toward Marcus, his work partner, who seemed to know all the siblings well. Maybe Dean had already found someone, Rory thought, and as he watched Marcus pointedly *not* look at Chance, he suspected that perhaps both partners were gazing their future in the eye.

At that moment, Prock walked up, with a lovely woman on one arm—and a car seat carrier on the other. Their two daughters were down in the pool, and Laure's sons were keeping an eye on them—and tormenting them as only older cousins could.

"Prock!" Rory said, extending a hand. "Good to see you again."

Prock made introductions, and Faith, his wife, shook his hand as well. "Prock told me about your adventure," she said on a laugh. "I'm awfully grateful to you for getting him out of that."

Rory had to laugh. "And we're grateful to Prock for keeping that refrigerator running. Gotta tell you, the whole thing would have crashed down around our heads if your husband hadn't known what he was doing."

Prock—who had set the carrier with the sleeping baby on the picnic table next to him—held his arms up like a victorious boxer gloating in the ring as he sang, "HVAC hero! He's got smart home supplies!" to the tune of an old rock song.

Faith smacked his arm and told him to stop it, but she was laughing so hard she almost couldn't stand.

Rory asked to look at baby Charlie, and he was charmed by the sleeping four-month-old, who had a head of frothy black curls and dusky skin from his mother and—according to Faith—his father's sweet, unruffled disposition.

The day progressed. There was swimming, laughter, deep conversations, verbal dogpiles, kids shrieking, and a couple of giant dogs who had to be shooed away from both hamburgers and ice cream. Before Rory knew it, the sun was slanting through the trees that shaded the far end of the yard. Rory found himself in this shady corner, watching as Val wrestled with his nieces in the pool. Anthony had quit the horseshoe game to swim, and now he'd hopped out and was standing at his side, wrapped in a towel, surveying the chaos, and Rory eyed him speculatively.

"So," he said. "You ready to have extended family?" He didn't mention the quiet attention his son had been paying to Reg Royal. Like his and Val's relationship, maybe it was better if there wasn't too much meddling.

"Absolutely," Anthony told him. "You ready to put a ring on it?" because apparently meddling be damned.

Rory almost choked on his hamburger. "I," he managed, "am too damned old—"

Anthony chortled. "Yeah, but Dad, you were too damned old to settle down just a couple months ago. Imagine what you won't be too old for tomorrow!"

Rory grinned at him and glanced back to Val, who was making his way toward them with a determined smile on his face but who kept getting waylaid by people—or animals—who absolutely needed his attention. He was probably the grimmest Royal, Rory realized, perpetually sober, listening to his younger siblings with the absolute attention of the kid who had to help the parents muster the troops. These things apparently didn't go away when the oldest grew up, they simply helped shape the man he became.

But the smile he shot Rory was pure, unforced, and dazzling.

Rory gazed at him, at the man who had become his present and his future, and felt his heart swell. Val would get to him in a minute, he knew. He wouldn't let family keep them apart for long because Rory *was* family. He got that now.

And while it had been a wait to find somebody Rory could really feel like this for, the wait had been worth it—*so* worth it. Rory understood now what letting someone into your heart could mean.

"Sorry about that," Val said, drawing near finally, this time with a full plate. "Here," he said, dumping a chicken breast onto Rory's plate with deft fingers. "These just came off the barbecue, and it's Sal's sauce. He forgave you for—his words—'being a wishy-washy ball-less wonder' and made sure you got the best piece."

"Thanks," Rory said roughly, his heart suddenly too full to find a retort to Val's brother—or even to speak.

"Well, it took longer than I thought to get here," Val told him, grimacing at his family. They seemed to have subsided for the moment, but Rory could sense a card game brewing at the table in the shade and wondered what this family liked to play.

"Me too," Rory said, laughing softly to himself. "But damn, son, we were worth the wait."

Val turned to him, grinning, obviously getting the other meaning, and leaned in for a kiss. "We are, aren't we," he said as Rory closed the gap between them to touch lips. Rory smelled sunscreen and cold water and fresh air, the heat and dust of the valley and the food on Val's plate, and ever so faintly, wet dog.

Their mouths met, and he was home, where he should be and planned to stay, whether they were in Val's house, his parents' backyard, or the moving comfort of Val's rig.

As he'd never known another human could be, Val Royal was his home.

# AFTERWORD

Still confused about the Royal clan birth order? Here you go!

Valedictorian—40
Laureate—38
Salutatorian—35
Proctor—32
Dean—29
Registrar—26
Chancellor—20

And just remember, if they'd had eight, he would have been named "Ambassador"!

Keep Reading for an Excerpt from
*Torch Songs*,
Book 4 in the Bonfires Series
by Amy Lane.

# Long Long Time....

"Oh my god," Roberta practically squealed. "Really? You want me to go as your plus-one?"

Guthrie Arlo Woodson tried to keep the melancholy out of his smile and mostly succeeded. "Yep, darlin'. The invite said I could bring someone, and I choose you!"

Roberta Querling sat across from him at the Washoe House, on the bar side, as the joint closed down, and now she lowered her voice even below the closing-time babble and murmured, "They, uh, know I'm just a friend, right?"

Guthrie worked hard to keep his laugh from being bitter. "Babydoll," he drawled, "these guys knew I was gay before I did." He shuddered. "I kept saying I was bi, and then I'd go home with a pretty girl and have a truly shitty time."

Roberta groaned. "I don't even want to know," she said—and she was right. There were things a man did to fake an orgasm that were a lie for the woman and not fantastic for a man's self-esteem. The taint of those days gave Guthrie a case of the cringes even two years after he came out to himself completely.

"And I don't want to tell you," he said, managing to make it roguish instead of ashamed, "but this is a bit of short notice. I appreciate it."

"What about the hotel room?" she asked. "Should we go halfsies?"

He shook his head and laughed a little. "No. Uhm, Seth is renting two houses next to each other, side by side. I told you he and Kelly are adopting Kelly's niece and nephew, right?"

She nodded, clearly as enthralled now as she had been two years ago when they'd auditioned for each other to form their little dive-bar band. Roberta was a violinist—and a good one—and she had better-paying gigs during the week, but she'd been a fan of rock and pop music her entire life. Since that's what Guthrie had been born playing, pretty much, she'd been happy to help him reassemble a band that had been torn apart by time and, well, his father's bigotry, so he could continue to do his favorite thing in the world.

There hadn't been a time in their acquaintance that Roberta hadn't appeared starstruck by Guthrie's friendship with Seth Arnold.

Of course, Seth Arnold was *literally* an international superstar, a young phenom who had taken the music world by storm in his first years in the conservatory by releasing a series of innovative videos featuring him performing multiple instruments and his own compositions or arrangements. Guthrie was pretty sure that now Seth had the hang of monetizing his channel (or more likely somebody had stepped in and started doing it for him and was being generously paid for their time), he was making roughly twice what Guthrie made in his day job *just* from YouTube, but that wasn't the sort of thing Seth paid attention to.

Guthrie had known Seth for six years, four of them playing together in Guthrie's dad's little honky-tonk band, Fiddler and the Crabs—with Seth as the Fiddler. During that time, Guthrie had learned Seth had two things that really caught his attention. One was music, and the other was his family, starring the love of his life, the boy he'd worshipped in high school and on through adulthood, Kelly Cruz. Kelly wasn't the *only* member of the family; Seth's dad was in his sights, Kelly's mom and sisters, and Kelly's late brother's two children, both of them suffering the effects of a mother who used narcotics during her pregnancy.

Seth adored the children like his own. Watching him play with them over Zoom calls was one of the things that gave Guthrie hope for the world, and he couldn't imagine a world in which his Fiddler didn't get a happy ending with Kelly as his husband and the two children living with them, cared for and beloved, in their happy home.

So hearing that Seth was renting two houses for his wedding in Monterey during the frigid-cold off-season didn't surprise Guthrie in the least. Being invited—and invited to bring a date—to stay in one of the houses and to attend the wedding and play with the family for a week— *that* was one of the proudest things in Guthrie's life.

What wasn't to be proud of by maintaining that friendship? Seth was a violin virtuoso who had brought the house down in Italy and New York and probably had a thousand other venues where he'd be invited as a soloist, and once he and Kelly were married and the adoption finalized, Seth would be bringing his husband and their children with him.

Guthrie loved that Roberta had a celebrity crush on his old friend, who had subsidized Kelly's struggling family with his income from Guthrie's father's band.

What he didn't love so much was that his feelings for Seth went way beyond crush, and he'd had them for six long goddamned years.

"So," Roberta said now, completely oblivious to the turmoil in Guthrie's heart, "we get to stay with the family in one of the houses?"

Guthrie shrugged. "Fiddler—erm, Seth and I go way back," he said. "He and Kelly had to overcome a *lot* of obstacles to have this moment in the sun. I'm proud that he invited me. But yeah. We're in with the family."

Roberta was a pretty young woman with long, straight brown hair that she pulled back from a long oval of a face with a band at her nape. She was a few years younger than Guthrie, right out of school, and still had some of the spots and the awkwardness that went with spending all her attention on her studies and very little on her fellow students. In a way she reminded Guthrie quite a bit of Seth, but Roberta had never had to hide in her own mind like Seth had. She still had some brain power left to observe other humans.

"You must be *really* good friends," she said softly, "for him to invite you like family."

Guthrie swallowed and looked out into the thinning crowd. He, Roberta, and two of her friends from her own conservatory/music days all performed at Washoe House three nights a week. They spent two other nights at a slightly more upscale place closer to San Francisco, and another night practicing, because they liked to play. During the day, Neil Chase, Owen Cuthbert, and Roberta all worked recording and teaching gigs in San Francisco, commuting from San Rafael, where Guthrie kept a small apartment as well. Playing with The Crabs was their happy place. It was fun music, with a lively, enthusiastic crowd, and while Neil, Owen, and Roberta were all top-notch musicians who could probably do *way* better, it was nice, Guthrie thought, for the three of them to play with an organization that didn't have reviews posted in the national press or frothing-at-the-mouth conductors who went on power trips designed to deconstruct even the strongest psyche.

Guthrie was under no illusions that The Crabs wasn't a step down for all three of them, just as he knew that for himself, it was the only thing that gave meaning to his life.

He hated to burden Roberta with the stupid, painful details of that life—but she was taking a week off from playing, practicing, and spending time with her family to be his plus-one so he didn't have to go in alone, and he thought maybe… just maybe… he could let her in a fraction.

But apparently she'd already seen a crack and shined her own light into it.

"Oh," she said softly.

"Oh what?" he asked, but he was watching Owen and Neil break down the instruments. The drum set was provided by the venue, thank God, because hauling around his own set was a colossal pain in the ass. He knew because he had to provide it for Scorpio, their other steady gig.

Her hand on his sleeve called him back to her, but he went reluctantly.

"Oh. You were in love with him," she said, like she knew for certain.

Well, it was a certain thing. "I was," he said, hoping the little lie would go unnoticed.

"Oh, Guthrie," she said, holding her hand to her mouth, her eyes watering. "No."

Apparently not. "Look," he said, touching her hand in return. "He knows. He's known since the beginning. For that matter, so has Kelly. They… they hung with me because I was a friend—and darlin', when I say friend, I mean *friend*. You can't get any better loyalty than Seth Arnold and Kelly Cruz. Don't ever doubt it. I do *not* want to repay that friendship by mooncalfing all over Seth during his wedding. He invited me—Kelly invited me—and I need to respect that means they both love me, and I am going to go hang out with their family and have the time of my life. Please come with me and make sure nobody gets hurt while I do that, okay?"

"Oh, Guthrie," she said again. "Nobody but you."

His own eyes burned. "And only you can know that," he said earnestly. "Please."

She squeezed his fingers and gave a watery smile. "Think he'll play for us?"

Guthrie laughed. "The boy plays like he breathes. Yeah. I think he will."

"Totally worth it," she said.

He was forced to agree.


And during the ceremony, when Seth stood on a promontory at Pebble Beach, overlooking a thunderous winter ocean, playing a composition he'd written for his beloved and nobody else, Guthrie still agreed.

When Seth was done—and his best friend, Amara, had taken his violin and put it tenderly in a slightly heated case while Seth turned to Kelly to say his vows, Guthrie knew his face wasn't the only one freezing with brine.

Roberta clung to his arm and damn near sobbed, so he got to comfort her, and that was nice. Gay or not gay, it did make him feel a little more powerful to be able to comfort a pretty girl.

The vows were short, and equal parts foolishness and mooncalfing, as Seth would have said. And they were perfect. Guthrie and Roberta had played their share of weddings, but this one…. Guthrie was just as glad Seth provided the music here, because anything either one of them could have done would have made them both seem underaccomplished in comparison.

And that wasn't Seth's intention. That's what made him the boy Guthrie couldn't get over. Seth had written and performed that composition to make Kelly smile at him. Kelly, who was a year younger than Seth, was a short, compact boy with coarse black hair he pulled back from his face in a half-tail for the occasion, and wide, almost guileless brown eyes that practically sparkled with mischief and joy. He stared at his new husband with a fond look that said he knew he was stupid with love but didn't care.

For his part, Seth, who was tall and who never *had* managed the knack of wearing clothes that fit, had trimmed his blond corkscrew curls tight to his head and returned Kelly's expression of profound stupid love with green eyes that were only ever focused when he was looking at Kelly. Those eyes in Seth's pale brown face—his mother had been Black and his father was once a blond, blue-eyed high school basketball player—were striking enough, but the faraway expression in them made him almost otherworldly in his beauty.

The fact that Guthrie knew that the two of them had overcome more tragedy than people twice their age in order to stand on this ice-fucking-cold romantic cliff and stare hopefully into each other's eyes made their love even harder to resent.

Guthrie had no choice but to be happy and proud for the two of them. To love them like the small gathering of family and friends around him.

When Amara's husband, Vince, was done with the short ceremony, they turned toward their parents, Seth to his father and Kelly to his mother, who both held out their arms. Seth's father deposited an almost pitifully thin little girl into Seth's arms. She clung to his neck and laughed excitedly, talking a mile a minute about cold and wind and pretty coats and "Set'" and "her music." Kelly took a limp, placid little boy, bundled in a warm winter-blanket sleeper. Even from fifteen feet away, Guthrie could see the baby's arms weren't as active as most children's would be at eight months, and Guthrie's throat tightened. Kelly gazed down at this baby with affection and love. He and Seth were twenty-five and twenty-four, and they were embarking on their new life together with two children with special needs—and Guthrie could only gaze at them as they posed for a joyous, unself-conscious picture, and think about what a happy family they made.

"I present to you," Vince said, his handsome, boyish face wreathed in smiles, "the Arnold-Cruz family. They've already kissed, so now we all get to hug them and then bundle up and go back to the houses for a hot drink and some good food."

To general laughter, Guthrie jostled up with the rest of the family to kiss the babies and hug the men and greet Vince and Amara, who had arrived that morning along with Guthrie and Roberta and he hadn't had a chance to hug them yet.

The five of them used to hang out in Seth's dorms and watch movies and eat pizza and talk about their lives together. It was damned good to see them.

He expected Seth and Kelly to be distracted and generally high with happiness by the time they got to him, but instead Seth focused on him, and Kelly gave him a super tight one-armed hug while the baby drooled on his good suit.

"You came!" Seth said happily. "I'm so glad you came. We didn't give you much time."

"And miss an opportunity to freeze my balls off?" Guthrie asked, eliciting warm laughter from both men. "How could I?"

"Speaking of which," Amara murmured, coming up between them and holding her arms out imperiously for the placid baby, "let's load into the cars and go back to the houses. You guys, I can't wait to catch up." She kissed Guthrie on the cheek and gave Roberta a smile. "And you are...."

"His totally platonic plus-one," Roberta said cheerily. "He didn't want to make the drive alone."

"Roberta plays fiddle in The Crabs," he told Seth, who cackled with laughter.

"You kept the band name!" he said, like this made him unutterably happy. "I'm so glad! Are your dad and Uncle Jock—"

Guthrie cut him off with a quick shake of his head. "Naw. Just me and some of Roberta's conservatory friends. We do five nights a week—keeps me out of trouble and lets me hold down the day job without any corporate fatalities."

Seth blew out a breath. "You're too good to have a day job," he said seriously, which, Guthrie admitted, could be yet another reason he loved the guy. Then right on the heels of the one thing came another. "You brought your guitar, right? You're gonna play for us tonight? 'Cause I'm saying, I've got some prime musicians here—Amara, Vince, you—" He grinned at Roberta. "And you, probably, cause you wouldn't play with Guthrie if you sucked!"

Roberta grinned, obviously enchanted. "I'm not bad," she said primly.

"Good." Seth nodded, taking her at her word. "You guys, me and Kelly are going to talk to all the people, and we're gonna dance and we're gonna eat and we're gonna have us a helluva party." He sobered. "I got us a house all lined up, and we're moving at the end of January. I'm gonna miss the hell out of everybody until we get to visit again, so you gotta make it good."

Guthrie nodded, a solemn oath, and held out his hand for Seth to shake. "I promise upon my honor," he said soberly.

"God, you're fun," Seth told him, shaking his hand.

They all broke up then to load into cars and minivans and rental mobiles—Guthrie watched as Kelly chivvied Seth into the passenger seat of an obviously new SUV after Seth had put the kids in the back, and laughed.

"What?" Roberta asked after they'd climbed into the cab of his ancient pickup truck, a vehicle so ugly Guthrie had almost expected to be stopped when they'd paid the fee for the lot at the state park where the wedding had been held. Across the street a few die-hard duffers were struggling through the bitter wind to capitalize on the famed golf-course's available tee times, but Seth and Kelly had managed to reserve a spit of sidewalk with a fenced-in promontory over a shoal of storm-tossed rocks. Guthrie had to admit, the scenery was right out of a Brontë movie. Who *wouldn't* be moved to confess undying love when right below their feet was proof of the mutability of life and the ever-present threat of mortality?

"Nothing," Guthrie said, slamming his door hard to make sure it shut. He cranked up the heater after he hit the ignition, because Roberta had worn a dress and her knees under her black tights were practically blue. "Just that he's traveled the world, he's overcome hardships, he's married the man of his dreams and is adopting two precious children, and that boy *still* hasn't learned how to drive."

Roberta let out a half laugh, because in California, that was practically heresy. "Why not? Does he have some sort of disability?"

Guthrie shrugged his shoulders. "Let's say the opportunity didn't present itself when he was younger, and our Fiddler is highly distractible. He's a sweet kid, but practicality ain't his strong suit."

"And I got to hear him play at his own wedding." Roberta gave a happy shiver. "And the week isn't over yet. Guthrie, I know you're probably eating your heart out, but I have to say thank you again, for being the most awesome friend."

"You know what?" Guthrie said, steering the truck around the 17 Mile Drive, careful not to go too fast around the curves. The ancient Chevy pickup was not exactly known for hugging the road.

"What?" she asked, huddling deeper into her wool coat and lush wool scarf.

"I may not actually be eating my heart out." He felt the words as he said them, a sort of letting go, a freedom from the burden of heartache that had plagued him for so long.

"Really?" she asked, sounding sort of excited.

"Yeah, darlin'. I… I mean, I love them both. I love Amara and Vince, and given how absolutely adorable Kelly's sisters were and how kind his parents seem to be, I could love them all too. But… but that's not the same as being *in* love, you know?"

"Yeah," she said carefully. "I know."

"Well maybe, after this, I can just love them. I don't have to worry about being *in* love with Seth. That would be load off my heart, you think?"

Roberta nodded. "Yeah," she said softly. "But you know what would put the cherry on the being-free sundae, don't you?"

He grimaced. "Can't we be happy with my heartfelt revelation right now?"

"Honey, I'm not going to be happy until you get laid."

WELL, IT didn't happen that long, long weekend—but Guthrie wasn't looking for that. Instead, all the things Seth had promised happened. People ate together, talked together, reminisced together. The musicians played together, and the friends and family danced together.

They even went to the aquarium together and on short, brine-tossed boat rides that made Guthrie feel like singing sea shanties and playing the theme from *Jaws*.

As far as he and Roberta were concerned, it was a sweet, happy holiday with people they came to regard as family by the time it was over.

On the last night—New Year's Eve—most everybody went to bed after the ball dropped, but the original core of movie-watchers from Seth's old school—Vince, Amara, Kelly, Seth, and Guthrie—all stayed up late, lounging in the front room in front of a gas-powered fireplace, drinking wine. The wine thing was new for Seth, and he only drank a little, but apparently Amara had been trying to teach him how to order and accept a glass of wine in a restaurant so it wasn't a production.

"Even if you hate it," she said soberly, "you're only sipping it anyway, so nobody questions if you don't finish the glass."

"Just don't order red," Seth said seriously. "Headaches. Oh my God."

Kelly snorted. "Hate to tell you all, but I've actually *been clubbing*. I order shots. I'm fine."

Seth grunted. "I tried once—it was in front of my conductor in Italy. He knocked it back, I tried to do the same, and I coughed so hard I threw up all over us both. It's a good thing we were in his kitchen. God."

"Which is why he came to me when we moved to New York," Amara said. Seth had been all over the world in the last four years, while

Kelly had been forced to stay home to help take care of his family, which Seth had subsidized with his music. Guthrie could tell the stories were their way of making up for lost time, but they were fun nonetheless.

"Yeah," Vince said. "I was with a dorm of three guys, and they were like, 'pub crawl!' So I learned to drink beer. I can tell you *all* about beer." He shuddered. "So much."

"Like, draft or bottled?" Guthrie asked, because those were the kind of bars *he* played at, but Vince—a beautiful native Hawai'ian man with skin a pale teak color and brown, fathomless eyes—shook his head.

"No, brother. I wish. This is, like, thirty taps in a place, and you go in and get a ten-shot flight and taste all these beers, and you have to *know* things. Like, 'Hmm, taste of citrus with a hint of plum and coffee!'"

Guthrie stared at him in horror. "Who?" he demanded. "Who? Who does this to beer?"

"Fuckin' heathens," Vince said, and he clinked his Sam Adams bottle with Guthrie, who had enjoyed it as an exotic taste when apparently it was like Coors to the people Vince hung out with.

Everyone else laughed, and the conversation went on. At its end, Seth and Amara had crashed next to each other, head on each other's shoulders, because they'd been friends from high school as well, and Vince curled up on the end of the same couch, his head in Amara's lush lap.

Guthrie smiled at the three of them as he and Kelly polished off the last two beers.

"How you doin', Guthrie?" Kelly asked. His eyes were a little glazed, but his speech wasn't slurred, and Guthrie had the feeling that Kelly was the one who could drink them all under the table.

"Fine," he said. He'd been nursing *his* alcohol, which was a trick you picked up when you'd been playing in dive bars since you were way underage. It was either that or his dad's route, which was full-blown alcoholism, and Guthrie wasn't a fan.

"Mm?" Kelly's eyes had sharpened, and Guthrie was forced to shrug.

"I've got a band right now," he said. It was his one good thing—he knew that.

"What about a *man* right now?" Kelly asked bluntly. "God, Guthrie. I know you had it bad for Seth. I couldn't even blame you. But neither of us want you to live alone forever because you"—his voice dropped—"fell in love with a guy you couldn't have. That's… that's not fair. You're a good guy, Guthrie. We want you to have more than a band for a minute."

Guthrie glanced away. Kelly was more right than he knew. Kids like Roberta, Owen, and Neil were too *good* to stay in The Crabs for long. They had places to go, real performances, spots in orchestras to achieve.

"What do you want me to say?" he asked finally, knowing there wasn't enough alcohol in the world to soothe over this rawness inside. "I'm…. Kelly, you know what I am. If… if your boy hadn't come wandering into that dive bar, looking for a job, I could have lied to myself my entire life. I could have slept with girls and told myself I wasn't the type to fall in love. I could have gotten drunk every night with my dad and Uncle Jock, and they could have yelled at me to get my shit together, and I would have known they were right, but I wouldn't have had any way, anywhere to reach higher. Your guy comes along and suddenly I'm, like, 'Hey, I can learn piano and get better at guitar! I can go to school! I can get a job with health and dental!'"

"You can fall in love with a guy, and it can last forever," Kelly said. "Man, I've been to school. I got the papers behind my name. Just like you, this wasn't a common thing in my family. And I can tell you right now, it's not the job or the health and dental—it's the guy you love forever and ever. That's the difference in your life. That's what makes it special."

Guthrie tried for condescension. "Maybe, sweetcheeks, I'm not special enough to get a special guy."

Kelly didn't blink. He simply stared at Guthrie until he shifted uncomfortably.

"What?" Guthrie finally asked.

"We love you, asshole. Seth worries about you. We know how to have friends from far away—you and me never stopped contact, not even when he was all over the damned planet. I want to hear there's a guy in your life. And don't tell me they don't fall in your lap. Keep your heart open for us, Guthrie. Learn to let someone in."

Guthrie swallowed, beaten and done. His eyes were burning, and it was all he could do not to sob his heart out on the shoulder of the guy *married* to the guy Guthrie couldn't seem to get over.

"It's hard," he admitted gruffly. "I… I know what it feels like now, when it's real. In your heart. Just like you two—I can't settle for anything smaller or dumber now."

"That's real good," Kelly said, nodding. "But don't let it hold you back. A kiss won't kill you, buddy. It's the way to see if there's sunshine in the corners."

Guthrie could only nod. He didn't remember much more about that night. They *all* fell asleep in the front room in front of the fire, bundled in blankets. Kelly took a recliner, and Guthrie lay in front of the couch, and when it was time to get up and leave in the morning, the five of them hugged and cried a little, because they were all old enough now to know times like that didn't come as often as they should.

But he kept Kelly's words in his heart: *A kiss won't kill you, buddy. It's the way to see if there's sunshine in the corners.*

He knew what to look for now. He'd look for sunshine.

# SCAN THE QR CODE
# BELOW TO ORDER!

Writer, knitter, mother, wife, award-winning author AMY LANE shows her love in knitwear, is frequently seen in the company of tiny homicidal dogs, and can't believe all the kids haven't left the house yet. She lives in a crumbling crapmansion in the least romantic area of California, has a long-winded explanation for everything, and writes to silence the voices in her head. There are a lot of voices—she's written over 120 books.

Website:www.greenshill.com
Blog:www.writerslane.blogspot.com
Email:amylane@greenshill.com
Facebook:www.facebook.com/amy.lane.167
Twitter:@amymaclane
Patreon:https://www.patreon.com/AmyHEALane

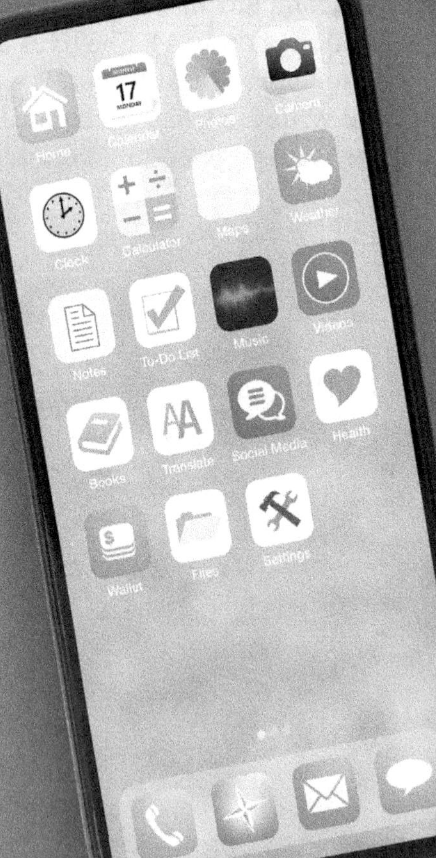


AMY
LANE



SWIPE
LEFT,
POWER
DOWN,
LOOK
UP

Busy soccer coach Trey Novak doesn't have time for the awkwardness and upheaval dating can cause, but when his cousin stands him up for a lunch date, he meets someone who changes his mind.

Dewey Saunders is dying to get a real job in his field and start the rest of his life, but a guy's got to pay rent, and the coffee shop is where it's at. When the handsome customer in the coach's sweats gets stood up, Dewey is right there to commiserate—and maybe make some time with a cute guy.

Trey's making hopeful plans with Dewey when his professional life explodes. He and Dewey aren't in a serious place yet, and suddenly he's promising to make sports a welcoming place for all people. When Dewey puts himself out to comfort Trey after an awful day, Trey realizes that they might not be in a serious place, but Dewey has serious promise for their future. If someone as loyal and as kind and funny as Dewey is what's offered, Trey would gladly swipe right for love.

# Scan the QR Code
# Below to Order!

SCTF
COVERT ★ BOOK 1
UNDER COVER
AMY LANE

Covert: Book One

For Judson Crosby, the transfer to the elite law enforcement branch of the SCTF is a great escape from the death sentence he earned as a whistle-blowing patrol officer. Calix Garcia, the fierce new guy, makes a perfect partner, catching bad guys while minimizing collateral damage. Crosby loves working with him.

Of course, he'd also love to work him over in a totally different way.

Garcia has waited his whole career for a solid, dependable partner like Crosby. But after six months fighting crime together, he's done fighting their attraction.

Their coming together promises to be everything they need… until a threat from Crosby's past comes back to haunt not just him, but their entire team.

When Crosby goes undercover to keep them safe, Garcia is frantic with worry. One false move could get Crosby killed and Garcia exposed. But they have to fight their way clear, because hiding your lover under the cover of darkness is no way to live. Crosby and Garcia will risk everything for the chance to live their lives in the light.

# SCAN THE QR CODE
# BELOW TO ORDER!

AMY
LANE

WEIRDOS

Not all
dogs are
Lassie.

If Taz Oswald has one more gross date, he's resigning himself to a life of celibacy with his irritable Chihuahua, Carl. Carl knows how to bite a banana when he sees one! Then Selby Hirsch invites Taz to walk dogs together, and Taz is suddenly back in the game. Selby is adorkable, awkward, and a little weird—and his dog Ginger is a trip—and Taz is transfixed. Is it really possible this sweet guy with the blurty mouth and a heart as big as the Pacific Ocean wandered into Taz's life by accident? If so, how can Taz convince Selby that he wants to be Selby and Ginger's forever home?

# SCAN THE QR CODE
# BELOW TO ORDER!

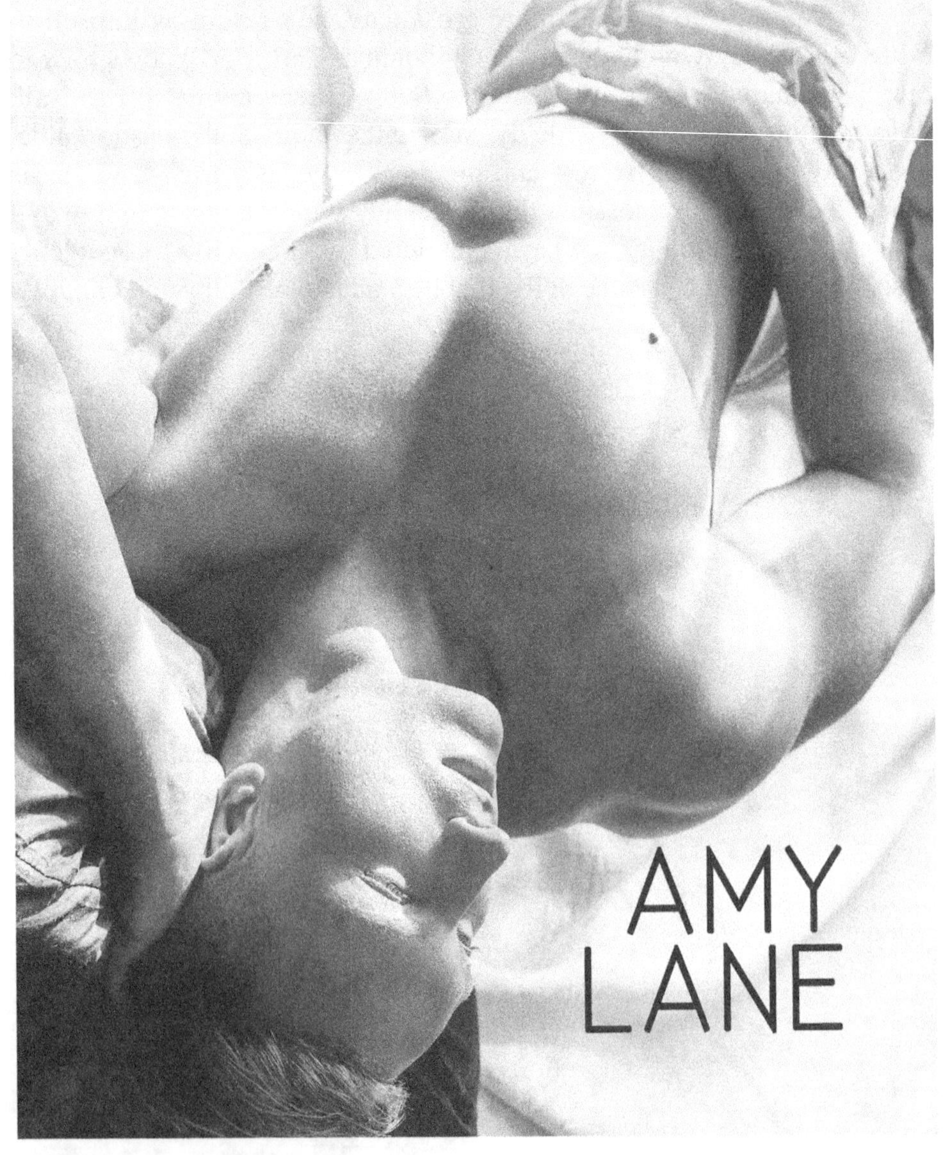
SHADES
of HENRY
AMY
LANE

A Flophouse Story

One bootstrap act of integrity cost Henry Worrall everything—military career, family, and the secret boyfriend who kept Henry trapped for eleven years. Desperate, Henry shows up on his brother's doorstep and is offered a place to live and a job as a handyman in a flophouse for young porn stars.

Lance Luna's past gave him reasons for being in porn, but as he continues his residency at a local hospital, they now feel more like excuses. He's got the money to move out of the flophouse and live his own life—but who needs privacy when you're taking care of a bunch of young men who think working penises make them adults?

Lance worries Henry won't fit in, but Henry's got a soft spot for lost young men and a way of helping them. Just as Lance and Henry find a rhythm as den mothers, a murder and the ghosts of Henry's abusive past intrude. Lance knows Henry's not capable of murder, but is he capable of caring for Lance's heart?

# SCAN THE QR CODE
# BELOW TO ORDER!

BONFIRES
AMY LANE

Bonfires: Book One

Ten years ago Sheriff's Deputy Aaron George lost his wife and moved to Colton, hoping growing up in a small town would be better for his children. He's gotten to know his community, including Mr. Larkin, the bouncy, funny science teacher. But when Larx is dragged unwillingly into administration, he stops coaching the track team and starts running alone. Aaron—who thought life began and ended with his kids—is distracted by a glistening chest and a principal running on a dangerous road.

Larx has been living for his kids too—and for his students at Colton High. He's not ready to be charmed by Aaron, but when they start running together, he comes to appreciate the deputy's steadiness, humor, and complete understanding of Larx's priorities. Children first, job second, his own interests a sad last.

It only takes one kiss for two men approaching fifty to start acting like teenagers in love, even amid all the responsibilities they shoulder. Then an act of violence puts their burgeoning relationship on hold. The adult responsibilities they've embraced are now instrumental in keeping their town from exploding. When things come to a head, they realize their newly forged family might be what keeps the world from spinning out of control.

# SCAN THE QR CODE
# BELOW TO ORDER!

FOR **MORE** OF THE **BEST** **GAY** ROMANCE